LORD ARMAND WAS CLOSE,
MUCH TOO CLOSE.

She could hear his breathing and feel the heat from his body as he stood behind her. She could sense his powerful muscles held in check. She could discern the scent of his warrior's body, of the soap he used before he shaved, of his woolen clothes and leather belt and boots.

The closest she had ever been to a man before was during a meal, when touch was by accident or conscious design. She could imagine all too well what the king would do if he found himself in Lord Armand's place. He, however, continued to stand perfectly still and made no attempt to touch her.

Her ears strained to hear anything from outside; all was silent. Perhaps it was safe to go out. Adelaide slowly put her hand on the latch, determined to leave, until he covered it with his own.

"Not yet," he whispered in her ear. "They may come back."

She couldn't disagree, even though it was a torment having Armand so close behind her, his hand slipping over hers like a caress....

MARGARET MOORE

My Lord's Desire

HQN™

ISBN-13: 978-0-373-77228-5
ISBN-10:   0-373-77228-9

MY LORD'S DESIRE

www.HQNBooks.com

Printed in U.S.A.

Also by Margaret Moore

Hers To Desire
Hers To Command
The Unwilling Bride
Lord of Dunkeathe
Bride of Lochbarr

And look for
The Notorious Knight
coming in July 2007

With many thanks to the veterinarians and staff of
the Guildcrest Cat Hospital for their
gentle kindness during Tommy's final days,
for their continuing excellent care of Eeky
and "the boys" and for the opportunity to add
Luis and The Count to our family.

My Lord's Desire

CHAPTER ONE

Wiltshire, 1204

"KEEP YOUR EYES open, Bert," the burly foot soldier ordered his younger comrade-in-arms at the gate of Ludgershall Castle. "I don't like the looks o' this fellow."

Bert, skinny and with spots on his youthful face, stopped watching the approaching rider to regard Godwin with surprise. "He's all by himself, ain't he? He can't be thinking o' attacking this castle single-handed. He'd have to be mad when we're up to our arses in soldiers with the king stayin' here."

"Fools and madmen have caused trouble before this," Godwin warned, "and this knight looks like he could finish off a dozen men before he fell."

"How d'you know he's a knight?" Bert asked. "Where's his men? His squire? His page? He's got no servants or baggage. He's probably another one of them *routiers* the king's hired."

Bert spat in disgust. Like most soldiers bound to his lord by land and loyalty, he detested mercenaries,

and those King John employed were the worst of
the lot.

Godwin shook his head. "Not him. Look at the
way he's sittin' that horse. The nag ain't much, but
only a well-trained knight rides like that, as if he's as
comfortable in the saddle as a lady at her sewing.
And he's got mail on, ain't he? And a sword, and
unless I'm going blind, that's a mace tied to his
saddle."

"Plenty of men carry maces," Bert replied, "and sit
up straight when they ride. Besides, what kind of horse
is that for a knight? It ought to be pullin' a hayrick. His
surcoat's seen better days, too. And look at his hair—
what knight has hair down to his shoulders? Fella looks
more like a Viking or one of them Scots from the north."

"Trust me, that man's a knight or I'm a nun."

"Well, supposin' he is," Bert allowed, "what's the
worry? We've had plenty o' knights coming and going."

"Not like this one," Godwin replied, stepping
out of the overhang of the massive barbican to call
out a challenge.

As the stranger obediently drew his sway-backed
nag to a stop, Godwin studied the man's stern, angular
visage and the grim line of his full lips. No, this was
no ordinary man, whether mercenary, knight or lord.

"It's Godwin, isn't it?" the stranger asked, his voice
deep and husky.

At the sound of the familiar voice and a closer look
at the man's lean face, Godwin gasped with recogni-

tion. He immediately lowered his spear and a wide grin split his face, making the scar on his chin curve, too.

"Forgive me, my lord!" he cried with both joy and relief. "What a surprise—a good one, mind. I was right happy to hear you wasn't dead."

"I am happy not to be," Lord Armand de Boisbaston replied as he swung down from his horse. He eyed the second guard, who still had his spear at the ready. "Am I to be allowed to enter Ludgershall or not?"

Godwin gestured for Bert to out up his spear. "This is Lord Armand de Boisbaston, a good friend of the earl's. He was last here, what? Three years ago, my lord?"

As the knight nodded, Bert did as he was told. "Sorry, my lord. That was before my time."

"No matter," Lord Armand replied. "You were wise to deny me entry until you knew I wasn't an enemy, especially if our beloved sovereign is within."

Godwin's eyes narrowed ever so slightly. *Beloved?* If what he'd heard was true—and he had no reason to doubt it—Lord Armand de Boisbaston had no reason to love the king, and every reason to hate him.

"Which way to the stable?" the nobleman inquired.

"It's along the west wall inside," Godwin answered. "Bert here can fetch a—"

"No need," Lord Armand interrupted as he reached for his horse's bridle. "I'll tend to my horse myself. The last time somebody else tried to brush him down, he got a kick for his trouble."

"Will your squire and servants be coming along with your baggage, my lord?" Bert asked. "We ought to know in case they don't get here before the changing o' the guard."

"My squire is dead, and everything I possess is in that pouch tied to my saddle."

Neither soldier knew what to say to that, so they didn't say anything.

"Is the earl within, or out hunting?" Lord Armand asked.

"He's in Wales, my lord," Godwin said, "on the king's business. He's not expected to be away for long, though."

"And Randall FitzOsbourne?"

"Oh, he's here, and a fine young gentlemen he is, too, I must say. Not like some of them courtiers who come with the king."

"Thank you," Lord Armand replied. "It's unfortunate the earl is away, but as it happens, I have business with the king, too." He started to lead his horse into the barbican. "It's good to see you again, Godwin."

"You, too, my lord," Godwin replied as he watched Lord Armand de Boisbaston, once rich and powerful, now neither, disappear beneath the heavy wooden portcullis as if he were a wraith newly risen from the dead.

LADY ADELAIDE D'AVERETTE slipped into the dim stable. Breathing in the air scented with hay and horse, she listened for voices, but heard only animals munching their hay and moving about their stalls.

Sanctuary! she thought as she pulled the door closed behind her.

That choice of words brought a smile of wry amusement to her lips, although it was true. She'd had enough of what passed for wit that morning, and more than enough of the fawning flattery of the men of the king's court. They must think she was a simpleton or vain beyond all reckoning if they believed she accepted anything they said as sincere, or that they wanted something other than her body in their beds.

As for the ladies, she was equally weary of their sly looks and snide, whispered remarks. She couldn't help being beautiful any more than they could help being devious and ambitious, seeking powerful, rich men for husbands or lovers.

Despite their treatment of her, she couldn't fault them for their plans and stratagems. In a world where men ruled, their husbands would determine if their futures were happy or sad, prosperous or impoverished.

Please, God, though, not her or her sisters, either. If they could prevent it, they would let no man have such power over them.

In her mind, she again heard the harsh, drunken voice of her father as if he were standing right beside her. "I'll marry you all off as soon as I can to the man who pays me the most. And if he wants to examine the goods before he makes me an offer, I'll strip you naked myself."

Shoving away that terrible memory, Adelaide found an empty stall and sank down upon a pile of clean straw. She removed her heavily embroidered cap, veil and the barbette that went beneath her chin, unpinned her hair and shook it loose.

A tiny mew at the far corner of the stall caught her attention. There, nestled on what looked like a bit of old blanket, lay a cat nursing her kittens, all save one. Apparently less hungry or more adventurous than its siblings, that one was moving toward Adelaide.

It was a cute little thing, mostly white with a black back, as if it wore a cloak. There was a black smudge on its nose and another just beneath its mouth, like a sort of beard.

Not wanting to distress the mother, Adelaide stayed where she was, content to watch the kitten explore its surroundings. It seemed quite fearless as it came toward her—and then she realized it was making for the veil lying on her lap. She returned her cap to her head and was putting the veil behind her when the kitten suddenly sprang for the end of it, landing in her lap. Laughing, but not wanting her silken veil torn, Adelaide shoved the veil and barbette behind her and petted the little kitten while keeping a watchful eye on its mother.

Another of the kittens—this one mostly black, with a white breast and white feet—romped toward her.

The white kitten began to wiggle free of her lap. At the same time, the large stable door creaked open and the unmistakable sound of a horse being led in from the cobbled courtyard broke the silence.

Not sure who it might be, and fearing it might be Sir Francis de Farnby or some other gentlemen of the court, Adelaide decided it would be wise to leave.

Before she could move, however, the white kitten leapt onto her shoulder like some kind of bird. The black kitten jumped into her lap, clearly following its sibling regardless of where it went. With a meow, the white kitten moved farther behind her head. She gasped as it dug its needle-sharp little claws into her back below the nape of her neck while the black kitten scampered back to its mother.

Her head bent, Adelaide twisted and turned and tried to get hold of the kitten, to no avail. Her cap tumbled to the ground while the kitten held on tighter, its claws digging into her skin, as well as her gown of scarlet damask.

"May I be of assistance?"

Adelaide froze.

This was no groom, and certainly no stable boy. Judging by the man's refined accent, he had to be a nobleman, although she didn't recognize his deep, husky voice.

She tried to raise her head, and the kitten clung on tighter. "Ouch!"

"Allow me, my lady."

A pair of scuffed, worn and muddy boots appeared in her line of sight and the weight of the kitten mercifully disappeared, if not the sensation of the painful little claws digging into her flesh.

"Please, be careful," she pleaded, her head still bowed in a position both awkward and embarrassing. "Otherwise the kitten might tear my gown."

"We can't have that," her rescuer agreed, his voice intimate and amiable, making her blush as if this were the sort of clandestine encounter she so assiduously sought to avoid.

She raised her eyes, hoping to see a bit more of the man standing in front of her. His gray cloak was made of wool and mud-spattered, and there was a hole in the hem large enough to stick her finger through.

"Come now, little one," the man murmured as he worked to free the kitten's claws from her garment.

Even as she tried to ignore the stranger's proximity, his deep voice and the warmth of his breath on the nape of her neck sent shivers down her spine— although not of fear. Of something else. Something forbidden and dangerous.

"You're free," he said, finally lifting the kitten from her. He brushed her hair away from the nape of her neck in a gesture like a caress. "Did it scratch you?"

God save her, no man had ever touched her like that. No man *should* touch her like that, and she should certainly not be enjoying it.

"I can't see any blood," he said. "Perhaps beneath your gown—"

"You're not looking beneath my gown!" she cried as she scrambled to her feet, snatching up her veil, barbette and cap and turning to face—

—the most attractive man she'd ever seen.

Long, chestnut-brown hair framed a handsome, mature face of angles and planes, sharp cheekbones and a strong, firm jaw. Dark brows slanted over quizzical brown eyes brightened with flecks of gold, like pinpoints of sunlight. His full lips curved up in an amused, yet gentle, smile that made her heart race as if she'd run for miles. The white and black kitten lay cradled in the crook of his arm, its eyes half-closed, purring loudly as the man rubbed its plump little belly.

Never before had Adelaide envied a cat.

"I assure you, my lady, I wasn't suggesting anything improper," the stranger said, a chuckle lurking beneath his rough voice. "I merely meant that you should have your maid tend to any scratches. A cat's scratch can be a serious matter."

Adelaide's mouth snapped shut as she realized she'd been staring at him like a besotted ninny. This was just a man, after all, not a supernatural being.

"I thank you, sir, for your help," she said with haughty dignity. "I'm sure any injuries I've sustained are minor."

His smile disappeared, and the light in his brown eyes dimmed.

This was as it should be. After all, *she* had not come to court to find a husband. She had come to court to do all she could to *prevent* being married.

A hiss came from behind her. The last of the kittens had finished nursing and the mother cat clearly thought it was time for all her brood to go.

The white kitten bounded out of the man's grasp and ran to join the others.

The handsome, well-spoken and therefore surely noble stranger gave Adelaide a rueful grin. "Alas, I've been abandoned."

Adelaide didn't want to smile, lest he take that for encouragement. She looked away—and saw a long scratch on the back of his hand. "You're bleeding!"

"Little devil," the man muttered as he examined his hand, exposing his wrist and mottled, red skin that had obviously once been rubbed raw. As if he'd been shackled. For weeks.

Adelaide raised her startled eyes to find the stranger regarding her steadily, with an expression that betrayed nothing. Although she was full of curiosity, she decided it would be best to say nothing and simply tend to his wound, as he'd come to her assistance.

She hurried from the stall to the nearest trough and dipped the corner of her veil into the water before returning to wash the scratch.

The unknown nobleman, as well as the cat and her kittens, were gone.

Adelaide stood dumbfounded, wondering where he'd gone and if she should seek him out, until she heard the all-too-familiar voice of Francis de Farnby. It wouldn't be good to be found here with a man— any man—and especially not a man as attractive as the unknown nobleman. She could easily imagine what the gossips of the court would make of *that*.

CHAPTER TWO

"ARMAND! You're finally here! I was beginning to think you'd gotten lost."

Delighted to hear the voice of his closest friend, Armand stopped rubbing down his horse and smiled as Randall FitzOsbourne limped into the stall.

As usual, Randall was dressed in a long, dark tunic that reached the ground, with a plain leather belt girded around his slender waist. He wore his hair, the color of newly cut oak, in the popular Norman fashion, although the cowlick on the left side of his head gave him a rakish look that was distinctly at odds with his gentle personality.

"Is that *your* horse?" Randall asked, running a wary eye over the ill-tempered animal that shifted at the sound of his voice.

"It was the best I could afford," Armand replied, tossing the rag he'd been using into a bucket on the other side of the stall. "I'm sorry if I gave you any cause to worry. This beast is not the swiftest, and I was longer at my uncle's than I planned."

"Success?" Randall asked, his sandy brows rising in query.

One hand stroking the horse as it snorted and refooted, Armand reached into his tunic and tossed a small leather pouch at Randall, the coins within clinking as he caught it. Randall had excellent coordination and would have been a formidable knight, had his club foot not made that impossible.

"How much?" Randall asked, pulling the drawstring open and peering within.

"Ten marks."

Randall's disappointment matched Armand's. "So little?"

"There was no love between my father and my uncle," Armand reminded his friend with a shrug of his broad shoulders. "I was fortunate he didn't set the hounds on me."

Randall sighed as he leaned back against the stable wall. "As bad as that?"

"Yes."

Armand saw no need to elaborate on the unpleasant reaction his arrival had elicited from his uncle when he went to plead for money to ransom his half brother, Bayard. He would not repeat the justifiable epithets applied to his vicious, lascivious, mercifully dead father, or the cold reminders that his uncle had already helped to pay for Armand's freedom; he had little to spare for Bayard.

"How much have you got now?"

"Two hundred and eight-four marks."

"So you still need two hundred and sixteen. I'm sure the earl would gladly loan you that amount, except that he's not here," Randall said with regret. "His steward, while a fine fellow, isn't likely to lend you so much as a ha'penny without the earl's leave."

"When is the earl expected to return?"

"A fortnight, I think."

Armand cursed softly.

"If you'd let me go to my father again—"

"No. As desperate as I am to have Bayard free, I'm not going to put you through that humiliation again."

As long as he lived, Armand would never forget the terrible treatment Randall's father, Lord Dennacourt, meted out to his only child when, in his desperation to rescue Bayard, he'd agreed to go with Randall and seek the ransom money, or a portion of it, from that wealthy nobleman. Judging by Lord Dennacourt's reaction, you would have thought Armand wanted to murder him and that Randall had deliberately crippled himself to thwart his father's plans.

Armand clapped a companionable hand on Randall's shoulder and, picking up his leather pouch, steered him out of the stall. "I've come up with another way to raise the money," he said with a good humor that wasn't completely feigned. "I believe, my friend, that the time has come for Armand de Boisbaston to take a wife."

Randall stared at him in amazement. "You'll marry to get the ransom money?"

"If I must," he replied, understanding Randall's surprise.

Before he'd sailed to Normandy on that ill-fated campaign, he would never have considered such a mercenary motive for taking a bride. Profit had been his father's reason for marrying again when Armand's mother had been barely a month in the grave, and that second marriage had been a disaster, a constant battle of wills and epithets, curses and blows. Armand had promised himself he would have affection, amiability and peace when he wed, regardless of dowries and lands.

But now, with Bayard depending upon him, he couldn't afford to think only of his own desires when it came to taking a wife. And he had to admit that his plan seemed more palatable now that he'd met that lovely, bashful beauty in the stable. It hadn't escaped his notice that she wore no wedding ring.

When she'd raised her eyes and looked at him, he'd experienced that almost-forgotten thrill of excitement and arousal, too. It was as if the recent past had never happened—until she'd seen his scarred wrist and he'd fled like a coward, or the most vain man alive. "I trust our king still enjoys the company of orphaned young ladies who are royal wards, as well as several wealthy, titled widows he can bestow in marriage on his friends, or those to whom he owes much?"

"Yes, he does," Randall replied as they entered the courtyard.

Several soldiers patrolled the wall walk and guarded the gate. Others not on duty lounged in the July sunlight, laughing and cursing as they exchanged stories. Ostentatiously ignoring the soldiers, a few young female servants strolled toward the well, whispering and giggling. Other servants, in finer garments, bustled about on business for their noble masters.

Merchants and tradesmen's carts arrived with produce for the castle kitchens; others, now empty, departed, their drivers cursing nearly as colorfully as the soldiers as they tried to pass.

Armand realized that Randall's expression was noticeably grim. "I'm very worried about Bayard, too," Armand said, speaking a little louder to be heard above the din. "I'm hopeful a marriage will mean I can free him soon."

"Perhaps."

These short, brusque answers were totally unlike Randall's usual responses. "What's wrong? Is there a scarcity of young, unmarried ladies or rich widows, or don't you think John will bestow one upon me? It's the least he can do after what I've suffered for him."

Armand had to strain to hear Randall's reply as they threaded their way through baskets of peas and beans outside the kitchen storeroom. "John might not like being reminded about his losses in Normandy."

"It wasn't my fault he lost his lands there and he should still be grateful for my service."

Randall's gaze flicked over Armand. "I agree John

should reward you, and I hope he will. But…well…" He delicately cleared his throat. "Are you planning on cutting your hair?"

"No, and you know why not," Armand replied, unable to keep the hostility from his voice as he contemplated the reason for that decision.

"What will you say to anyone else who asks?"

"The truth."

Randall took hold of Armand's arm and pulled him behind the nearest farmer's cart. "For God's sake, Armand, do you *want* to be accused of treason?" he demanded in a fierce whisper.

Armand shook off his friend's grasp. "I'm no traitor. I swore my oath of loyalty to John and I'll keep it, although I rue the day I put my honor in his hands. It's because of John that I nearly died in that dungeon. It's because of John that my squire and several good men did, and it's John's fault my brother is still imprisoned in Normandy."

"Even so, you must take care, Armand, especially when you're not completely recovered from your injuries—or are you?" Randall's gaze darted to Armand's right knee that had been struck hard with a mace and left to mend on its own while he was imprisoned.

"Almost," he replied, although his knee ached like the devil most of the time. His arms were still weak, and his voice was a little rough from the lingering cough he'd suffered for over a fortnight. Still, he was much

better than he'd been the last time Randall had
seen him.

"But not yet, so you *must* be careful," Randall persisted. "John sees conspiracies everywhere, and your
oath may not protect you. And your estate alone
would be enough to encourage greedy, ambitious men
to poison John against you. If you're accused of
treason, what will happen to Bayard then?"

Armand's jaw clenched before he answered,
although he knew his friend was right. He'd have to
be cautious in this nest of vipers. "I'll be careful."

"Good," Randall replied with genuine relief. "Now
let's get something to eat. John and the queen are still
abed, so you won't have to see them right away."

"Thank God. Otherwise my appetite might disappear completely."

"I'M GLAD you're feeling better," Adelaide said to
Eloise de Venery as they sat on a stone bench in the
castle garden later that morning.

Sweet, kind and pretty, Eloise was Adelaide's one
true friend at court. She was also genuinely good,
trustworthy and blessedly free of ambition.

Nearby, several of the courtiers were playing a
game of bowls on the flat, lush lawn that formed the
center of the garden. Their goal was to get their ball
nearest to the one in the center, and to block or knock
away any others that were closer.

Around the outside of the garden were walks

bordered by beds of flowers and sweet-smelling herbs. Roses climbed the walls, and several alcoves and nooks had been created with vines and lattices.

Lord Richard D'Artage was about to take his turn. He was the most vain peacock at court, spending hours every morning on his hair and clothes. There were rumors that he had padding in the shoulders of his tunics, and that his hair owed its color as much to art as to nature.

Other young noblemen looked on and offered their advice, whether it was welcome or not, and more than one was somewhat the worse for wine. Several ladies were also in attendance, including the ambitious, sharp-tongued Lady Hildegard, with her piercing eyes and pointed chin.

Adelaide was quite happy to watch the other courtiers play their games, whether it was bowls, or bantering, or maneuvering for power. She preferred to be ignored, although her damnable beauty made that all but impossible.

Eloise gave her a sheepish look. "I wasn't really sick this morning. I just didn't want to be near Hildegard for a while."

"Understandable," Adelaide said. Hildegard was no favorite of hers, either.

Eloise sighed. "She always manages to upset me. I wish I were more like you, Adelaide. Nothing she says bothers you."

"Because I don't care whether Hildegard likes me

or not," Adelaide truthfully replied. Only the king's opinion of her mattered, as he was the one who held power over her fate, as well as that of her sisters.

Eloise still looked upset, so Adelaide sought to lighten her mood. "Randall FitzOsbourne was watching you dance last night."

Eloise's head shot up like an eager puppy's, and then she flushed and looked down at the stone walk at her feet. "Oh, I don't think so. He must have been looking at someone else."

"He certainly *was* looking at you," Adelaide assured her. "Perhaps tonight you should speak to him."

"I couldn't! What would I say? He'll think I'm being too forward."

"I doubt that. You're the most modest woman at court. I'm sure he likes you. Unfortunately, he's as shy and modest and unassuming as you are. Perhaps if you were to speak to him first—"

"I just couldn't! Besides," Eloise woefully continued, "since his friend's arrived, he probably won't even remember I exist."

"What friend is this?" Adelaide asked, trying to sound nonchalant despite the excitement that coursed through her. As far as she knew, there was only one new arrival at court—the man she'd met in the stables. She'd heard of no others.

"Lord Armand de Boisbaston," Eloise said. "You weren't here when he was last at court, or I'm sure you'd remember him. He's a very handsome man."

That had to be the knight she'd met in the stable. "I think I may have seen him," Adelaide said, oddly reluctant to tell Eloise about her encounter with the man in the stable. "Does he have long hair?"

"My maid said it's nearly to his shoulders. Marguerite was fluttering about like a loosed pigeon when she told me about him. Wait until the ladies of the court hear he's come back. They'll be just the same. I wonder why he hasn't cut his hair, though. He used to be quite neat and tidy in his appearance before he went to Normandy. Did *you* think he was handsome?"

"Yes."

"I'm surprised it's taken him so long to return to court. He's been free for weeks now."

"Free?" Adelaide prompted, remembering the scars on his wrist.

Eloise lowered her voice to a whisper. "He commanded one of John's castles in Normandy. They were besieged for months waiting for reinforcements, but John never sent any. Lord Armand finally surrendered when the French king threatened to fire the town and kill everyone in it. Afterward, Lord Armand and the knights who were with him, as well as their squires, were imprisoned until ransoms could be paid. Those who paid quickly were freed in a fortnight or so. Others weren't so fortunate. It took months for Lord Armand's friends to raise the funds. His family's estate was left rather barren after equipping an older half brother to go on crusade with Richard the

Lionheart. The poor fellow died before he even reached the Holy Land. Lord Armand's younger half brother is still imprisoned in Normandy waiting to be ransomed."

"He has…had…two *half* brothers?"

Eloise nodded. "Raymond de Boisbaston had three legitimate sons by two different mothers, and from what I've heard, probably a few bastards, as well."

"If the son resembles his father, I can understand why women would be eager to go to his bed," Adelaide mused aloud, thinking of Lord Armand's smile and bewitching brown eyes.

Eloise nodded at the courtiers playing bowls. "The other unmarried noblemen aren't going to be happy that Lord Armand has returned."

"He has no wife then?"

Eloise shook her head.

Adelaide tried not to be pleased, or relieved, by that knowledge. After all, marriage was something to be avoided, unless she wanted to be subject to a man's whims and commands, and treated as less important than his dogs or his horses. She would have no man beating her for birthing "useless" girls instead of sons.

And if he were handsome and had a voice that seemed to promise pleasures that were surely sinful, he would surely never be faithful.

"Maybe John will give him a well-dowered wife as a reward for his loyalty and suffering," Eloise suggested. "Then he could use the dowry to ransom his brother. Maybe that's why he's come to court."

"Perhaps," Adelaide agreed, glad she'd been implying that her family was relatively poor by dressing simply. The only jewelry she wore was her mother's crucifix. It was old, and although made of gold and emeralds, it was a modest piece compared to the jewellery other ladies of the court flaunted.

"Oh, how unfortunate!" Lady Hildegard cried as Lord Richard rolled his ball and missed. "The ground must be uneven, or I'm sure you would have won."

"Too bad, Richard. You nearly had me," Sir Francis de Farnby, the winner of the game, said with self-satisfied triumph. He was more attractive than Lord Richard, with fair hair, broad shoulders and a narrow waist; however, like Lord Richard, he was well aware of his personal attributes and his family's wealth and prestige. He was the sort of man who expected everyone to be as impressed with him as he was with himself.

Adelaide stifled a frown as he sauntered toward them.

"Ah, my lady, I feared the fairies had captured you and taken you for their own this morning," he said when he reached them, ignoring Eloise. "You seemed to vanish into thin air."

It was all Adelaide could do not to roll her eyes and tell him she would vanish from his sight right now if she possessed the power. "No doubt you missed Lady Eloise, too. Are we not fortunate she's feeling better?"

Francis glanced at Eloise, who gave him the sort of benevolent smile she reserved for very small children and very stupid adults.

"Yes, of course," he said, turning back to Adelaide, and quite oblivious to Eloise's lack of admiration. "Where did you go? I searched high and low for you. I nearly called out the guard."

"I went to the stable."

"If you wished to ride out, my lady, you had but to ask. I would gladly have accompanied you."

No doubt he would have tried to get her off her horse, the better to seduce her, too.

"I wasn't dressed for riding and that wasn't my purpose," she replied. "I find the company of horses soothing."

The kittens had been an unexpected source of amusement, and as for the arrival of Lord Armand de Boisbaston...

"I doubt the horses appreciate your exquisite beauty and grace as much as I," Francis said, his tone softly flattering and his expression adoring.

Oh, God save her from fawning, foolish—

"By all the devils above and below, if it isn't Sir Francis de Farnby," a slightly raspy, familiar male voice declared nearby.

Adelaide's face heated with an unstoppable blush as Lord Armand de Boisbaston strolled toward them, followed by Randall FitzOsbourne.

Lord Armand had divested himself of his cloak,

surcoat and mail. He now wore a plain leather tunic
with a glossy black sheen, a white shirt beneath it
laced at the neck, as well as black woollen breeches
and the worn boots free of mud. His belt was wide,
likewise of leather, and his scabbard and broadsword
hung at his side.

Between his clothes and his hair, he looked more like
a barbarian than ever, or a man who saw no need to
adorn himself with fine garments to make an impression.

The courtiers who'd been discussing the game fell
silent, and Eloise didn't seem to know where to look.

"You appear surprised to see me, Francis," Lord
Armand said as he came to a halt beside Adelaide.
"I'm delighted to see *you* looking so well, but then,
when one is far from battle, one is more inclined to
keep one's health. Won't you introduce me to these
two lovely ladies?"

His gaze flicked toward Adelaide and although he
gave no outward sign of recognition, a sense of familiarity, even of intimate acquaintance, sent a frisson of
warmth and excitement through her—an unwelcome
sensation. After all, she was no desperate woman
eager for a man's approval. She would rather that he
hate her, or at least dislike her.

"This is Lady Eloise de Venery and Lady Adelaide
D'Averette," Francis said through thinned lips. "My
ladies, may I present Lord Armand de Boisbaston,
whose vanity and presumption are apparently

undiminished by his recent incarceration, and despite surrendering the castle he was charged to defend." He looked pointedly at Adelaide. "I would caution you, my lady, to beware this man's honeyed tongue."

How dare Francis mock a man who'd risked his life for his king when *he'd* never done anything more dangerous than participate in a tournament? "He doesn't seem to be speaking very sweetly of you, my lord," she very sweetly noted.

A furrow appeared between Francis's brows as if he was displeased, or perhaps confused by her response. "That's because I'm not a beautiful lady. Armand de Boisbaston's reputation, however, is well-known."

"Indeed it is," Randall FitzOsburne declared, the words bursting out as if he would explode if he didn't speak. "He's the best and bravest knight in England!"

"You flatter me too much, Randall," Lord Armand protested with a smile that had nothing of modesty about it. "William Marshal is the best and bravest knight in England, and Europe, too. If I could claim but a portion of his skill and honor, I'd consider myself fortunate."

"Honor?" Francis scoffed. "I believe you left that in Normandy."

Anger flared in Lord Armand's brown eyes. "At least I had it once to lose."

"Do you insult me, my lord?" Francis demanded.

Didn't Francis notice the ire in the tightness of the man's features? Adelaide wondered. The little line of

anger between the slanting brows? Did he really want
to come to blows with this man?

"I merely made an observation based on your ref-
erence to my sojourn in Normandy," Lord Armand
coolly replied, the tone of his voice at odds with his
obvious rage. "I cannot be responsible for how you
interpret it. You seem to have developed a rather thin
skin since I've been away, Francis. Perhaps you've
been spending too much time at court."

"While you seem to have forgotten how to dress
for it. My servants are better attired than you. Have
you not even a knife with which to trim that unkempt
mop of hair?"

"Since I was forced to give nearly all that I possess
to regain my freedom after fighting for the king, I
have no finer clothes to wear. As for my hair…"

Lord Armand glanced first at Adelaide, then smiled
at Eloise. "Do I look so very awful?"

Eloise blushed and lowered her eyes, and shook
her head.

He turned next to Adelaide. "What about you, my
lady? Would you say my hair looks like an unkempt
mop?"

Adelaide reminded herself that she was at court for
a reason, and it certainly wasn't to fall under a handsome man's spell. If Eloise or Lady Hildegard or any
other lady of the court wanted Lord Armand, they
could have him.

"No, I would not," she replied. "It does, however,

make you look quite savage. Should we next expect to see your face painted blue like a Pict? Or will you be wearing the horned helmet of a Northman? Is there some reason for this unusual hairstyle, my lord, or do you simply enjoy shocking people and being the center of attention?"

As Francis guffawed, the expression that came to Lord Armand's face made her want to squirm.

"Someday, perhaps, my lady," he said, "I will tell you why I haven't cut my hair since I was taken prisoner. I doubt, however, that you'd understand."

Adelaide blushed with shame, and she wanted to apologize, but she didn't dare. She had a reputation to maintain, even if it wasn't one she particularly relished.

"Pay no heed to what he says, my lady," Francis said. "And *you*, my lord, had best take care how you speak to one of the king's wards."

Lord Armand didn't look the least bit worried. "Tell me, Francis, while I was in the Comte de Pontelle's dungeon, where were you?"

Francis straightened his shoulders. "I, too, was serving the king."

"I'm sure you were, in your own way," Lord Armand agreed with more than a hint of mockery in his voice and eyes. "We cannot all bear arms in battle."

"And some of us can barely walk," Francis shot back, his gaze darting to Randall FitzOsbourne, who blushed bright red.

That was truly a low blow. Randall FitzOsbourne couldn't help being crippled.

The slight smile remained on Lord Armand's face, but his eyes filled with renewed rage and his hand went to the hilt of his sword. So did Francis's.

Eloise blanched and Randall FitzOsbourne looked worried. Adelaide, however, was quite sure Lord Armand could defeat Francis in a contest of arms, and Francis deserved to be humbled.

"By the teeth of God, is something amiss among my courtiers?" the king called out.

They all turned to see John striding toward them. Everyone had been too intent on the exchange between Sir Francis and Lord Armand to notice his arrival.

As always, John was expensively and ornately dressed, in a long tunic of ivory cendal, heavily embroidered around the neck, cuffs and hem. His belt was gilded, and he wore a large gold brooch with a ruby in the center. Rings sparkled on his plump fingers, and his hair shone with oil. The odor of expensive perfume wafted from him, overpowering the more delicate scent of the roses nearby. The queen and several of his *routiers* followed, trying to keep up with the king's brisk pace.

Regardless of the presence of his queen, the king leered at Adelaide when he came to a halt. "I suppose these two bold cockerels are glaring at each other because of you, my lady."

"Your Majesty," she replied, keeping her tone and

expression carefully neutral, "I was merely passing the time of day with Lady Eloise when these gentlemen approached me."

"I see." The king ran a speculative gaze over Lord Armand, who was a full head taller than he. "We were informed of your arrival, Lord Armand. You're most welcome at our court."

"Thank you, sire," Lord Armand replied. He took a step toward John. "I hope—"

"We can guess what you hope," the king interrupted with a hint of pique, "and we do not intend to discuss it when the noon meal is about to be served."

John turned back to Adelaide. "For the sake of peace in the hall, you must sit beside me at table, my lady."

Knowing she really had no choice, trusting she could continue to be neither encouraging nor obviously discouraging to the notoriously lascivious king, Adelaide smiled and said, "It would be my honor, Your Majesty."

CHAPTER THREE

"I'M SORRY. I truly thought I'd be able to keep my temper," Armand said to Randall as they watched the king and his companions, now including Lady Adelaide, leave the garden. "Unfortunately, the very sight of de Farnby is enough to annoy me."

It didn't help that Francis was talking to the bashful beauty, who proved to be anything but bashful. Indeed, her lively responses had been very disconcerting.

"Francis annoys everybody," Randall consoled. "At least you didn't attack him. That would have been a disaster."

Armand eased himself onto the stone bench Lady Adelaide and her fair-haired friend had recently vacated. He stretched out his right leg and massaged his aching knee. "I notice Francis manages not to annoy the king."

"He flatters the king and amuses the queen."

Armand knew he should curb any interest in the sharp-tongued Lady Adelaide, as well as stifle the desire that leapt into life when he saw her, given his reasons for marrying and the sort of placid wife he hoped to have. He also had no idea how rich or poor Lady Adelaide's family might be. After all, there were other unmarried ladies at court, and if there were none so beautiful, or with such shining, soft eyes, they might be richer, and that was what he needed to remember.

Nevertheless, he couldn't resist asking a little more about the dark-haired beauty. "Francis flatters Lady Adelaide, too, yet she doesn't seem susceptible to his oily charm. Is that because she's set her sights on a richer prize?"

Sitting beside him, Randall looked around to make sure they were alone. "You mean the king?"

That wasn't what Armand meant, yet it wouldn't be surprising if John had enticed, bribed or compelled that young beauty into his bed. "Is she his mistress?"

"Not yet, I don't think, although nobody knows for certain."

"In this court, they'd know," Armand replied, trying not to betray any relief, or to feel it, either.

"It's very difficult to say what *that* lady's plans are," Randall said, "or who, if any man, she likes or wants. She gives nothing away and acts the same to all."

"Perhaps she doesn't want to limit her choice of wealthy husbands."

"I don't think we can fault her for that," Randall said. "She has two unmarried sisters who are wards of the king, as well, although they aren't at court, and the family isn't very rich. If she makes a good marriage, their chances to do the same improve considerably."

"What about her friend, Lady Eloise?" Armand asked. "Is her family rich?"

Randall hesitated a moment, and didn't look at Armand when he answered. "Yes, her family is richer. Her dowry should be more than enough to pay Bayard's ransom. I haven't really inquired." He swiftly got to his feet. "We had better get to the hall if we want to eat."

Randall's manner and his sudden desire to leave was more than enough to tell Armand that even if Lady Eloise were the richest woman in England and panting after him, he shouldn't consider her for a bride—not unless he wanted to upset Randall.

"I suppose I could try for Lady Hildegard," Armand mused as they made their way toward the garden gate.

"Things have changed since you've been gone," Randall replied. "She's got her eye on Lord Richard."

Armand raised a brow as he held the gate open for his friend. "Don't you think I could persuade her that I would be a better husband?"

"I don't doubt you would be," Randall replied. "But Lady Hildegard is as ambitious as any man. Lord Richard, for all his vanity, is from a very wealthy family, and wealth means power."

"Then I must choose another," Armand said with a shrug as they crossed the yard between the garden and the hall.

"At least you have a choice," Randall said with

more bitterness than Armand had ever heard him express before.

"Any woman should be delighted to have your good regard," he said. "You're a kind, clever fellow, and as loyal as they come. Just because you can't dance a jig or ride off to war is no reason to believe you're not deserving of a bride."

"Thus says the most handsome knight in the king's court."

"Who's fortunate to be friends with the finest man at the king's court."

That honest response made Randall smile, something Armand was glad to see as they entered the great hall.

The Earl of Pembroke had been poor in his youth, but as the furnishings, gorgeous, colourful tapestries and banners of the earl's household knights hanging in the hall now testified, he was poor no longer. After years of loyal and devoted service to the Plantagenets, he'd been given Isabel de Clare, the richest heiress in England, for his bride.

A clean, bright wood fire burned in the central hearth, warming the chamber that could be chilly even in summer. Well-made, heavy trestle tables had been set up for the meal, including one on the dais for the king and queen and their chosen companions, their chairs sporting silken cushions for their comfort. Pristine white cloths covered the tables above the salt for the courtiers and were set with silver goblets and spoons. Below the salt, tankards and wooden spoons had been put out for the soldiers and body servants of the nobility.

The rushes on the floor had been sprinkled with fleabane and rosemary, the scents mingling with the smoke drifting up to the louvered hole in the roof and the perfume of the courtiers. The ever-present hounds roamed the hall, anticipating scraps tossed their way from the meal to come.

The beleaguered master of the hall rushed from table to table and servant to servant to ensure that all were in place and ready to perform their duties.

As they made their way to a table, Armand and Randall passed tumblers and jugglers stretching their limbs and practicing for the performance they would give during and after the meal. Nearby, minstrels tuned their instruments, and a bard was mumbling to himself, obviously practicing, too.

Armand caught sight of Godwin and Bert, and inclined his head in a greeting. The soldiers grinned and tugged their forelocks in return.

The priest, an elderly, pinched-faced fellow with a fringe of white hair, said a grace that was notable for its pleas for God's mercy in these terrible times. As Armand said his amen, he reflected that with such a king, asking for God's mercy was no doubt a wise precaution.

"There seems to be a bevy of unmarried ladies here," Armand observed as they took their seats. He nodded at one of the noblewomen sitting opposite them, closer to the king. Her long features struck him as unfortunately reminiscent of a horse. "Who is she?"

The young lady caught him looking and giggled and blushed as she whispered to another young woman beside her. That lady met Armand's gaze quite brazenly.

God help him, how could he have forgotten what life at court was like? The games of love, the little intrigues. The suspicions. The jealousies.

Forgotten or not, he needed a richly dowered wife, so he had to play these games. He raised a goblet in salute and said, through clenched teeth, "Well, Randall? Who is she?"

"That's Lady Mary de Chearney, and the blond woman beside her is Lady Wilhemina of Werton," Randall answered. "I believe both have dowries large enough to pay Bayard's ransom thrice over, but I've heard Lady Mary's father has his eye on a Scots earl for her, and I think Lady Wilhemina's brother plans to marry her off to a very rich, very old Welsh nobleman with several estates in the March."

Relief filled Armand, and then annoyance. He mustn't think of his own pleasure when it came to marriage. He must remember Bayard, languishing in a dungeon until his ransom could be paid.

Shyly sliding Armand a glance and a smile, a maidservant placed a platter of fine white bread before them. Armand took out his eating knife and cut off the heel of the loaf. Let others praise the roasted meats and exquisite sauces to come, the pottages spiced with herbs from far-off lands and puddings made of rare ingredients. As he'd sat in that dungeon, it had been bread he'd missed. He'd dreamed of having a whole loaf to himself, washed down with honest English ale.

The maid's smile reminded him of another appetite that hadn't been whetted since his release. He'd not had the energy for some time, and lately, all his efforts had gone to raising the money to free his brother. Nor had he met a woman who stirred his desire—until Lady Adelaide.

His gaze drifted toward that lady, sitting serenely beside the king. Had she been acting a part in the stable, trying to attract his interest before she learned who he was? Or had she been acting in the garden, when she had made sport of his appearance?

Randall cleared his throat as another servant set down the trenchers of slightly stale bread that would be used as plates. Later, when they had been soaked with the gravy and sauces, they would either be fed to the hounds, or given to the poor waiting at the castle gates. "I think Lady Eloise would be your best choice for a wife. Her dowry should be enough, and she's a very sweet girl."

Had there ever been a better friend? "Bayard wouldn't want your happiness to be part of his ransom."

"Oh, I have no interest in her *that* way."

Armand gave Randall a look that told him exactly what he thought of that response.

His friend sighed as he took a piece of bread for himself. "What does it matter if I like her or not? She won't want a cripple."

"If that's all she sees when she looks at you, then *she's* not worthy of *you*."

Randall tossed his bread to one of the waiting hounds. "You don't know her. She's the kindest, most amiable lady at court."

Armand's brows rose. "Am I looking at a man in love?"

When Randall didn't answer, Armand knew the truth, and it made him feel...strange. It was as if Randall, who was usually the one left behind, had ventured into a foreign land without him. "If you care for her that much, you should ask for her."

Randall's lips thinned into a stubborn line. "I may not be a mighty warrior, but I do have my pride."

"You fear her family will reject you?"

"I'm afraid *she* might."

The minstrels struck up a cheerful tune, and more servants arrived bearing roasted venison, beef, eels soaked in ale and a thick pottage made of liver and kidneys, leeks and bread crumbs. Armand cut himself a slice of beef and put it on his trencher. The pottage he would not have. Although it smelled good and was likely tasty, the look of it reminded him too much of the slop he'd been fed in that cell. "So you haven't told Lady Eloise how you feel?"

"I've hardly spoken to her at all."

Armand paused with a piece of roasted beef halfway to his mouth. "Then how can you be so certain of your feelings?"

"I just am," Randall said as he ladled some of the pottage onto his trencher, speaking with a conviction that took Armand aback.

Randall pointed to his chest. "I feel it in my heart. I fell in love with her the moment I saw her."

Before today, Armand would have said such a thing was impossible, or a happy delusion at best. But then he'd walked into a stable and discovered a woman with a kitten clinging to her back. A beautiful woman who looked at him with the most amazing eyes he'd ever seen, a few tendrils of hair encircling her perfect features, her lips parted as if begging for his kiss. She'd made his heart race and a vitality he hadn't felt in months rip through his body.

He forced his attention back to Randall's dilemma as a second course of duck stuffed with a mixture of eggs, currants, apples and cloves arrived, as well as roasted chicken filled with bread and onion and spiced with rosemary and sage. A carafe of thick gravy accompanied both, and Armand was liberal in its use. "What of Lady Eloise's family? Perhaps if you were to approach them first…?"

"Lady Eloise has no family. She's one of the king's

wards, so he'll decide who she marries. Unfortunately, I have nothing to offer John for the privilege."

Armand was well aware that the king accepted bribes for the bestowing of a bride, as well as for the guardianship of young male heirs whose estates could be picked clean before they came of age. "Did your father not provide you with money before you came to court?"

"Some, but what I had is gone."

Armand stopped eating as a terrible thought seized him. "You didn't use any of your own money for my ransom, did you?"

"A little," Randall admitted.

Armand swore under his breath. "I'll pay you back. Every ha'penny."

"I know you will."

His appetite gone, Armand muttered, "I should have surrendered to the French the first week. I should have realized that after what happened with Arthur and the men at Corfe, the French would show no mercy. We should have fled the castle when we could, and given up without a fight."

"Don't blame yourself for what happened, Armand," Randall said. "You followed the orders of the king as best you—or any decent man—could."

Armand surveyed the finely dressed men sitting in the Earl of Pembroke's hall, eating his food and drinking his wine. One or two, like that dark-haired, bearded fellow, he didn't know. A few had fought in

Normandy; most had not, preferring to pay a scutage instead. Lording over them all was the king, lascivious and going to fat, his face glistening with grease from the duck and roasted goose on his trencher.

To think that he had done his duty to maintain such a king and such a court.

The very least John could do was give him a rich wife.

ADELAIDE would rather have been nearly anywhere than sitting on the dais beside King John. She could take some comfort from the fact that the king bathed more often than many a nobleman, but that was the best thing she could say about him.

She looked down the hall at Eloise, seated at the far end of a table and wedged between Lady Jane and her querulous, elderly mother.

Lucky Eloise. Lady Jane talked whether one listened or replied, and her mother was interested mainly in her food. You could eat and think without having to participate in any conversation; it was as close to being alone in the hall as it was possible to be.

"So, my lady, another bold knight has come to court and no doubt will be seeking a smile from your pretty lips," the king remarked. "What do you think of Lord Armand? A handsome fellow, is he not?"

Adelaide's every sense was suddenly on alert, as if alarm bells were pealing from the watchtowers. It wasn't like the king to compliment another man.

"If one prefers that sort of rugged charm," she replied, giving the king a slight smile and pretending that the jugglers who were keeping a series of brightly painted wooden balls in the air and passing them back and forth were distracting her.

"Do *you,* my lady?" the king pressed.

She had to turn to him then and she encountered a searching gaze that made the sweat start to trickle down her back.

In spite of her discomfort, she let her smile grow and willed her eyes to tell John that there was no one more interesting, important or fascinating than he. That would be an unspoken lie; what came from her lips, however, was the truth. "I find myself wishing to do something about his hair and find him garments more appropriate to your court, sire."

She *did* want to do something with Lord Armand's hair. She wanted to touch it. She longed to run her fingers through the unruly waves and comb it back from his handsome face. And although she should have been paying close attention to the king and his queen to ensure she made no misstep in either look or speech during the meal, she'd been imagining Armand de Boisbaston attired in garments more appropriate to the court—rich fabrics cut to accent his magnificent, well-muscled body. She'd spent the better part of the first two courses trying to decide if he'd look better in scarlet or in blue.

"Even so poorly dressed, he is a fine-looking man,

is he not?" the young queen interjected with a cunning smile as the final course arrived at the table, a meat pie of rabbit and pork colored with saffron and spiced with cinnamon.

Adelaide gave the queen a smile. She didn't like the spoiled, often petulant girl, but at least Isabel was no Eleanor of Aquitaine. Isabel had very little power at court; John even took the Queen's Gold for his own use, something the awe-inspiring Eleanor would never have allowed.

"If one considers personal attraction to lie solely within outward appearance," Adelaide replied. "Many women prefer a man of learning and intellect."

Adelaide knew well that John considered himself a learned man. In many ways, he was, and had he been trained to a career in the law. Adelaide had sometimes thought, he might have been a worthy attorney. Sadly, his interest in the law, like so much else in him, had been corrupted by greed and ambition.

"They say Lord Armand is quite learned, too," the queen noted. "He speaks Latin like a Roman, or a cleric."

"You seem to know a good deal about him, Your Majesty," Adelaide placidly observed.

The king cut his wife a glance. "Yes, you do."

"It is my duty to know all about the men who have sworn their oath of loyalty to you, my husband," the queen calmly replied.

John made no answer, but it was plainer than words

that he was annoyed. He might treat his vows of marital fidelity lightly and expect the wives and daughters of his noblemen to be eager for his bed, but when it came to his queen, it was quite a different matter.

"I suppose he will be asking for money," the queen said, "as if he should be rewarded for losing Marchant."

The king sniffed. "He is welcome to ask."

Adelaide bunched her linen napkin into a ball on her lap. It was no wonder the king's barons loathed him. He seemed to treat their loyalty and risks on his behalf as no more than his due. He made light of their sacrifices, and demanded bribes and payment for what he should bestow as justly earned rewards. He ignored the rules of chivalry, and many believed he'd killed his own nephew with his bare hands. Even if he hadn't, Arthur had certainly disappeared and was very likely dead.

Her appetite quite gone, Adelaide glanced at the king's plump, bejewelled fingers. Were they capable of squeezing a boy's throat until he died?

If he could order a boy blinded and castrated to prevent him taking the throne, what would he *not* do?

She couldn't suppress the shiver that ran down her back. And to think this man had the power to compel her to go to his bed, if he chose to use it.

"My lady is cold?" the king asked, leaning closer.

It was all Adelaide could do not to shy away. "There must be a draft."

"Perhaps dancing will warm you."

The thought of touching John made her feel ill—
and she found her excuse. She put her hand to her
head and gave him a woeful smile. "I feel a little
unwell, Majesty. I believe I had best retire."

The king frowned, but mercifully didn't command
her to stay. "Very well. We hope that you'll be feeling
better tomorrow."

Adelaide bowed her head and said no more as she left
the dais. Sensing the eyes of the other courtiers upon her,
she knew they were wondering if she'd already shared
the king's bed. She had heard that wagers had been
made, and those who believed the king hadn't yet succeeded had placed bets on when he would.

Despite the secret anguish that speculation brought
her, she held her head high and her lithesome back
was as straight as a barge pole. She was Lady
Adelaide D'Averette, and she would never willingly
submit to any man's domination.

Not even the king's.

CHAPTER FOUR

"So I DECIDED to use the excuse of an aching head to take my leave of the king," Adelaide said as she strolled beside Eloise in the garden after breaking the fast the next morning.

The day was warm and sunny, with a light breeze that stirred the leaves of the vines and made the red and white roses nod. In a lovely light blue gown trimmed with delicately embroidered green leaves and with her blue silken veil floating about her face, Eloise looked like the very spirit of summer. Adelaide was more plainly dressed, as befitted her supposed lack of fortune, in a gown of russet wool, with only a simple leather girdle around her waist.

"I also told Sir Oliver I was feeling a little ill this morning when he asked me if I was joining the hunt," she said.

"I'm so relieved most of the court went," Eloise replied. "It's so much more peaceful and quiet when they're hunting."

By silent mutual agreement, they went into one of the many little alcoves and sat upon a wooden bench.

"Did you speak to Randall FitzOsbourne last night?" Adelaide asked.

Eloise flushed and studied the white rose bushes around them. "No, I didn't get the chance."

"Eloise…!"

"I was going to," her friend protested, clasping her hands in her lap, "but before I could, Lord Armand asked me to join him in a round dance. It would have been rude to say no, and when we finished, Randall was gone."

Eloise frowned and spoke with uncharacteristic bitterness. "I should have retired when you did. Lord Armand only asked me to dance because Lady Hildegard was marching toward him with a most determined look in her eye. He didn't want to dance with her so he asked me instead."

A sudden, silly surge of disappointment pricked Adelaide as she wondered if that was really true. She didn't doubt that Lord Armand wanted to avoid the predatory Hildegard, but she could also believe he had an additional reason for asking Eloise to be his partner. Eloise, however, was so modest and unassuming, she was probably quite blind to a man's genuine interest.

"Even if Hildegard was bearing down on him like an attacking knight, he didn't have to ask you to dance," Adelaide pointed out.

"I wish he hadn't. He never said a word to me the entire time. And I'm quite sure asking me to dance doesn't mean he likes me *that* way. After he danced with me, he asked Jane. The poor thing was so flustered, she forgot the steps and ran into Hildegard, who said something that made her burst into tears. I don't know what Lord Armand said to Hildegard after that, but I don't think she'll be chasing after *him* again. She'll have to content herself with Lord Richard, if she can, and I wouldn't be overly confident of that, either, if I were her. You should have seen the way he looked at *you* when you left the hall last night."

Adelaide frowned and said with all sincerity, "I truly hope John doesn't make me marry Richard. Why, he'll be more concerned about his boots than he'll ever be about his wife."

Eloise started to laugh in agreement, then glanced up at the sun above the nearest tower.

"Oh, saints preserve us, it's nearly the noon," she cried, jumping to her feet. "Marguerite should have returned with my clean shifts by now. Pardon me, Adelaide, but I must see if they're all right. The last time she did the washing, two of them were torn."

With that, Eloise gathered up her skirts and rushed away toward the garden gate without waiting for Adelaide to say another word.

Adelaide watched her go with a bit of relief. She hated talking about marriage. Such conversations inevitably reminded her of her parents' unhappy union. Her father had been a harsh, overbearing tyrant who was often in his cups, and her mother had been frail and delicate, too weak to defend herself or her children when he was in a rage. As long as Adelaide could remember, her mother had been sick in body and sick with fear.

She would never forget the shock she'd felt the day she'd dared to come between them. For the first time, she'd seen a grudging admiration in her father's eyes, and he'd never again laid a hand on her, or her mother and sisters, if she was nearby.

That day she had learned that strength need not be physical, that resolve and boldness could be strengths, too.

She'd also realized that both her parents were weak. If her father had not the law and the dictates of society to bolster his rule, and if her mother had had the determination to stand up to him, their lives might have been very different.

Approaching footsteps interrupted her unhappy thoughts. The gait was uneven, as if the person limped, like Randall FitzOsbourne.

Eloise was so shy, she might never speak to him, even though it was obvious she liked him very much. If Eloise wanted to marry—and she did as eagerly as Adelaide did not—Randall FitzOsburne was better than many a husband would be.

Prepared to do whatever she could to help her friend be happy, Adelaide left the alcove—and discovered Lord Armand de Boisbaston walking down the garden path.

As startled as she, he came to a halt a few feet
away. Then he crossed his arms and leaned his weight
on his left leg as he stared at her with those brown,
gold-flecked eyes.

She blurted the first thing that came to mind. "I
thought I heard somebody limp—I thought you were
Randall FitzOsbourne."

"Obviously, I'm not."

She felt an almost physical pain at his brusque
response, although it was no more than she deserved
after what she'd said to him yesterday.

She simply couldn't let him continue to think she was
insolent and rude. "I'm sorry if I insulted you yesterday,
my lord," she said. "I was impertinent and I wouldn't
be surprised if you never wanted to speak to me again."

Lord Armand's brows rose.

"I doubt I can truly appreciate what you've endured. I should have accorded you the respect to
which you're entitled, and I deeply regret what I said."

His body relaxed and a smile dawned upon his
handsome face. She was pleased to see it, even if it
sent another unwelcome thrill throbbing through her.

"In light of your apology, my lady," he said, "I'll
tell you why I haven't cut my hair."

He gestured at the nearby bench and although it
was rather hidden from the path, she answered his
silent request and sat upon it.

He joined her and explained. "I want my appearance to remind the king that things have changed

since I went to Normandy, that myself and others paid a heavy price for trying to hold his lands there. I don't want him to be able to delude himself that everything is as it was before."

"Now I'm even more sorry for what I said."

"Dwell no more upon it, my lady," Lord Armand replied, his answer like a warm blanket on a cold day. "It's forgotten."

Then his lips lifted in a devilish little grin and his eyes shone with merriment. "Although the notion of painting my face blue and leaping out at Francis in the dark does have a certain appeal."

Adelaide had to smile, too. "I'd like to see that myself."

"I gather, then, you don't particularly care for Francis?"

She felt as if they were veering onto treacherous ground. "He's a knight in the king's household," she answered carefully.

"That doesn't mean you have to like him."

She decided it would be better not to talk about the other men of the court. "I hope the kitten's scratch is healing, and you suffered no lasting effects?"

"No. And you?" he asked.

"A few small scratches—nothing of consequence." She slid a glance his way. "You left the stable rather abruptly."

His discomfort at her observation was obvious. For a moment, she wished she hadn't mentioned it, until he gave her a wry little grin and said, "I was embarrassed by the scars on my wrist. I'm as proud as any man, my lady, and some consider surrendering cowardice."

"I don't," she truthfully replied. "What good would it do to have a knight like you dead?"

The look that came to his eyes made her heartbeat quicken, and her whole body pulse with something that could only be lust. Many men had said ridiculous things to amuse or flatter her, and to arouse this sort of sensation, she didn't doubt. None of them ever had, yet Lord Armand had done so without a single word.

Again, a warning sounded in her mind. This time, though, it had little to do with her future, and everything to do with what she was tempted to do right then and there.

Fortunately, before her wicked impulse could triumph over her rational mind, a door banged open on the far side of the garden, followed by a burst of feminine laughter.

"Lord Aaarrr-mand!" Hildegard called out, sounding as if she'd been sharing a cask of wine with someone. "Come out, come out, wherever you are, or you're going to have to pay a forfeit for abandoning us!"

Lord Armand grimaced. "God's blood, I thought I'd gotten clean away."

Adelaide knew exactly how he felt. "Come with me, my lord," she said, rising and taking his hand in hers. "There's a little hut at the far corner of the garden where the servants keep their tools. It's well hidden behind some climbing roses."

He made no objection, and as they hurried down the path, she noticed that he favored his left leg.

"Here," she said, a little out of breath as they reached the wooden building. She pulled open the door and ushered him inside. "If they come this way, I'll tell them I haven't seen you."

"You'd lie for me?"

"To Hildegard, I would."

He was about to close the door when they heard other voices close by. It was the king and his companions, obviously back from the hunt.

"God's teeth!" Adelaide muttered under her breath. She didn't want to see them any more than Lord Armand wished to converse with Hildegard.

Without a word, Lord Armand yanked her into the hut and closed the door. The building was hot and stuffy and smelled of damp earth, but that wasn't why Adelaide found herself breathing rapidly, and she knew it.

Lord Armand was close, much too close, in this dark, confined space. She could hear his breathing and feel the heat from his body as he stood behind her. She could sense his powerful muscles held in check as he, too, tensely waited. She could discern the scent of his warrior's body, of the soap he used to soften his whiskers before he shaved his jaw clean, of his woollen clothes and leather belt and boots.

The closest she had ever been to a man before was during a meal, when touch was by accident or conscious design—the sort of scheme she consciously and continually thwarted. Indeed, she could imagine all too well what Francis, the king and several other men at court would do if they found themselves in Lord Armand's place. He, however, continued to stand perfectly still and made no attempt to touch her—which was good, because she didn't dare leave their hiding place. She couldn't risk being discovered in this situation by anyone.

She couldn't move, either, lest she knock over the tools leaning against the wall or hanging from pegs.

Her ears strained to hear anything from outside; all was silence. Perhaps it was safe to go out—

"I wish I could kill them all, each and every one, and Philip most of all," the king declared, sounding as if he were less than three feet away.

She instinctively shrank back, colliding with Armand. It was like hitting the castle wall, except a stone wall wouldn't put its hands on your shoulders to steady you.

She squirmed, silently commanding him to let go. Which he did. Thank God.

"He would kill me if he dared, that French fop," the king continued. "As for Hugh the Brown, he should thank me for taking Isabel off his hands. She's a spoiled little brat."

"A very pretty little brat," Francis replied. "You

certainly showed Hugh you were a man to be reckoned with when you stole her away from him. He shouldn't have tried to make an alliance with her father."

The king chuckled, sounding a little farther away. "Yes, I got the better of him there, didn't I?"

"As you will of all those who try to defeat you," Francis assured him, his voice even more distant.

Adelaide slowly let out her breath, and Armand did the same. She put her hand on the latch, determined to leave, until he covered it with his own.

"Not yet," he whispered in her ear. "They may turn back."

She couldn't disagree, although it was a torment having Armand so close behind her, his hand slowly slipping from hers like a caress.

She never should have led him there. She should have let him take his chances with Hildegard, as she should have taken hers with the king and Francis and whoever else might be with them. It wasn't as if she hadn't done so before. Instead, she found herself trapped in this little hut with this handsome, incredibly virile man.

She put her ear to a crack in the door. She could hear nothing. Surely it was safe to leave now. Once again she put her hand on the latch.

Hissing a curse, Armand clapped a strong hand over her mouth. His left arm encircled her waist, pulling her back hard against him. She struggled and twisted but he held her in a viselike grip, his arms as confining as iron bands.

"Shhh," he whispered, the sound as soft as wind passing through the grass.

"Then it's decided," said a man outside the hut, his voice low and from somewhere close by. "Both must die."

Adelaide stilled.

"First the archbishop, then Marshal," confirmed another man whose voice she likewise didn't recognize.

"Why not the earl first?" a third man demanded in a harsh whisper. "He's the stronger."

"The archbishop is old. It'll be easy to make his death look like an accident or illness."

"When?"

"You don't need to know. Just be ready to move when the archbishop is dead."

They heard the sound of foliage being moved, followed by retreating footsteps.

For a moment, Adelaide stood limp in Armand's grasp, too stunned by what she'd heard to move. Those men, whoever they were, were planning assassination.

Startled into action by that realization, she fought her way free of Armand's grasp and wrenched open the door. She hurried down the path in the direction she thought the men had gone, determined to find out whose voices they'd heard.

The garden was deserted. There was no sign of

anyone—not the men they'd heard, or the king and his party, or Hildegard and the ladies.

Armand ran after her and grabbed her arm. "Where the devil do you think you're going?"

"We have to find out who they were!"

He stared at her incredulously. "Don't you know?"

"No," she snapped in frustration. "They were talking too quietly and it may come as a shock to you, my lord, but I haven't spoken with every single man, servant, clerk or clergyman who inhabits this castle or travels with the king. And now you're letting them get away!"

"What would you do if you caught them?" he demanded, his voice low, but firm. "Accuse them of plotting murder? Upon what evidence—a whispered conversation overheard in a garden?"

"While you would let them get away?" she retorted. "God knows I have no love for John, but they're planning the assassination of the two men most capable of keeping him from destroying England."

"I'll go to the king. Forget what you've heard."

"I'm not a child!"

"Nor are you a knight sworn to protect the king," he replied. "That is my duty, my lady, not yours."

"I may not be a knight," Adelaide returned, "but I have no wish to allow men to overthrow the kingdom by murder, especially of those two fine men."

"No, it's too dangerous," Armand persisted. "It's

my duty to protect women, too, not put them in harm's way. I will not allow you to involve yourself in this."

"It may have escaped your notice, my lord," she retorted, getting angrier and more impatient by the moment, "but I'm already involved in this. As for danger, every time I'm away from my chamber, every minute I spend at court, I'm in danger of one sort or another. How easy would *you* find it, I wonder, to tiptoe around John's desire or that of other men, seeking never to enflame their lust, yet knowing to reject them outright could be more dangerous than facing a lance charge?"

Armand's brow contracted as he considered her words, and she was prepared to argue more. Men wanted to believe that without them, women were weak and helpless, and almost useless, too, except to bear children. She did not agree, and she wasn't going to let him dismiss her.

But instead of arguing, he nodded. "Very well. We'll both go to the king."

"We can't," she said as another possible explanation for the scheme came to her. "John might be involved."

Armand looked at her as if she were demented.

That wasn't going to dissuade her, either. "John hates being told what to do, or listening to advice, even if it's sound. He heeds the Earl of Pembroke because he knows Marshal would sooner die than be disloyal. He respects the archbishop more than most clergymen, but that isn't saying much. If those two men are dead, he'll be free of the two people whose counsel he feels most compelled to heed. In his mind, he might finally be free."

Armand ran a hand through his long hair and a scowl darkened his features. "God's blood, I can believe it. Perhaps you're right and we shouldn't go to John until we know more about this plot. But in the meantime, I must warn Marshal. Randall has many friends among the clergy. He can send word to the archbishop."

Adelaide saw a danger in this plan, too. "We should alert Marshal and Hubert, but only if you can do so without arousing suspicion or telling anyone else what we've heard. I realize Randall's your friend and I'm sure he's a trustworthy fellow, but the fewer who know of the conspiracy, the better. Men who seek to achieve their ends by murder won't hesitate to kill anyone who threatens their plans."

She waited for Armand to protest that he knew best.

"Very well. I'll get word to the archbishop myself."

Relieved that he wasn't going to argue, she said, "While I talk to any of the courtiers I don't know well and try to discover who we heard."

Again she waited for him to protest, but again he didn't. "As you're doing that, I'll try to find out if anyone's leaving Ludgershall today. I have some friends among the guards I can ask."

"Good," Adelaide replied, pleased and still somewhat surprised that he was so agreeable. "Now we must think of a way to meet and share what we've learned."

Lady Jane came bustling down the path toward them, her head bowed in thought.

Armand de Boisbaston abruptly tugged Adelaide into his arms.

And kissed her.

CHAPTER FIVE

ADELAIDE was too shocked to resist as he held her in his warrior's arms and his lips moved over hers with confidence, as well as desire. His embrace set her blood alight with excitement and powerful longing. Other men had tried to kiss her, and their fumbling, clumsy attempts had been repellent. But this this was as different as the sun from the moon, night from day. This was...delightful. Exciting. Wonderful.

She wrapped her arms around him, instinctively returning his kiss with equal fervor—until she heard Lady Jane's gasp, followed by the swish of a woman's skirts and her swiftly retreating footsteps.

Appalled by her own shameful conduct, as well as his, Adelaide pushed Armand away. "What do you think you're doing?"

"Kissing you," he replied with aggravating calm. "If people think I'm wooing you, no one will wonder if we want to be alone."

He made it sound as if he'd done nothing very much at all, although he most certainly had. "Did you give any thought at all to my reputation when you came up with that astonishing plan?"

"In truth, my lady, no," he said, and he still did not look sorry. "I was thinking I needed a way to be alone with you, just as you said, and that way came to mind." He had the gall to smile. "Was it as terrible as all that?"

"Yes," she hissed. "How dare you do such a thing? How could you put me in such a position? For months I've walked a narrow path among the men of this court, and then you come here and in *one day* destroy my reputation."

"Not destroyed, surely," he protested. "After all, it was just a kiss."

"Just a kiss to you, perhaps, but it's different for a woman, as you should know." She straightened her slightly askew cap. "I take it you aren't often at court, or you'd appreciate how even the most innocent encounter can soon be exaggerated by gossip and rumor."

All trace of appeasement disappeared from his features. "You aren't the only one who'll pay a price, my lady. I came here to find a wealthy bride. I can't do that if the court believes I'm in hot pursuit of you."

"If your hasty act has thwarted your plans, you have only yourself to blame," she replied. "You should have considered the ramifications of your actions before you kissed me."

"Well, I didn't—and it's too late now. We're both just going to have to make the best of this."

"Easy enough for you to say," she charged, shoving her hands into the long cuffs of her gown. "You're not a woman whose life can be ruined by rumor and gossip."

"I've had to deal with rumor and gossip since I surrendered Marchant," he replied, his left hand gripping the hilt of his sword. "And shouldn't our own lives be of little consequence when the peace of the kingdom's at stake? The important thing is to find out who's planning to murder the archbishop and the earl, not to protect our reputations."

He had her there, and because he did, she had little choice but to agree to the role he had assigned her.

"I don't want a rebellion any more than you do," she snapped with frustration and anger. "Therefore I shall go along with your plan until we can discover the identity of the conspirators—but *only* until then."

With that, she turned on her heel and marched out of the garden.

THAT NIGHT, after the tables had been cleared and taken down so that the courtiers could dance, Armand took another drink of wine and watched Lady Adelaide clap hands with a dark, bearded knight. She'd already danced with three other men. Apparently her attempt to find the conspirators involved flirting with every single male at court.

God help him, what had possessed him to kiss her?

It had been a stupid, impulsive decision—if one could consider giving in to his overwhelming desire a decision.

His explanation had come after, although that hadn't been totally impromptu. He *had* been thinking of ways a man and a woman could be seen talking together, and wooing came to mind. Then he'd noticed Lady Jane.

"What's the matter?" Randall inquired solicitously. "Is your knee troubling you?"

Armand stopped watching the vivacious, beautiful Adelaide who kissed with such heart-stopping passion, and turned to his companion. "Yes," he replied, for that was partially the truth. His knee did hurt.

Meanwhile, Adelaide trotted past them, the bearded man's arm around her slender waist.

She'd made him forget everything and everyone while they kissed, including Bayard. Damn the woman—and damn that black-haired knave dancing with her. "Who's that with Lady Adelaide? I don't recall seeing him at court before."

"That's Sir Oliver de Leslille. Most of his family's estates are in Ireland. I must say I'm rather surprised Lady Adelaide accepted his invitation. She's never danced with him before."

Randall's wistful gaze drifted toward the minstrels, and the young lady sitting near them.

"Why don't you go talk to Lady Eloise?" Armand suggested, taking his mind from his own troubles for a moment. "She's all by herself and would surely welcome an intelligent conversation."

Randall blushed to the roots of his hair. "Oh, I couldn't. I wouldn't know what to say."

"You know a lot about music. Talk about that."

A stubborn set came to Randall's lips. "Why don't *you* ask her to dance? You have before."

"I give you my solemn word that although Lady Eloise seems a very sweet and charming young woman, I only asked her to dance to avoid dancing with Lady Hildegard," Armand sincerely replied.

Randall appeared to struggle between relief and annoyance. "You used her to get away from Hildegard?"

"Wouldn't you? And it should comfort you to know Lady Eloise wasn't happy to be asked, either. I'm sure she would have preferred to refuse, but she didn't want to offend me."

Randall smiled, and as he got up to go, Lady Mary came sidling up to them.

"I hear you were a very naughty boy this afternoon, my lord," she said, addressing Armand as Randall beat a hasty retreat.

Armand forced himself to smile, although obviously Adelaide had been right to worry about rumor and gossip. It was also true that his reputation had suffered since the surrender of Marchant, but to judge by Lady Mary's bright, eager eyes, that shouldn't affect his chances for an advantageous marriage. "Was I?"

Lady Mary waggled a long, bony finger at him. "Sneaking out of the hall like that and depriving the ladies of your company."

She must not have heard about the kiss. "I was overwhelmed by all the beauty and clever conversation."

Lady Mary looked as if she didn't believe him, as well she should not, but he continued to smile nonetheless.

"Where did you go?" she asked.

"To see my horse."

That wasn't exactly a lie. He had gone to the stable, although much earlier in the day, to feed and water and brush the nag. The poor creature had been so pleased to see him, he'd felt guilty for not coming sooner. Afterward, he'd encountered Hildegard and escaped her as soon as he could—only to be forced to take refuge in that hut with Lady Adelaide. Which had been a different sort of torment.

"Oh, yes, I've heard about your horse," Lady Mary said. "Very mean-spirited and prone to biting."

"Not if he's shown the proper respect and affection."

Lady Mary lowered her voice and slid him a glance that managed to be both brazen and coy. "Like his master?"

"I don't bite."

"Pity," she murmured, her eyes glowing with seductive interest.

No doubt she hoped to arouse him, or at least encourage him. Unfortunately for Lady Mary, after that kiss with Adelaide, she could strip naked and he wouldn't care.

What the devil was wrong with him? He had come here to get the ransom for Bayard, and by God, he would. "Would you care to dance, Lady Mary?"

When she eagerly assented, Armand led her toward the other dancers in the center of the hall with a smile fixed upon his face, but a look akin to martyrdom in his eyes.

LATER THAT NIGHT, Adelaide made her way up the curved stairs toward her bedchamber in the east wing of the castle apartments. She hadn't been this exhausted since the day her father had died, still cursing God and her poor dead mother for not giving him sons.

How many men had she danced with tonight? Fifteen? Twenty? And none of them had sounded like those men in the garden.

Normally, she rarely danced, for she felt on display when she did, and she wanted to avoid raising the ire or jealousy of the other ladies.

Tonight, she hadn't even refused Sir Oliver's invitation, although his dark-eyed scrutiny always made her uneasy, and his voice was nothing like those they'd overheard. It was too deep, and he had an Irish accent—his inheritance from his mother, he'd said.

Of course, accents could be feigned, and perhaps the conspirators had somehow disguised their voices in the garden, or later in the hall.

Why would they do that, unless they'd feared being overheard? And which, then, were their natural voices—those in the garden or the hall?

It was also possible that the plotters were not even nobles. Servants crossed the garden to get from the courtiers' apartments to the hall all the time; no one would look askance at a small group of servants talking together for a moment.

As for Armand's impertinent, improper, unwelcome kiss, his reason for it *was* plausible, and yet...

A sound echoed in the narrow stairwell—a soft, slight scraping, as if something had rubbed against the step or wall, like a heel or the edge of a scabbard.

Adelaide quickened her pace, hurrying to reach the guest chambers where she could expect to find servants waiting for their masters and mistresses to retire, including the maidservant the steward had assigned her.

She missed her footing on one of the low, worn steps and fell on her hands and knees. A strong hand grabbed her arm and started to pull her up.

Panicking, she swung hard and hit a face.

Armand de Boisbaston's face.

"God's teeth!" he growled, putting a hand to his cheek.

"You scared me!" she exclaimed, her heart beating like a startled bird's wings. "I thought you might be one of the assassins."

"If I was," he said through clenched teeth, "it might

be because you aroused my suspicions with your behavior in the hall tonight. I gather it's not usually your habit to converse with every male in the hall, or dance with any man who asks, but you were certainly the merry gadabout tonight. You couldn't have drawn more attention to yourself if you tried."

Adelaide didn't appreciate his criticism and raised her chin. "I thought time was of the essence, so I talked to as many men as I could. Are you truly distressed to think I put myself at risk, or are you upset because a mere woman might prove to be more useful in such a matter than a mighty warrior?"

"I'm upset because you deliberately put yourself in danger."

"If I can prevent a battle for the throne, then I'll put myself in danger. And where was all this noble concern for me when you kissed me and risked my reputation?

"What have *you* done to determine who is plotting against the archbishop and William Marshal, my lord, except talk to Randall FitzOsbourne and dance with Lady Mary? Have you already determined, as I have, that it was most likely *not* any of the noblemen in the hall this evening that we heard? Have you, too, concluded that it must be a high-ranking servant, clerk or soldier to speak with such an accent and yet not be in attendance on the king?"

"I've not been idle," he impatiently replied. "I spoke with Godwin, one of the soldiers here, and he told me three men left Ludgershall before the evening meal—a clerk from Salisbury with a message for the bishop, a steward from a castle belonging to Sir Francis de Farnby, and a tailor from London who'd brought some samples of cloth for the queen."

"I hardly think a London tailor could be the perpetrator of such a plot."

"If he *was* a tailor," Armand shot back.

That gave her a moment's pause before she continued just as defiantly. "Perhaps the conspirators are *not* gone, and since they may still be here, we should continue to look for them, in any way we can."

"I will not allow you to put yourself in jeopardy."

She wasn't going to let him, or any man, intimidate her, or tell her what to do. "You have no right to rule me, my lord, so I don't need your permission, your protection, your approval or your help to do what I must do. Now, if I have your *gracious* leave, I am going to bed, and tomorrow, I may very well discover I have to speak to several of the king's clerks. That, I *will* do, whether I have your permission or not."

She swept her skirts behind her and continued up the stairs, determined to prove to Armand de Boisbaston that she was no flighty, foolish woman overwhelmed by his looks, his kiss or his masculine arrogance.

While pretending to fall in love with him because *he* had made that necessary.

ARMAND GLARED after Adelaide a moment, then turned and marched back down the steps to the hall. God's blood, of all the high-handed, stubborn women! She was *precisely* the sort of female he would *never* marry!

He was so angry and engrossed in silently denouncing Adelaide, he didn't see the shadow that shifted in the flickering torchlight when he left the stairwell.

Or the person who made it.

CHAPTER SIX

"WHERE ARE YOU off to, Godwin?" Armand asked the soldier as they crossed the courtyard together after breaking the fast the next morning.

Instead of a gambeson and helmet, Godwin was dressed in tunic, shirt and breeches. He'd also been whistling a jaunty tune as he skirted several puddles left from the previous night's rain.

"I just finished my turn on the walk and now I'm on my way to the village," Godwin replied.

"May I join you? I've had a yearning for some fine ale, and the earl's told me many times about an alewife here who makes a good brew."

That was certainly true. However, Armand also didn't want to remain in the castle where Lady Adelaide would be, and it was possible that one or two of the conspirators might be staying in the village.

It had been enough of a strain breaking the fast in the hall with her—acting as if he wanted nothing more than to win that lady's love, gazing at her from afar as if she were the goddess of his fortunes, all the while knowing her answering smiles were only intended to make their ruse believable.

At least he hadn't had to sit beside her. Even if he had, though, surely he would have been able to control himself better than he had last night.

"Aye, that would be Bessy," Godwin replied with a chortle. "I'm surprised you never tried some of Bessy's best before. It's a full-bodied brew—just like her."

"I never stayed in Ludgershall long enough before," Armand admitted as they went through the barbican and headed for the village.

As the sun warmed his back and sparkled on the water of the small river that wound its way through the lower meadow known as Honey Bottom, he noted that Ludgershall was clearly prospering under the rule of the Earl of Pembroke. Several two story half-timbered buildings, with stalls for merchandise below and living quarters above, lined the green. A smithy belched smoke into the crisp morning air, and several elderly men had gathered beneath the wide oak beside it, sheltered from the summer sun. Other cottages were spread along the road before giving way to farmers' fields.

The aromas of smoke and cooking meat, chickens and pigs, wet wool and mud, all combined to remind Armand that he was back in England, and free. He'd spent many happy hours in the village on his family's estate, avoiding his stepmother.

His cell in France had been as dark as dusk during the day, as chill as autumn, and black as pitch at night.

He'd had no candle, no rush light, no torch—nothing to relieve the gloom. That had preyed on his mind as much as his regrets, his fears for his men, and his concern about Bayard, who'd been commanding another of the king's castles before it, too, had fallen.

The sight of the tavern, with its sign portraying two stags' heads swinging outside the door, brought his thoughts back to the present, and the pungent scents of ale, straw, beef stew and bread filled his nostrils as Godwin led the way inside the low building.

Several farmers were seated in a corner, deep in discussion about the wool crop. A traveling merchant napped in the corner near the hearth, a plate containing a heel of bread and the remains of a thick stew near his elbow, his mug of ale clutched in one hand and precariously perched on his large belly. Two young men were sprawled at another table watching the sleeping merchant like two foxes eying a single hen, quietly making bets on when the mug would tip and spill the ale.

A pleasant-looking, buxom woman in a loose-fitting gown belted with a large apron greeted Godwin warmly and nodded at a table and bench not far from a large cask of ale that had already been tapped. "Sit ye there, boys, and I'll fetch you a mug of my best."

It had been a long time since anyone had called Armand de Boisbaston a boy, yet he was far from offended; indeed, he quite liked her familiar address. It made him feel like a youth again.

Because he also wanted to speak to Godwin about something important, he was pleased to note that the bench and table she indicated were in a corner of the room. They wouldn't be overheard by the other customers or anyone passing by the small windows, for the shutters were open to let in the fresh summer air.

"Would you like a bite to eat, too?" Bessy asked.

Godwin grinned. "Aye, some bread and stew for me. What about you, my lord?"

Armand shook his head. He'd rather save the money, although the aroma wafting in from the kitchen made his mouth water.

"As you will," Bessy said with a toss of her light brown hair before heading to the kitchen.

"Well, my lord?" Godwin asked as he slid onto the bench. "Was I lying? Isn't Bessy something?"

"She is," Armand agreed.

Godwin chuckled and leaned closer. "I tell you, my lord, if I could get her to marry me, I'd be a happy man."

"You'd have both a pretty wife and a business that seems to be prospering," Armand agreed. "She must be busy these days with all the people visiting Ludgershall while the king's in residence."

"Aye, she is. Merchants and tradesmen from London and all over England have been coming here." Godwin lowered his voice. "She could do without them *routiers,* though. A bad lot, the bunch o' them."

Armand thought of another pretty woman who had to endure men's unwanted attention, and felt a twinge of regret that he hadn't come up with a better plan to confer with her.

Bessy set down two frothing mugs of ale and shook her head when Armand went to pay. "You're Armand de Boisbaston, aren't you?"

"I am."

"Thought so. I heard about your hair. No charge for you, then, my lord. Keep your money for your brother's ransom. He come here once and did me a bit of service. There was a rough lout who wouldn't pay for his meal. He paid up quick enough when he had the tip of your brother's sword at his throat." She grinned at the memory, then frowned when Godwin's hand went to the purse at his belt.

"Nor you, neither, Godwin," she said. "Your ale's free till Christmas for fixing my roof."

She winked at the soldier, and then hurried off to take more bread to the farmers.

"She's very generous," Armand noted.

"Aye," Godwin murmured as Bessy lifted the mug from the slumbering merchant's hand without waking him.

As the pair of young men chastised her for spoiling their entertainment, she gave them a maternal smile and said, "Mind your manners, boys, or I'll make Moll stay in the kitchen."

They groaned and Armand turned to Godwin. "Who's Moll?"

"Bessy's daughter, and as pretty as her mother."

At nearly the same time, a young woman appeared in the doorway leading to the kitchen. She was very pretty, in an apple-cheeked, robust way. She held a plate of steaming stew in her hand, with a small loaf on the side, and although she didn't look at her two young admirers, Armand realized she was well aware they were there.

She smiled at Godwin as she set the food before him and acknowledged Armand's presence with a little dip, although as she did, she slid the two young men a glance. She had an even saucier swing to her hips when she strolled toward them afterward.

"A young unmarried woman like that can cause a lot of trouble in a village," Armand said.

"Oh, she's a good girl, is Moll," Godwin replied as he ate the stew with gusto. "And it's no secret she's sweet on the smith's son. They'd be married by now if he wasn't livin' with his parents. He's started buildin' a house, though, so it's likely they'll marry before the winter."

"Those two lads will be disappointed."

"Not much. They just like to tease her."

And indeed, their easy banter with the young woman belied any serious intent on their part.

After looking around to make sure no one was paying any attention to them, Armand leaned closer to Godwin and got down to business. "I'm glad I met you this morning, Godwin. I have a message for the earl, and I'd like you to take it."

Godwin stopped eating and regarded him gravely. "Of course, my lord, if the steward will give me leave."

"I think he will," Armand said. "I need to send another to Canterbury, as well. Is there someone you could recommend to take it, someone who's as trustworthy as you?"

Godwin's expression was thoughtful, as well as proud. "Bert's a good lad and he can't read, so even if I'm wrong, he wouldn't know what was in the letter."

Satisfied, Armand nodded. "I'll write the letters and speak to the steward as soon as we return."

"What ho within!" a jovial young man shouted outside to accompaniment of laughter and the stamp of horses' hooves. "Bessy my love, I'm parched!"

The door to the tavern burst open and five young noblemen came stumbling into the taproom, laughing and swearing. Leading the pack was the already drunk Sir Alfred de Marleton, followed by Lord Richard d'Artage. Then came Charles de Bergendie who Armand knew by reputation; he was said to be a worthy opponent in a melee, despite his youth. Sir Edmond de Sansuren and his brother, Roger, brought up the rear. Armand knew nothing bad of those two, except that they seemed to follow whoever was of a mind to lead them. Apparently, they were following Alfred today, at least as far as wine was concerned.

Bessy marched into the room just as a sixth young

man joined the band of drunken knights—the dark-haired, bearded and seemingly sober Sir Oliver.

"Well, now, what have we here?" the alewife asked, one hand on her ample hip.

Although she smiled, Armand was quite sure she was neither pleased nor impressed with these potential customers, whether they were noblemen or not. Her daughter, meanwhile, sidled toward her mother, and the door to the kitchen.

"Some very thirsty fellows," Sir Alfred said with a sodden grin. "We thought we might find something to assuage it here."

"Aye, you *might*," Bessy answered.

Alfred leered at Moll. "Oh, I think we will. And we're hungry, too."

He lunged for Moll, grabbed her arm and pulled her toward him. "Very hungry," he murmured, running his hand over her bodice, "and here's just the morsel to sate us."

As Moll emitted a screech of fear, Armand jumped to his feet. Godwin rose, too, his hand on the hilt of his sword. The two lads, their faces red with anger, likewise got up. The group of farmers stood more slowly, but their expressions were just as angry. The merchant, awakened by the commotion, looked about wildly, his hand going to the handle of the dagger visible in his belt.

"Are you forgetting that you are a knight, sworn to protect women and children?" Armand demanded of the young noblemen, his stern gaze on Alfred, who was holding the frightened Moll in a grip that made her wince.

"I don't have to listen to you," Alfred declared. "You're no saint, and neither's Lady Adelaide, from what we've heard."

Then he kissed Moll's cheek, making her squirm with disgust.

"Let her go," Armand commanded. He didn't raise his voice, but when Armand de Boisbaston issued an order in that tone, he didn't have to.

Scowling but obeying, Alfred shoved Moll away. She ran to her mother, who glared at the knights as if she wanted them boiled in oil.

She probably did.

"The girls of this village are not doxies for your amusement," Armand said to the swaying Alfred and his friends. "If your oath of chivalry is not enough to make you behave as an honorable man should, I remind you that this estate belongs to the Earl of Pembroke, one of the most chivalrous men alive, and not a man you want for an enemy. What do you think he'll do if he hears you've been abusing his tenants?"

Sir Edmond threw out his chest like an indignant pigeon. "Our father—"

"Is one of the king's valued counsellors," Armand interrupted. "What do you think *he'll* say when he finds out you've risked the ire of William Marshal?"

All trace of bravado fled Edmond's face. "You'd tell him?"

"If I must."

Edmond nearly tripped over his own feet trying to get to the door, his brother hard on his heels. Lord Richard shrugged and started after them, while Sir Oliver stayed where he was, watching them all as if this were a performance staged for his benefit.

Armand coolly regarded the three remaining knights. "I suggest, my lords, that you return to the castle at once."

"You can't make us go," Alfred slurred.

Armand raised a brow. "Can't I?"

Alfred felt for his sword. "You wouldn't dare attack me!"

Armand held his arms away from his body. "Am I attacking anybody?"

As Alfred continued to try to locate the hilt of his sword, he cried, "You don't scare me!"

"Then I appeal to whatever remains of your honor. Your behavior here has been a disgrace."

"I've done nothing to be ashamed of! Why, I hardly touched her! You'd think I'd raped her, the way you're acting." His own words seemed to encourage him. "And since when are *you* the arbiter of chivalry and honor? You seduced Lady Adelaide. It's all over the court that you two were making love in the garden."

It took a great effort not to strike the sot for his

insolence, and to wipe the smirk off his face. "We did not make love in the garden."

Alfred and Charles stared at him with blatant disbelief, while Sir Oliver's face betrayed nothing.

Albert straightened his shoulders. "Well, nobody but the lady can vouch for that. *Everyone* knows you surrendered Marchant."

"What do you know of battle, bravery or defeat?" Armand asked, trying to hold on to his patience. "I surrendered after being besieged for months, when there was no hope of relief, and even then, only after the French king threatened to destroy the village and kill all the people in it. Would you rather I let Philip kill an entire village of innocent peasants? And have I not paid for my failure, if failure it was?"

Alfred didn't meet Armand's steadfast gaze. "I think...I think I'm a little drunk," he muttered.

"Yes, you are, although that's no excuse for your disgraceful behaviour," Armand said, his anger lessening. Young men in their cups often said and did things they later regretted, as had he, although he'd never accosted a woman. "Go back to Ludgershall and sleep it off."

He headed to the door, making it clear he intended to see that Alfred did as he was told, and believing there was hope for these young fellows yet, if they had other examples of honorable behaviour than the king and his sycophants.

"The rest of you, as well—back to Ludgershall," he ordered, holding the door open and waiting for them to pass.

Charles likewise made no protest, and left.

His head bowed, Alfred dutifully departed. For a moment, Armand thought the Irishman was going to refuse, but then he shrugged his shoulders and strolled out the door as if Armand's order was just a suggestion and he had nothing else to do.

Insolent pup!

Godwin also started to leave, until Armand waved him back. "Stay and finish your stew."

"Thank you, my lord," Godwin replied with a grin, and the women smiled gratefully as they bade Armand farewell.

As Armand was ensuring that the young knights returned to the castle without further incident, Adelaide walked briskly across the courtyard. In her hand she held a scroll, a letter to her sister Gillian that one of the king's clerks had written for her.

She didn't really need any man's aid to write a letter. She and her sisters had been taught to read and write by their father's steward, one of the many secrets in their father's household while he'd been alive. Her father had believed that educating women was a waste of time and effort, and by the time she was old enough to realize there was such a thing as reading and writing, her mother had been so worn out

giving birth to her sisters and other babies who had
not lived, she had no strength to teach her.

Adelaide, however, had not wanted to remain
ignorant. As she'd pointed out to her father when
he was in a rare, peaceable humor, being able to
read and write would increase her value to a potential husband.

His good humor had died in an instant, and he'd
thrown his goblet at her. "Think you know better than
me, girl?" he'd shouted.

Thankfully his steward, Samuel de Corlette, had
heard the exchange. Afterward, he'd told Adelaide
she was right to want to learn. "After all," he'd said,
smiling kindly, his face lined with furrows of stress
from dealing with her father all those years, "your
father will not live forever."

So he had not—and the day he died, not a single
person had mourned his passing.

It had been different when kind-hearted, patient
Samuel had died. He'd been born the bastard son of
a Norman foot soldier, but he'd been more honorable,
noble and kind than most noblemen she'd met, and
everyone at Averette had been saddened by the loss.

Here at Ludgershall, the clerks had flocked about
her like so many busy bees when she'd appeared in
their chamber and asked if any of them had a moment
to spare to write a letter for her. All had smiled and
several had offered, while she'd dithered and
demurred and apologized for taking them from their

worthy labors. She'd been able to hear most of them say something in response.

None of them had sounded like the men in the garden.

She wondered where Lord Armand was. She hadn't seen him since they'd broken the fast that morning, when he'd given a masterful impersonation of a lovestruck suitor, looking at her as if she held his happiness in her hands.

But any man who got so angry at her couldn't truly want her. Which was a comfort.

She hoped he was trying to find out who they'd overheard, and not merely pursuing a rich wife. She could appreciate his desire to free his brother but—

"My lady! Where are you off to in such a great hurry on this lovely summer day?"

Subduing a grimace, she halted and turned toward the stable where Francis de Farnby leaned against the door frame. She should have paid more attention to her surroundings so she could have avoided him; unfortunately, it was too late now.

"Good day, Sir Francis," she said. "You aren't hunting with the others?"

He shook his head. "Too muddy, and I think some of them had other sport in mind."

He obviously thought she should find his allusion to whoring amusing, which was even more proof that he was not a gentleman, in spite of his rank and wealth. She also supposed he expected her to be either impressed or curious as to why he'd stayed behind.

As if she cared. "If you'll pardon me—"

He hurried toward her and gave her an ingratiating smile.

"Actually, I was looking for you. I thought perhaps you'd decided to spend more time with the stallions."

His choice of words and the look in his eyes was enough to make her sneer, but she refrained. "I was preparing a letter for my sister at home."

"That would be Gillian?"

"Lady Gillian, yes. So if you'll excuse me, Sir Francis, I must ask the steward about a messenger."

"I'll walk with you."

Short of bluntly telling him to go away as she would have preferred, she had no choice but to allow Francis to accompany her as she headed toward the solar where the steward would likely be. Although as she disliked Francis, the king seemed to enjoy his company, and she didn't want to risk making an enemy of him.

"Writing to your sister seems to agree with you, my lady," he noted with another obsequious smile. "You look more beautiful than ever."

"Thank you." She would be polite, but she didn't have to be encouraging.

"I hear your younger sister is away from home."

"She's visiting friends in the north."

"I trust she'll have a sizeable escort when she

returns. These are dangerous times for young noble-women."

The tone of his voice made her feel as if a skeletal fingertip had run down her spine, and she clenched the scroll tightly. "I believe it has never been a perfectly safe time to be a young noblewoman."

"Surely you feel safe among the court?"

"Sometimes I fear court is the most dangerous place of all," she admitted with a smile that was only slightly strained.

"It need not be. You have the king's power within your grasp, if you would reach for it."

The idea of reaching for anything where John was concerned was so repugnant, it was all Adelaide could do not to curl her lip and say so. "I have no such ambition," she replied as they passed the chapel. "And need I remind you, the king is married."

"So what of that?" Francis replied. "His mistresses are richly rewarded and he would see that you were well married when he was done with you."

"To whom would you suggest I be given, my lord?" she asked, raising an interrogative brow as she paused near the outer steps that led to the solar. "You?"

Francis pulled her behind one of the hayricks, out of sight of the people in the yard.

Despite his action, Adelaide felt not fear, but indignation. After all, she had only to scream for help to arrive.

"You can cease acting the virtuous maid with me, my lady, and with the king, too," Francis said as he backed her toward the wall. "It was a fine performance while it lasted, but those days are at an end."

"I *am* a virtuous maid."

Francis sniffed with scorn, his face uncomfortably close to hers. "That's not what I heard. Should I go to Lord Armand and ask *him* about your virtue? And here I was thinking you were angry with Armand last night, or trying to make him jealous."

Francis trapped her against the wall, one hand on either side of her face, his nose inches from hers. "You've kept me and half the court dangling after you like fish on a line, yet you gave your maidenhead to that dog the first day he got here. What did he do, sing you a tale of woe about his terrible imprisonment? Complain about his ill treatment and the king's reluctance to come to his rescue as if he were a maiden waiting for a knight to save her?"

"Sir Francis, let me go, or I'll scream," Adelaide warned.

"God's blood, you women are all alike!" he charged, pressing closer. "A handsome face, a tale to make you weep and you throw off your clothes like any whore offered a coin."

"Are you calling my wife a *whore?*"

CHAPTER SEVEN

BEFORE Adelaide could even gasp, Armand leapt from the wall walk above, grabbed Francis by his tunic and threw him hard against the wall.

"Wife?" Francis cried, as shocked as she as he tried to regain his balance.

"As good as," Armand said, his expression fierce. "Lady Adelaide has agreed to marry me."

What in the name of the saints—! First that kiss and now this?

"I don't believe it!" Francis retorted. "The whole court would know if that were true. You have to get permission from the king to marry one of his wards. You haven't."

"I'm going to speak to the king now that he's returned from the hunt," Armand said, taking Adelaide's hand in his firm grasp. "Come, beloved. You see the trouble our secrecy has already caused?"

Not giving her a moment to reply, he pulled her around the hayrick, back into the courtyard that was now crowded with snorting horses, barking hounds, boisterous men and soldiers, as well as several ladies who'd been hunting that morning.

Adelaide didn't care if all the host of heaven were assembled there. She could have dealt with Francis. He was a dog who barked loudly, but lacked teeth, a coward who would never physically assault one of the king's wards.

Even so, she had been relieved when Armand had appeared like an avenging angel—until he'd made that incredible, false assertion that they wished to marry. That would surely reach the king's ears, and soon.

Was he truly that ignorant of John's temper, or was he always prone to blurt out the first thing that came into his head, a tendency she herself had to fight?

"Why did you tell him we wanted to marry?" she demanded as they skirted the noisy crowd.

"Because our kiss has been turned into something more serious than wooing," he grimly replied. "It seems gossip has us making love in the garden."

Her grip on his hand tightened with dismay. "I warned you about the scandal that kiss could cause. You should have denied we made love, since it isn't true."

"Whatever regrets I have for my hasty decision yesterday—and I assure you, I *do* regret it—we have no choice now but to try to lessen the damage."

"You could have done that without saying we wanted to marry," Adelaide pointed out, halting in the shadow of the chapel's porch. He stopped, too, as she pulled her hand from his grasp.

"Unfortunately, my lady," he said, crossing his arms, "claiming that we hope to marry is the only way to retain even a portion of your honor. You know as well as I do that we could deny that rumor from now until the day we die, and people would still believe we made love in garden."

She opened her mouth to protest, except that he was right. She was as trapped by that kiss as she'd been by Francis's arms.

"And that is not the only reason I said what I did," he continued. "My father was a lascivious, dissolute man, and I will not have people believe I'm following in his immoral footsteps."

"While I appreciate your concerns," she answered, sympathizing with that last reason although she was still upset, "you've again acted without considering all the consequences."

"There was no time to *consider,* my lady," he replied. "As for the consequences, I had no choice but to offer you the protection of my name and reputation."

As if she should be grateful for his most reluctant sacrifice, although he himself had made it necessary. "I don't need your protection," she returned. "I didn't ask for it and I don't want it."

"Whether you want it or not, it's necessary, and I am bound by my oath as a knight to give it. Otherwise, what do you think will happen if Francis or another of his ilk comes upon you alone?"

He was, unfortunately, right about her possible fate

if men believed her a loose woman, but she wasn't about to express overwhelming gratitude for the protection he offered. After all, it was his fault she needed it. "So now, thanks to you, my situation at court has become even more perilous."

"Not if you're betrothed to me. Or would you rather I'd left you with Francis?"

"I could have dealt with him myself."

"As you were?"

"As I've been doing for weeks, until you kissed me."

"I admit that kiss was a terrible mistake—but I repeat, my lady, what's done is done, and unless you want to start sharing the beds of courtiers, we have little choice but to become betrothed. I also point out, *my lady,* that you are not my first choice of bride. I wanted a gentle, demure wife."

He abruptly grabbed her shoulders, hauled her close and kissed her.

Upset by his words, angry at his presumption, she bit his lip hard enough to make him stop, although not enough to bleed.

Hissing a curse, he slid his mouth toward her ear. "The king is coming this way. Even if you hate me, woman, act enthused, unless you want John chasing you again. I'm your best chance to prevent that."

If it was a performance he wanted, by God, she'd give him one that would leave his efforts in the dust.

She relaxed against him, supple as a willow branch, and with sensuous deliberation, caressed his lips with her mouth. She ran her hands up his broad back, then into his thick, waving hair.

Her body didn't know this was supposed to be a ruse. Her blood heated like iron in a smith's forge, molten and searing, throbbing with an excitement as old as mankind. When his tongue slid between her parted lips, she swayed with genuine longing, and a need that seemed to spring up from within her with all the power of nature itself.

"By the teeth of God, what have we here?" John declared. "Have you no respect for a sacred edifice?"

As they broke the kiss and turned to face the pompous king, Armand struggled to regain his shattered self-control. The sight of Adelaide being accosted by that slimy snake Francis had roused his ire, while her kiss had aroused...something different.

"We're sorry to have caused any offense, sire," Adelaide replied as coolly as an empress, and as if she weren't seething with wrathful indignation, although he was sure she was.

However upset she was, and however justified, he was right. If people believed they'd already made love, unless they were betrothed, she would be the prey of every lustful courtier at Ludgershall, whether they were married or not, including the king.

And he would appear to be the same sort of lustful scoundrel his father had been.

"As a matter of fact, my liege, we were coming to seek an audience with you," he said, managing—

just—to sound equally calm. "Lady Adelaide and I would like your permission to marry."

Fortunately, Adelaide didn't protest. Perhaps the appearance of Francis sidling toward the king's party made her appreciate this new, necessary lie.

The king's eyes narrowed with suspicion, as well they might. John was not a wise man, but he was no simpleton, either. "This comes as quite a surprise, my lady."

"It did to me, as well, sire," she agreed, "but Cupid's arrow aims where it will, and we are powerless against it."

"As Your Majesty can attest," Armand added.

One explanation John had given for his sudden marriage to Isabel had been his overwhelming love for the young lady, although not a single soul believed it. Their marriage had prevented Hugh the Brown from gaining control of a vast territory; as for the very young lady, it had made her a queen.

"I see," the king replied, his gaze flicking between them. "This warrants some discussion better conducted in private. Isabel, await me in the hall."

Turning on his heel, John gestured for Adelaide and Armand to follow him.

"Eloise will wonder why I didn't tell her about the betrothal," Adelaide whispered as they hurried to keep up with the king. "I don't suppose you thought of *that*. And what will you tell Randall?"

God's wounds, Armand thought, what a web of deception they were weaving—and all to save a worm like John. Unfortunately, his oath as a knight would permit no less. "We need an excuse."

"You mean another lie."

He ignored her disgusted tone. "We can say we wanted to wait until we had the king's permission."

"Aren't you a clever fellow?" she muttered as they reached the earl's solar, and it was not a compliment.

The solar was another well-appointed chamber, with a brazier for warmth when it was colder, and large, unlit candles in a bronze stand polished to a high gloss. A cabinet containing tithe rolls and other estate records stood in one corner. John waited beside an oaken trestle table while Armand opened the wooden shutter covering the window to provide more light. There was not a speck of dust on any of the furnishings.

As Armand returned to stand beside Adelaide, John settled into the earl's chair and rested his elbows on the waxed table.

"So, my lord, you have fallen in love with this lady and wish to marry her?"

"I have and I do, sire," he said as if he meant it.

"I love her, too," John replied, "as a father loves his daughter, and as a father with a daughter, I do not let her go lightly."

Armand could guess where this was going. The king required an inducement to approve of their betrothal, and in John's case, that meant a bribe.

He was partly responsible for the predicament he and Adelaide were now in, and he could guess how he would feel if he were in Adelaide's place, forced to listen to them haggling over her as if she were no more than a horse or dog. He would spare the proud Adelaide that humiliation if he could. "Perhaps, sire, it would be better if we had this conversation alone."

He felt, rather than saw, Adelaide's sharp glance. "Majesty," she said, "since my future is in the balance, I—"

"Lord Armand is right," the king declared. "He will come to you and let you know our decision. You may wait for him—" he gave her a chilly smile "— in the garden."

So, he'd heard the rumors, too, probably while he was on the hunt.

Adelaide made a graceful obeisance before turning toward Armand. "Adieu, my lord."

It had been obvious from the moment he'd jumped from the wall walk that she was upset, angry and indignant. Yet beneath those obvious emotions he'd sensed her relief that he had come to her aid, as well as the iron will to hide even that slight sign of vulnerability.

As she walked away now, more regal and dignified than John could ever hope to be, he suddenly realized that as he wore chainmail to battle, her cold demeanor and haughty bearing were her armor on this different sort of battleground, hiding and protecting the kinder, more compassionate Adelaide he'd met in the stables that first day.

"You're a fortunate man to have won that particular lady's regard," the king said, reminding Armand where he was, and why. "I've already had several offers for her hand."

"I am indeed fortunate, sire," Armand replied, looking at the man whose selfishness, greed and ambition had caused the deaths of so many good men, and put women like Adelaide in jeopardy. "I confess I was surprised to discover that she wasn't already betrothed."

"Thus far, it hasn't suited my purposes to bestow Lady Adelaide's hand on anyone, nor has the lady herself seemed anxious to wed."

"Apparently, she's changed her mind."

"So it seems," John dryly replied. "So the question becomes, how much are you willing to give to have her?"

"Whatever is necessary," Armand said, "although I hope you'll remember that I've suffered in your loyal service and that my brother, also your loyal vassal, continues to endure imprisonment until his ransom can be paid."

"Ah, yes, your brother Bayard. He remains in France, then?"

Rage welled up within Armand. Of course Bayard was still in France. He would be there until his ransom was paid—and John knew it.

In spite of his rising ire, however, Armand kept his voice even and his expression as calm as possible. "Yes, sire."

"You plan to pay the ransom?"

Considering John's acrimonious relations with his own brothers, he shouldn't be surprised John asked that question. "Yes, sire, as soon as I'm able."

"Yet I note you've found time to woo and win the most beautiful woman at court—although you seem to have accomplished that with remarkable speed."

"Our love has been a delightful surprise."

The king was clearly sceptical. "I'm sure. How much is your brother's ransom?"

"Five hundred marks."

The king's beady eyes gleamed in the light streaming in through the arched window. "I gather you haven't got the money, or you'd have already paid for his freedom."

"That is so, Majesty," Armand replied. "I've only managed to raise about three hundred marks."

Whatever faint hope Armand had had that John would offer to pay the rest of the ransom, or even the entire amount, were quickly dashed.

"Pity. I'm sure the earl would loan you the rest if he were here. Alas, he's not." John's expression grew speculative. "If Bayard dies, you won't have to give him a portion of your father's estate. It would all be yours."

Armand still hid his rising anger. "My father

always made it clear that Bayard was to have the portion of the estate that was his mother's dower. Since it was his mother's, I have no complaint."

"You're a very generous fellow, Armand. Have you no fears that this half brother of yours will try to take your father's estate from you?"

"He knows he has no right to it, and he's a man of honor, sire."

"Well, well, if you're content, so be it. And now you wish to marry Lady Adelaide, one of the most beautiful women I've ever seen. Cold, though, to my thinking. Is she cold?"

"She's warm enough for me, Your Majesty," he answered carefully.

John barked a laugh. "So I assume, for otherwise I'm sure you could win a richer prize."

The king became serious again. "Indeed, I am in sore need of funds myself. It's going to cost a great deal of money to regain my possessions in France. If you are to marry Lady Adelaide, I will require your three hundred marks."

Armand's hand went to the hilt of his sword. "Sire, that is all the money I have."

John got to his feet. "I suggest you take your hand from your blade, my lord. I remind you that I hold the fate of you, your brother and the woman you claim to love in the palm of my hand."

Armand had no intention of attacking John. If he did, he would have only a brief moment of satisfaction before he was arrested, and nothing more. Bayard would still be imprisoned and Adelaide's honor compromised.

"There is no need for alarm, Majesty," he assured the king.

"Good," John replied, "especially if you want Lady Adelaide. What is your game with her, I wonder? From what we hear, you've already plucked that particular rose, although other men have tried and failed. That should be enough to content you."

For a single moment, as he once again envisioned Bayard in a cold, dank cell, Armand was tempted to keep his money and let Adelaide go—until he thought of the way Francis had treated Adelaide that morning.

Surely if Bayard knew the circumstances, he would say that a woman's honor and safety must come before a knight's. He would agree that Armand had to do the right thing by Adelaide and marry her, even if he had to linger awhile longer in captivity. "I would have Lady Adelaide for my wife, even if it costs me three hundred marks and means my brother, your loyal servant, must suffer more."

Apparently not caring a whit for Bayard's fate, the king smiled much as Armand imagined a snake would smile if it had lips. "There is one other condition you must meet, my lord, before I will agree. You must reaffirm your oath of fealty to me in the hall tonight."

God's blood! As if his loyalty was suspect, despite his service in Normandy!

"And you will do so on bended knee."

As enraged as he was, and although his pride protested, Armand knew he had little choice but to agree, unless he wanted to throw Adelaide to the jackals of the court. "Very well, sire."

John's eyes gleamed with lust. "I'll expect the lady to be grateful, too."

The king had finally gone too far.

Armand crossed his powerful arms and let his ire show on his face. "You demand money needed to secure my brother's release, you ask me to humiliate myself before your court, and to that I have agreed— but I will *never* share my wife with any man, be he king or commoner."

John tapped his chin with a bejewelled finger and regarded Armand with arrogant animosity, reminding Armand that whatever else John was, he was a Plantagenet, a family rumored to be descended from the Devil. "You would refuse a direct command of your king?"

There were some things no honorable man could countenance, and there were some things not even John should dare to do. "That one I would, and I would have the backing of the church and many a man at court if I did."

Fortunately, John reconsidered, or else he decided Adelaide wasn't worth the possible trouble, for he laughed and said, "By the teeth of God, it must be love, indeed! Therefore I shall ask no more than that you to bring me three hundred marks before the

evening meal and swear your oath again to me
tonight."

But there was hostility in John's eyes, too. "Otherwise, my fine and haughty lord, you may find
yourself in an *English* dungeon."

CHAPTER EIGHT

RANDALL WAS WAITING for Armand when he left the solar.

"What's going on?" he asked as he limped after his enraged friend. "One moment you're looking for a wealthy bride, the next you're closeted in the solar with John seeking permission to marry Lady Adelaide. She's very beautiful, of course, and a good friend to Lady Eloise, but her family's poor. I just about fell over when I heard where you'd gone and why."

Armand paused to give Randall a chance to catch up, and also to give himself time to calm himself. Only once before in all his life had he been this angry—when he'd learned John wouldn't be sending the reinforcements he needed to save Marchant.

"We didn't want to say anything about the betrothal until John agreed," he said, using the lie he'd suggested to Adelaide. "As for our haste, I can't put my feelings for Lady Adelaide into words," he continued as they headed toward the garden at a slower pace.

"So that's why Lady Eloise was equally ignorant," Randall said.

"You spoke to Lady Eloise?" He might be able to take some comfort from this bizarre situation if it helped Randall gain the woman he loved.

Randall blushed like the most bashful maiden in Wiltshire. "I was driven to it."

"And what does Lady Eloise think of our betrothal?"

"She approves, although she was hurt that Adelaide hadn't told her anything, either." Randall paused to catch his breath, reminding Armand to slow down. "Where are we going?"

"To the garden. Adelaide's waiting there to hear the king's answer."

"I don't suppose John simply said yes," Randall proposed as they walked on.

"I have to pay him three hundred marks. Unfortunately, Bayard will have to wait a little longer."

"That's terrible!"

"But not surprising. Can you give me the loan of sixteen marks to add to the money I've collected for Bayard's ransom?"

"Of course."

Armand put a smile on his face. "Then wish me joy, my friend, for I'm to be married to the Lady Adelaide."

ELOISE FAIRLY POUNCED on Adelaide when she found her waiting in the garden for Armand.

"Is it true?" she asked, her hazel eyes alight. "Are you betrothed to Lord Armand?"

"I don't know," Adelaide answered honestly, still trying to come to terms with Armand's brazen and unexpected announcement. "I'm to wait for Armand here, and he'll come to me and tell me if the king has agreed. Will you keep me company while I wait?"

Otherwise, she might give way to tears—not of sorrow or dismay, but frustration. Once again, her fate lay in a man's hands.

"Of course," Eloise said, slipping her arm in Adelaide's and strolling down one of the cobbled paths with her. "I must confess I didn't believe you wanted to marry Armand de Boisbaston until Randall FitzOsbourne told me Armand hadn't said anything to him about your plans, either. He wondered why else you would both be with the king, and I had to agree. And now I find it's true after all."

"I wanted to tell you, but we decided to keep our hope a secret until we had the king's permission to marry," Adelaide said. She hated having to tell Eloise a falsehood, and her anger toward the unknown conspirators increased. They had made this dishonesty necessary.

Eloise's expression grew worried. "I hope you won't hold what I said about dancing with him against me."

"Of course not," Adelaide assured her as they turned and walked back along the path toward the gate. "I would have been annoyed, too, if I thought any man had asked me to dance simply to avoid another woman."

"Are you going to ask him to trim his hair?"

"I think not. I rather like it."

That was actually true, she realized. She liked Armand's long hair. It made him seem like one of the warriors of ancient days—a wild Celt, or a Saxon king.

"Well, even with that hair, he's a very handsome man. And so chivalrous! Why, Randall told me things about his defense of Marchant that brought tears to my eyes! He shared all the meager provisions equally and kept his men's spirits up right until the last, telling them there were no finer soldiers in all of Europe, and that he was proud to serve with them. They would all have died for him, you know, down to the last man, so Randall says. After Lord Armand was forced to surrender, he starved himself for days trying to keep his squire alive. The poor fellow died in his arms anyway. Randall told me the first place Armand went after he was freed—even before trying to raise his brother's ransom—was to his squire's father. He prostrated himself before the old man and begged his forgiveness for failing his son."

Adelaide could easily imagine Armand rallying his men, sharing what remained of the food and wine, cheering them even when things were grim. She could also picture him doing all he could to save his squire's life until he cradled the poor boy's limp body in his arms.

"Randall had tears in his eyes when he told me. He's such a kind-hearted fellow, and loyal, too. I think he would die for Armand if he had to."

Whatever else happened, this unfortunate business seemed to be bringing Eloise and the kind, gentle Randall together. "I'm glad to hear that Armand is an even finer man than I supposed," she said.

The garden gate opened and Adelaide's breath caught but instead of admitting Armand, Hildegard and her two most ardent acolytes, Lady Mary and Lady Wilhemina, entered. Behind them, and at a pace to match her infirm mother, came Lady Jane. Lady Ethel glared at Adelaide as if she were a criminal, while Jane gave Adelaide a surreptitious little smile as she sat beside her mother on the nearest bench.

"So, here is the *virtuous*, the *clever*, the *honorable* Lady Adelaide who's finally caught a husband by playing the whore," Hildegard sneered, a superior look on her waspish face.

"To think you surrendered just like that," she continued as she snapped her fingers, "after leading half the men of the court on a merry chase for months."

"Lord Armand is the first man I've met who made me want to yield," Adelaide replied evenly, serenely smoothing her skirts.

Hildegard looked as if she wanted to spew venom, while Lady Jane stifled a sigh.

"If any lady here has tried to get a husband by giving her body, it's you, Hildegard," Eloise charged, stepping in front of Adelaide. "Why, I would need the fingers of both hands to keep track of the men you've lain with in the past few months. It's no wonder Lord Richard isn't keen to marry you, although you've been sharing his bed for the past three weeks."

Hildegard's face turned as red as a cardinal's robe. "At least men find me attractive. No one's anxious to court *you*."

Adelaide gently moved Eloise out of the way. "I'm not surprised Eloise's finer qualities aren't apparent to you, Hildegard, since you lack *all* the virtues."

Crossing her arms, Hildegard ran an insolent gaze over Adelaide. "Who are you to act as if you rule here? You have no power at court, especially now that you belong to Lord Armand."

"I *belong* to no man!"

"Oh, yes, the high and mighty Lady Adelaide belongs to no one. She makes her own rules and acts as if everyone else is beneath her or a fool. She plays the queen although her father was nothing but a poor knight with a small estate who beat his wife to death—"

"He did not!" Her father was guilty of many things, but not murder.

"Yet we are to admire and respect you," Hildegard continued as if Adelaide hadn't spoken. "Well, I do not and I never will. I'm sure Armand de Boisbaston will rue the day he marries you!"

"He will not," Adelaide retorted, determined to

refute Hildegard's hateful words. "I shall be the best, most loving wife a man could desire."

"Hussy!" Lady Ethel cried out, pointing a shaking finger at Adelaide. "Disgusting! Disgraceful!"

Adelaide couldn't help blushing; nevertheless, she didn't take her attention from Hildegard. "How can I expect a woman like you, who thinks only of herself, to know anything about love?"

Hildegard raised her pointy little chin. "I know a great deal about it."

"I'm not referring to what you do with your body, Hildegard," Adelaide replied. "I'm referring to your heart, assuming that you have one."

Hildegard's face turned purple with rage—a most unbecoming sight. "I hate you!"

"Do you? Oh, dear. I shall have to cry myself to sleep over that   provided I remember."

Hildegard's mouth moved noiselessly for a moment, then she turned on her heel and strode to the gate. She opened it with so much force, she nearly tore it off the leather hinges.

After darting a hostile glance at Adelaide, Mary and Wilhemina followed, trotting to catch up with their angry friend.

Meanwhile, Lady Jane rose and helped her mother to her feet. "Let's get some wine, Mama," she suggested a bit warily, as if she feared Adelaide might quarrel with her, too. "I do believe it's become rather chilly out here."

Adelaide went to open the gate for them, but neither lady said a word as they went by.

Adelaide stifled a sigh of dismay. She'd always liked and admired Jane for her patient devotion to her grumbling, querulous mother.

Eloise gave Adelaide a comforting smile. "Lady Ethel would have us all in convents until we marry if she had the power."

"Not you," Adelaide replied as they walked back into the garden, happy to talk about something other than Hildegard or Armand.

"Oh, especially me, I think. She keeps telling me what a fine nun I'd make. I must confess, I don't know how Lady Jane manages to be so good to her. I think I'd have run off years ago."

"You know you'd be just as dutiful," Adelaide replied as they sat on the bench Jane and her mother had vacated.

She wondered how much longer Armand was going to be, and what the king had decided.

"So would you," Eloise said. "You cared for your father, and he was hardly a loving parent."

"I did my duty," Adelaide replied, as the gate flew open and a resolute and obviously angry Armand strode into the garden, followed by Randall FitzOsburne.

Adelaide suddenly felt as if she were again thirteen years old, with her sisters huddled behind her as their father stalked toward them in one of his rages. She jumped to her feet and her heart began to pound.

Every sense seemed heightened as she raised her hand, palm out. "Stop there, my lord!"

He halted abruptly, his angry expression altering to one of confusion.

He wasn't her enraged father coming to take out his frustration and rage with harsh, undeserved denunciations and the occasional blow. Her father was dead and buried, and she was supposed to be in love with this man.

"Alas," she cried, clasping her hands together in a gesture of despair. "Has the king refused?"

What would happen to her if he had?

As Armand's full lips curved up into a smile, it was like watching a player don a mask before a performance. He crossed the space between them in one long stride and pulled her into his arms. "Good news, my love! The king has given us permission to marry."

And then he kissed her. His lips brushed gently, tenderly over hers, kissing her as a true lover would, or as she imagined a true lover would.

She tried not to feel anything, but it was hopeless. She would have had to be dead, or nearly. Instead, she felt remarkably alive as he pressed her close.

She knew she ought to resist, but his kiss was like the key to a hidden part of her, opening the door to feelings, yearnings and desires she'd never known she possessed.

Instinctively responding, her hands slid up his back, feeling the taut muscles beneath her palms. He shifted slightly, bringing more of his body in contact with hers, increasing the powerful, exciting passion he aroused.

Dangerous passion, because it was nearly impossible to control. And regrettable, too, because of a solemn vow she could not break.

Despite that promise, she wanted him to do more than kiss her. She wanted him to sweep her off her feet and carry her into one of the alcoves, or better yet, that little hut, and make love with her. She wanted to let him take her, to love her until she was sated beyond reckoning.

She didn't want to be married, and she had promised she would not, but she wanted that. No other man had ever made her feel as he did—that she alone was what he wanted, and that even if she weren't beautiful, he would want her still.

And when he had her in his bed, *she* would be the one rewarded.

Nevertheless, she put her hands on his chest and gently shoved him back. "My lord, my love! Please! We aren't alone." She nodded at Eloise standing beside Randall.

"How unfortunate," he said with a seductive smile. "Otherwise, my dearest one, I would carry you into that alcove and give the court more cause to gossip."

That suggestion should appall her, not excite her.

Both ashamed and dismayed by her reaction, she replied sternly. "My lord, such activity has already caused me enough embarrassment. I believe anything more should wait until our wedding night."

"Which cannot come too soon for me," he said softly, with another look that made her feel as if she'd been into the wine. "However, if I must restrain myself, I shall."

He turned to their friends. "Would you please wait for us by the gate? I wish to discuss the terms of our betrothal with my bride."

While Randall and Eloise did as he asked, Adelaide struggled to subdue her emotions. She wondered what John had demanded in exchange for his permission. Given his appetites, she was sickeningly sure of what he would want from her. That would be another reason to be angered by Armand's hasty declaration that they wanted to be married. "Terms?" she said when their friends were out of earshot.

Armand's expression hardened, all pretence of love or any tender feeling gone. "I am to again swear fealty to John, in front of the whole court, as well as pay him three hundred marks."

"Is that all?"

"All?" Armand repeated incredulously. "God's blood, my lady, *all?* I am to humiliate myself by repeating my solemn oath as if the first were a lie, or as if I've betrayed the king who left my men and me to die in Marchant. And while you may value yourself at more than three hundred marks, it means my brother must linger even longer in a French dungeon. That's money I can ill afford to lose unless you can provide the rest. Can you? Just how poor are you, my lady?"

"It's your fault more than mine that you find yourself in this situation," she replied defensively. "*I* didn't kiss *you,* my lord. *I* didn't announce that we were betrothed, or wanted to be. Nevertheless, I have gone along with your actions because I have little choice, and we have yet to discover who's plotting against the earl and archbishop."

She paused and drew in a ragged, but calming, breath. "As for your brother's ransom, I haven't been completely truthful about our family's wealth while I've been at court. I had no wish to make myself more sought after. It's very likely my sister can send us three hundred marks from Averette, although it will take some time for her to do so. When does the king require his payment?"

"Today, and I am to swear the oath tonight."

"So soon? Then we have no choice but to use your ransom money." She reached into her girdle and pulled out a scroll. "I'll write another letter to Gillian asking her to send three hundred marks."

"And she'll do it, just like that?"

"Yes. She trusts me." She thought of his suffering in that dungeon and all he had endured in the king's service. "Perhaps Gillian can even send the entire amount of the ransom. I'll ask her. After we break the betrothal, you can pay us back."

Armand's dark brows lowered. "Break the betrothal?"

"Surely you don't think we should really marry?"

Apparently, he did. "I've agreed to John's terms."

"I agree we must *ask* to be betrothed because of what you've said and done, but I don't want to marry you."

He looked at her as if she'd insulted him. "As terrible as marriage to me appears to be to you, my lady, marriage is the only way for either of us to retain our honorable reputations."

He couldn't be serious…yet judging by his expression, he certainly was.

That could not be. "Regardless of rumor or gossip or the attentions of lascivious men, I will not be tied in the bonds of matrimony to a man I scarcely know for the rest of my life."

He looked baffled, as most men probably would be to hear such a determined pronouncement from a woman.

"I have no desire to be *any* man's chattel," she clarified further.

"A husband would surely be a better master than the king," Armand replied.

"Better, perhaps, but still a master."

Armand obviously couldn't accept what she was saying. "Marriage need not be a yoke, or a wife a slave. I assure you, I would never be a tyrant."

"There speaks a man, who is by law and society already deemed to be worthy of ruling me simply by virtue of his sex. Can you promise me, my lord, that I will be happier as your wife than I would be as the king's ward? That you will treat me as more than another of your possessions? Can you even assure me I will be any safer from the king's lust?"

For John paid no heed to the marital status of any woman he wanted.

"If you're *my* wife, you will be safe. John won't dare to touch you."

She stared at him in wonderment…but John's lustful behavior was not her main reason for avoiding matrimony. "And would you always treat me with respect? Would you listen to my opinions, or would I be merely worthy to share your bed, bear your children and run your household? Would I be your partner, or a glorified servant?"

"I would treat my wife with all the respect, deference and regard she's due."

"And *you* will be the arbiter of that?"

"Who else?"

Who else indeed—and thus he proved himself no different from other men, despite his fine words. "Regardless of the ruin of my reputation, I will *never* marry you, my lord. Once we discover who's involved in the conspiracy, our betrothal *will* be broken."

"What if the king refuses to allow us to break the agreement?" he countered. "He might insist we marry."

"Since neither of us wish it, I'll persuade him that it would be in his best interests *not* to insist."

"I don't doubt you could do that," he replied, "but he might demand something from you in return."

"It will be nothing he hasn't tried to get from me before—with no success."

"What if, this time, he threatens your sisters to force you to comply?"

He had hit upon the one certain reason she would ever give herself to the king. Nevertheless, she wasn't going to capitulate completely, to John or to him. "Then naturally we'll have to pretend to accept the king's decree while delaying and prevaricating until John grows frustrated and breaks our betrothal himself. After all, if our betrothal is broken, he could still marry me off to someone else—or try to. If I must, I'll announce I'm taking the veil."

Armand stared at her with a mixture of surprise and disbelief. "You'd become a nun?"

"Only as a last resort. I have no desire to shut myself away from the world."

"To break a betrothal is different from simply ceasing to woo," he grimly pointed out.

"I realize that, and it's unfortunate that you said we were betrothed, but we need only pretend to be betrothed until we can discover who we overheard in the garden."

Crossing his arms, he leaned his weight on his left leg. "And after the conspirators are known, I'm to simply throw you back to the wolves of the court?"

"I've been dealing with those wolves for quite some time—and to some I will now be a much less tasty morsel." Perhaps there could even be some benefit to her in all this, she realized, despite what he'd done.

"To some, but not to all."

"What other choice do we have?"

As she expected, he had no answer to that.

"Now, my lord, our friends are waiting, and I have a letter to write. And you must take your money to the king."

Armand glanced over his shoulder at Randall and Eloise, who were talking quietly together. "Yes, our sovereign awaits his bribe."

He lifted her hand to his lips. "Until this evening, then, my lady." His lips slowly curved up into a smile devoid of mirth or joy—a smile for show. "When we must continue as we apparently began, the slaves of our desire."

ANNOYED, determined and most of all, frustrated, Armand struggled to hide his true emotions as he left the garden. He hadn't asked Randall to leave the garden with him, but Randall bade farewell to Eloise, and now did his best to match Armand's irate strides as he marched toward the chamber they shared.

To think he'd come to Ludgershall with one firm purpose—to get the money to ransom his brother—only to find himself embroiled in a bizarre, aggravating mess that was robbing him of what money he'd already collected, and Lady Adelaide acted as if being betrothed to him were akin to being banished to a lepers' house.

As Randall silently watched, no doubt ascribing Armand's state to anger at the king's demands, Armand went to his narrow cot and shoved it away from the wall.

"It's too bad you have to pay John so much," Randall ventured. "Are you sure I can't—?"

"No," Armand snapped as he knelt beside the wall.

He took a deep, calming breath and glanced over his shoulder at his friend. "All I need is the loan of sixteen marks. I wouldn't even need that if John didn't want the money today. Fortunately, Adelaide's family may not be as poor as we've been led to believe. She thinks her sister might be able to provide that much from the family estate, and perhaps even the whole amount of Bayard's ransom."

He began to work one of the stones free, bits of loose mortar falling to the floor. He'd not completely wasted his time in that cell. He'd become adept at scraping away mortar and removing stones and then replacing them before his jailor came with his meager meal, or to remove the bucket. It hadn't yielded a way to escape, but it had helped to pass the long, mournful hours after his squire had died.

"That's wonderful!" Randall cried.

It would be, Armand thought, if he weren't worried about paying back the money, or what might happen to Adelaide when they announced their broken betrothal.

No matter how sure she was that she could deal

with the consequences, he was just as sure it would be more difficult than she thought. She—obviously and not surprisingly—had never spent time in the company of men in a barracks or tavern. She'd never heard the way they spoke of women when there were no women nearby, save serving wenches or whores.

Armand laid the stone on the floor and reached into the wall.

Muttering a curse, he frantically felt around the empty space.

"What's wrong?" Randall asked.

Armand sat back on his haunches and stared at the hole. "My money's gone."

CHAPTER NINE

"ARE YOU an *utter* fool?"

Leaning back against the cold chapel wall, Francis stared down at his boots and didn't answer his accuser. He shivered—because the stones were cold, he told himself, not because he was afraid.

"I didn't touch Lady Adelaide," he muttered. "And how was I to know they were betrothed, or as good as'? God's blood, Armand just got here!"

"He works fast, I'll give him that," Francis's companion agreed with a smirk, his face more visible in the flickering light of the votive candles burning at the feet of the statue of the Virgin nearby.

"I never thought John would agree, either," Francis said. "He's been after Adelaide as much as anyone."

"No doubt our sovereign remembers Armand's a well-trained, honorable knight who, unlike you, has been proven in battle. However John seems to favor you now, Francis, never forget that. John will drop you like a hot rock if he has to choose between you and Armand when he goes after his lands in France again, as he surely will, the greedy, ambitious dolt."

Francis shifted, trying not to breathe too deeply. The air was heavily scented both with the lingering odors of incense and his companion's perfume. "John's servant tells me Armand has to pay three hundred marks for the betrothal and he also has to swear fealty again before the entire court tonight."

Francis's cohort whistled through his teeth and shook his head. "That's madness."

"It's as if he's *trying* to set Armand against him," Francis agreed. His expression altered. "What, you don't think so?"

"I think John intends Armand's humiliation to serve as a reminder to us all that he still has good men who've pledged themselves to his service and who'll continue to do so no matter what he does, as a warning to those of us who waver in our loyalty."

"Provided Armand will swear," Francis replied, tucking his thumbs into his swordbelt. "He's a proud bastard. I'd be willing to wager he won't."

"Not even when the reward is Lady Adelaide's hand?"

"I think there's more to this betrothal than love, whatever Armand says. What's he really up to?"

"You don't think the man could truly be in love?"

Francis laughed with scorn. "In less than a se'ennight? No."

"Perhaps he merely wanted to rob the king, or you, of that luscious prize."

"That I can more easily believe." Francis fingered

the hilt of the sword. "If Armand does swear, we'll have to kill him, too."

"All in good time," his co-conspirator assured him as he looked around the chapel, empty save for Francis and the trappings of faith. "All in good time. Now where the devil's Oliver?"

"Here, my lord," a low voice replied as the man himself stepped out the shadows.

Francis started. He'd checked the chapel carefully when he'd entered to await his fellow plotters. He'd not seen Oliver, and the man couldn't have arrived afterward, for there was only one entrance to the chapel, and it was in plain sight.

If Oliver had been hiding there, he was even more skilled at subterfuge than they knew.

"Marcus has gone?" their leader asked the Irishman.

"Yes. He'll be glad he doesn't have to play the holy brother for a while. I wouldn't be surprised if he heads to a brothel in Canterbury before he attends to the archbishop."

"You gave him the poison and told him how to administer it?"

Oliver nodded. "Wine should easily mask its taste."

"You're certain no one will be able to tell what brought on the illness?"

Oliver smiled with cold satisfaction. "I've used it before, my lord. My father didn't last the night, and a most learned physician said it was his heart."

FOR ONCE, Adelaide was relieved to part from Eloise as they went to change for the evening meal. Eloise kept talking about the betrothal, while Adelaide would prefer not to think about it, or Armand, if she could help it.

Sighing wearily, she entered her small chamber, which barely had room for the curtained bed, dressing table and chests containing her garments, and closed the door behind her.

"My lady?"

She whirled around to see Armand standing by the arched window. A thrill of undeniable excitement shot through her, followed quickly by annoyance. Betrothed or not, he shouldn't be here.

Before she could speak, he said, "I've been robbed."

"What?" she gasped, instinctively moving toward him. "Robbed? Here in Ludgershall?"

"Yes, here in Ludgershall," he replied, running an agitated hand through his hair. "The money was well hidden in my chamber. Only Randall knew where it was, and I would trust him with my life."

"You searched?" she asked as she felt for the stool beside her dressing table and sat.

"Of course. Randall and I tore our chamber apart. Then we went to the steward to report the theft. De Chevron was shocked, too, and he's agreed to search the servants' quarters."

"What about the chambers of the courtiers?"

"Believe me, my lady, I suggested that," Armand

said as he started to pace, "but de Chevron wouldn't allow it. He said only the earl could command such a thing. He would inform the earl of the theft, but until he hears back from his lord, he won't risk insulting any of the earl's guests."

"Do you think John will wait for the money if he hears it's been stolen?"

Armand's expression didn't give her hope. "My meeting with John didn't end well. I think he'll imprison me if I don't bring him the money today."

"On what charge?" she demanded.

"Treason."

Surely not even John would stoop so low. "He wouldn't dare!"

"He's dared to commit greater injustices."

That was unfortunately true, but it only added to Adelaide's outrage. "I won't let him put you in prison!"

Her declaration brought a weary smile to Armand's face. "As delighted as I am to have your backing, I have no other way to pay him, unless you have three hundred marks at your immediate disposal you haven't told me about?"

She sat back down. "I've sent my letter to Gillian, but it will take at least three days for it to be received and for her to send the money I've asked for."

"Then I fear our betrothal is already at an end," Armand said. "I truly regret what's happened, my lady, and the trouble it's going to bring you." He sighed. "And I had best prepare myself for another stint in a cell."

As angry and upset as she'd been by Armand's actions, she didn't want him imprisoned, or the conspirators to succeed, or Bayard de Boisbaston held in a dungeon any longer than necessary. "I have something worth three hundred marks."

Lowering her head, she reached behind her neck to take off her mother's crucifix.

"My lady, no."

"Have you another three hundred marks hidden anywhere?" she asked.

He looked anguished as he shook his head, and his reluctance made her decision somewhat easier to bear. "Then we have no other choice."

Yet in spite of her intrepid words, her satisfaction that he realized this was no small sacrifice on her part and her belief that this was the right thing to do, her fingers trembled as she undid the clasp. This was the only thing of her mother's she possessed.

When Armand came behind her and lifted her veil to get it out of the way, she tried to ignore the sensation of his fingers brushing the nape of her neck. "My lady, I wish you didn't have to do this," he said, his deep voice low and full of regret as he lifted the crucifix away and came around to face her. "I would I had something of equal value that I could give the king instead, but since I don't, I give you my most solemn vow and promise that I will repay you as soon as I possibly can."

How was he to know the crucifix meant far more to her than its monetary value?

He went to the door, then paused on the threshold to look back at her. "Adelaide, are you certain about what we're doing? We could break this bogus betrothal now, if you would rather."

Not willing to let him see her pain, afraid he would think her weak, she regarded him with all the dignity she could muster. "But then we couldn't be seen together, or what would people think? That, having given you my virginity, I cannot let you go? That I am grovelling for your favor like a lovesick fool? Heaven forbid, my lord. My pride must bear what it must if we're to foil this plot."

She crossed the floor and closed his hand around the crucifix.

When she spoke again, her voice was softer, although no less determined. "Rest assured, I can bear much when the lives of William Marshal, the archbishop and your brother are at stake. They are more valuable than this."

He looked down at her, and it seemed to Adelaide that her sacrifice was worth it for the gratitude and respect in Armand de Boisbaston's eyes.

"Someday," he said, "the others will know what you've done for them."

"It will be enough that *I* will know," she replied.

"And *I* know," he reminded her, kissing her lightly on the cheek before he went out the door.

After he was gone, Adelaide put her palm where he had kissed her, and told herself again and again that what she did was necessary, and no more.

ALTHOUGH Armand's rage had abated when he was with Adelaide, it returned in full force as he marched toward the king's quarters, and thought of her sacrifice, for the crucifix obviously meant much to her. He'd seen the anguish in her beautiful eyes and noticed the way her hand had trembled as she'd tried to remove it. Her pain smote him to his soul and doubled his guilt, for he was responsible for the rumors that made it necessary for her to lose this possession upon which she set such store.

The necklace she had given him to bribe the king, made of gold and emeralds, was old, and finely wrought, delicate as Adelaide's features—far, far too good and beautiful for John or his queen.

Yet he allowed none of his dismay to show on his face as he approached Falkes de Bréauté outside the king's chamber, more than half expecting that insolent lout to try to prevent him from meeting with John.

Instead, de Bréauté immediately opened the door, albeit with a smirk on his face and an impertinent bow.

The king's bedchamber was dim, and stuffy, too, enshrouded by thick tapestries that made it seem more like a tent than a room. The afternoon was fair, yet the painted wooden shutters were closed tight. Three bronze braziers full of glowing coals heated the room to an almost unbearable degree. Heavy, costly carpets covered the stone floor, muffling any footfalls.

It took a moment for Armand's eyes to adjust to the gloom, and when they did, he discovered why the room was kept so hot and close. John lay in an immense wooden tub cushioned with linens near the braziers, indulging in one of his frequent baths, his arms along the rim and his eyes closed as if in ecstasy. Two body servants attended him; otherwise, he was alone.

If he were an assassin, Armand thought, especially one prepared to die to achieve his goal, this would be the perfect chance to do the deed.

But he wasn't an assassin, and he had sworn to protect this man with his life.

"Ah, Lord Armand," John said, opening his eyes and giving him a satisfied smirk. "I assume you have the money."

"Your Majesty, I regret I do not."

The king frowned and shifted to a more upright position, making the water slosh over the rim of the tub and splash upon the floor.

As one of the servants hurried to wipe it up, Armand said, "My money's been stolen."

John's expression relaxed back into a smirk. "Has it indeed? How unfortunate for you, and the lady, too."

Armand wondered if John was behind the theft. Sadly, he could well believe John would stop at nothing to retain control over one of his noblemen. Yet if John was involved in the theft, there was nothing Armand could do about it. The money was as good as gone into the ether, and no one would ever be charged.

Thank God, and thanks to Adelaide, he had a way to triumph over John, at least in this instance.

"Fortunately, I have something else that's worth at least three hundred marks, sire," he said, holding up the crucifix.

The king gestured for one of his servants to bring it to him. "I recognize this," he said, examining it. "This usually graces the neck of Lady Adelaide."

"Until now, Your Majesty," Armand agreed.

John handed the crucifix back to his servant as if it were no more than a cheap trinket. "Put that with my other jewels. And if anything of *mine* goes missing, you will pay for it with your life."

Blanching, the servant nodded and scurried away to do John's bidding.

Armand waited for the king to dismiss him, but instead, John ordered the remaining servant to bring them both some wine.

"Sit, my lord," the king ordered, pointing to a nearby chair.

Armand obeyed and accepted a golden goblet of wine from the middle-aged, slender servant.

"So, Lady Adelaide pays for the privilege of marrying you," the king remarked after he'd sipped some of the excellent wine. He watched Armand's face like a cat stalking a mouse. "I'm shocked she would part with that even for you. It belonged to her mother, I understand."

Adelaide must have loved her mother dearly, and for that, Armand envied her. The only mother he could remember was his stepmother, who'd never liked him. She'd seen Armand and his older brother as impediments to the inheritance of her own child.

Thank God, Bayard had not felt the same. He'd been a good friend and comrade while they were growing up. Now Bayard lay helpless in a dungeon in Normandy, thanks to this pale, plump monarch sitting in a tub like a piece of salted pork.

The king closed his eyes and leaned his head back against the rim of the tub, exposing his neck as if daring Armand to slit it. "Lady Adelaide's mother had a most unhappy life, I understand. Her husband was said to be a vicious tyrant. I've been thinking Lady Adelaide wasn't keen to marry because Lord Reynard gave his daughter an aversion to men. Evidently I was mistaken."

Perhaps Adelaide's father hadn't managed to completely ruin his daughter's opinion of men, but he was probably responsible for her aversion to marriage.

"My own father never liked Lord Reynard," the king continued, "but then, he rarely liked or trusted anyone, and he was hardly an exemplary husband himself."

Armand took another drink rather than comment on John's father.

"Now that I'm a king myself, I begin to understand him better. A king can't trust anyone." John opened his eyes and sat up, looking directly at Armand. "It's a very lonely life, being a king."

Armand's fingers clenched the goblet. He'd heard the stories about John's brother, Richard, and his preference for men. While John had had many mistresses, Armand also knew some men sported with both sexes.

John barked a harsh and scornful laugh. "No need to look so stricken, my lord Armand. You aren't the sort of lover I like. Your bride is much more to my taste."

Armand slowly and deliberately set his goblet down on the table near him. "And I have told you, sire, I will not share."

"So I recall. However, Lady Adelaide has sisters whom I hear are just as beautiful. I expect you to invite them to the wedding."

He waved a dismissive hand in the direction of the door. "Now go to your bride, my lord. We'll see you in the hall when you renew your oath."

Armand didn't trust himself to answer as he made a brief bow and left John soaking in his tub.

THAT NIGHT, the hall seemed more crowded and splendid than ever, as well as filled with an air of suppressed excitement. The flambeaux flickered, and fat beeswax candles by the dozens burned in bronze stands or from great iron rings hoisted high above the people's heads. Perfumes scented the air, mingling with the odor of the heavy fabrics and the rushes on the floor. Servants hovered near the corridor to the kitchen, awaiting the signal that would tell them to begin to set up the tables and bring the food.

A large, ornately carved chair had been placed in the centre of the dais like a throne, and a smaller one of lighter, ancient design was beside it, no doubt for the queen.

Groups of courtiers came together and broke apart like flotsam in the tide. The tapestries undulated as the people passed, as if they, too, were anxiously waiting.

By now, everyone had heard of the ceremony about to take place. Adelaide had overheard enough excited whispers to know that several of the courtiers were expecting Armand to refuse to repeat his oath, regardless of his professed love for her. More than one wager had been made to that effect, for there were likewise several who expected Armand to do as the king commanded.

She spotted Eloise beside Randall FitzOsburne, who stood anxiously biting a fingernail, and started toward them.

Where was Armand? What if he'd decided the humiliation would be too much to bear? She could hardly fault him if he did, but if that were so, she hoped he hadn't given her mother's crucifix to the king.

As for the smirks, sneers, jabs and snide remarks she'd have to endure, they were going to come either now, when Armand didn't arrive, or later, when the betrothal was broken.

"Do you think he'll do it?"

Adelaide froze. She'd heard that very voice, speaking in just that soft, low tone, when she was hiding in the hut with Armand close behind her.

CHAPTER TEN

ADELAIDE QUICKLY TURNED—and found herself facing the scornful Hildegard.

"Well, if it isn't Lord Armand's betrothed," Hildegard said. "Where is he, I wonder? Riding hard for home, happy to escape your snare, perhaps? After all, why should he tie himself to a poor little nobody like you when there are so many more worthy, wealthy women at court?"

Adelaide wanted to shove Hildegard out of the way so she could see who was behind her, but that would be difficult to explain. Besides, the people were moving so much, jostling for positions near the dais, her chance to discover who possessed that soft, low voice had probably passed.

Angered at the lost opportunity and by Hildegard's nasty words, Adelaide met Hildegard's hostile gaze with one of her own. "He will come. He loves me, and I love him."

Hildegard snorted. "If you say so."

"I do."

There was a commotion by the door and, out of

the corner of her eyes, she saw Randall straighten like a hound on the scent. It was either the royal party, or Armand.

It was Armand.

Adelaide watched with relief, as well as a twinge of regret for her lost crucifix, as Armand came forward. He was dressed in a woollen tunic of unrelieved black, dark breeches and his boots had been well polished. His hair was combed, but not trimmed. It still looked wild, seductively savage, reaching to his broad shoulders.

There were other warriors here who'd led men into battle and fought for their king, yet there was such an air of command about Armand de Boisbaston that even those with more experience or higher rank made way for him.

Just as many of the young women looked at him with desire.

Suddenly it felt thrilling to have him claim her for his bride, and disappointing to realize it was just a sham.

Then she remembered her vow and the reason for it, and tore her gaze away from the dark knight to another source of disruption. The king, dressed like a peacock in a long, heavily embroidered robe, his hair smoothed and cut in the Norman style, his fingers jewelled and his plump face smiling, led in his diminutive, juvenile queen.

As the king sat on the thronelike chair, he immediately spotted Armand, and the smugly satisfied smile that grew upon his face filled Adelaide with even more disgust. That they should endure so much for such a man—yet what choice did they have, unless they wanted rebellion and war?

She began to make her way through the crowd toward Armand. So did Randall and Eloise.

Francis was on the other side of the hall, watching the proceedings with a frown and furrowed brow. Lord Richard and Sir Alfred stood together near the corridor to the kitchen. With a chill in her heart, she noted the hostility in Sir Alfred's face as he watched Armand.

What if Armand was in the same danger as William Marshal and Hubert, the archbishop? After all, he, too, was loyal to the king and would stand between John and any who tried to take the throne.

"My lords and ladies," the steward called out before they reached him, "the king bids you witness the swearing of allegiance of Lord Armand de Bois-baston to John, by the grace of God, King of England, Lord of Ireland, Duke of Normandy and Aquitaine and Count of Anjou. My Lord Armand de Boisbas-ton, come forth, make your obeisance and swear fealty to your liege lord."

Armand strode forward, a king among men in dignity and worth, if not by title.

He paused a moment and, like everyone around her, Adelaide held her breath. Was he going to refuse, after all? Was he going to remind the king that he had already sworn such an oath and nearly died in John's service? Was he going to declare that he would not humiliate himself by doing so again? Would he forfeit their betrothal, bogus though it was?

Slowly, his back straight, Armand went down on his knees and held out his hands to the king, who grasped them in his own.

If this act had been intended to humiliate Armand, the king has seriously miscalculated. Looking at this tableau, no one could doubt who was the stronger man, in personal attributes, honor and nobility, even if he knelt before the other.

A sigh seemed to arise from the gathering, as all, including Adelaide, relaxed.

Nearby, Sir Oliver caught her eye and held it. In the past she would have found his scrutiny unnerving. Now, she smiled, no longer the least bit intimidated, although she didn't care to examine why.

Then Armand spoke, his deep voice firm and strong. "I swear before God and this court that I will be the faithful vassal of John, by the grace of God, King of England, Lord of Ireland, Duke of Normandy and Aquitaine and Count of Anjou."

He had done it.

"In return for this oath and the faithful service you have already performed," the king declared, his gaze sweeping the hall until it lit upon her, "I give you in marriage my ward and the jewel of this court, Lady

Adelaide D'Averette. Come forward, my dear, and claim your husband. I suggest you hurry before another of these ladies tries to take him from you."

Adelaide went to stand beside Armand, and she smiled at the king. "Woe betide the lady who tries to take him from me," she said, speaking loudly enough for all in the hall to hear.

The king laughed and released his hold on Armand's hands. "Rise, my lord, and take your bride. Never let it be said your king is not a generous man, for truly, I could have gotten much for her."

Again John laughed, and while those nearest him joined in, their laughter was strained at best. This was too close to the truth to be funny to anyone save John.

Armand did as he was directed, holding out his arm to Adelaide, who lightly placed her hand upon it before they bowed to the king. "Thank you, Your Majesty, for bestowing such a bride upon me," he said.

The king leaned forward and spoke softly. "I expect you both to remember my generosity and be grateful." Then he reached up and fingered his newest ornament—a crucifix of gold and emeralds.

Adelaide had to bite her lip to hold back the angry tears that started in her eyes. It disgusted her to see his fingers, like pale worms, stroking her mother's necklace.

To think this was the man whose reign they were trying to save. They should forget what they'd heard about a conspiracy and let it take its course...except that the deaths of the archbishop and William Marshal would be the price.

"Majesty," Armand said, his voice low but astonishingly stern and determined. "Must I remind you that my bride is not an object to be shared, even with you?"

She had never heard anyone speak to the king that way, not even William Marshal. She could believe Armand would truly protect her from John, or any other enemy.

That realization made her feel…odd. Not weak, but stronger and more confident than she'd ever felt before.

The king smiled, although it didn't reach his eyes. "You are excused."

After another brief bow, Armand and Adelaide left the dais. As they headed toward Randall and Eloise, Armand nodded in response to the congratulations from the other courtiers. So did Adelaide, until Francis appeared like an unwanted guest during a busy harvest.

"I must also add my congratulations to the happy couple," he said with the most insincere of smiles.

Adelaide gave him her brightest and most meaningless smile in return. "Thank you. We are very happy."

"Yes, we are," Armand said, his low, seductive voice sending ripples of excitement through her body. His gaze was so full of seemingly genuine desire, it took her breath away.

Francis was no longer quite so smug. "Have a care,

my lord, that you don't forget yourself and take your bride in the hall the same way you did in the garden."

Lady Jane, nearby with her mother, gasped at the crudeness of his comment.

"What?" Lady Ethel demanded. "What did he say?"

"I can't repeat it, Mama," Lady Jane said with unexpected vigor. "Such language in the king's court!"

Armand, meanwhile, ignored everything but Francis as he, too, continued to smile, although his eyes held scorn and derision. "If you can't be civil, Francis, might I suggest you keep silent?"

"You seem to have lost your sense of humor, my lord," Francis replied.

"Several weeks in a dungeon does tend to rob one of good humor, especially when good men die while others who have much less to offer live in ease and comfort," Armand answered, his voice like the slash of a whip.

Francis raised his brows and regarded them with apparently genuine remorse, unless one happened to be looking directly into his eyes. "Forgive me for upsetting you or your lady, my lord. I meant no insult."

"Have no fear, Sir Francis," Adelaide said, stroking Armand's muscular arm and telling herself that was also part of the ruse. "I'm sure anything you say tonight will be forgotten tomorrow."

Armand's arm shot around her and he pulled her close against him. "I've already forgotten," he said with a low, husky chuckle that made her feel as if she were melting like butter in the summer's sun.

She might have forgotten more than Francis if the steward of the hall had not then ordered the servants to prepare the hall for eating.

Armand let her go. "Come, my lady, I'm famished for food, as well as your sweet kisses."

She nodded wordlessly and let him lead her to a table.

Yet even though she was nearly overwhelmed by the lust-inspiring power of the proud, handsome knight beside her, she scanned the hall and all those gathered in it. Which one of these men was the conspirator she'd heard again tonight?

Whoever he was, she'd have to find a way to tell Armand that at least one of the traitors was still in Ludgershall.

ADELAIDE PICKED her way through several courses, including a salad of greens dressed with vinegar, oil and spices, three kinds of fish done in a light sauce of leeks, followed by roasted lamb and beef, as she awaited an opportunity to talk to Armand.

Unfortunately, he seemed more inclined to speak with Eloise, who sat on his left, while Randall sat to Adelaide's right. Between Armand's lack of attention and the volume of the minstrels' music, she didn't dare risk raising her voice to tell him what she'd heard, nor could she hear much of what her friend and Armand were talking about.

So she tried to enjoy the feast. Marshal had ordered

his steward and servants to do all in their power to
feed, entertain and keep the king comfortable. The
steward of Ludgershall was fulfilling that command
admirably. How much food, money, wine or ale
would be left in Ludgershall after the king departed
was a different matter; Adelaide doubted there would
be much at all until the next harvest. But then,
Marshal and the bulk of his men would move with the
king, leaving this household a chance to recover
before its master and his entourage returned.

Armand reached out for another piece of bread, and
his arm brushed against hers. She tried to ignore the
sensation of his touch, just as she told herself it didn't
matter that Eloise's dowry was more than hers would
ever be. After all, Eloise didn't like him. Or at least, she
hadn't. Armand undoubtedly improved upon acquaintance, and he was an astonishingly attractive man.
There were women with even larger dowries here, and
several of those ladies were watching him so atten-
tively, she wouldn't be surprised if they started to drool.

She should say something to Armand here and now
about hearing the conspirator again. She could lean
close and whisper in his ear. Didn't lovers whisper
like that? No one would take it amiss—and was that
not precisely why they were feigning their betrothal?

"What do you expect of him, my lady?"

Adelaide nearly knocked over her wine at
Randall's sudden question, asked with such suppressed fervor as she was about to speak to Armand.

"Forgive me, but you hardly know him, my lady," he said. "I don't doubt you believe you love him. I know love can strike like a thunderbolt. And Armand's a fine man—the best of men, in fact, although he hasn't had the most loving of families. But he's fiercely loyal and he'll always treat you well."

She thought of the passion in Armand's kisses, even if he wasn't in love with her, and the way he restrained his anger when it was roused. "I don't think Armand's wife will have any cause to doubt his devotion, or to fear him."

"I hope you likewise intend to be a good and loyal wife to Armand," he said.

"When I marry," she replied and despite her vow not to marry at all, "I will never dishonor my vows, of that you may be certain, and when I give my heart, it will be given for life."

That brought a grin to Randall's face. Between that and his cowlick, he looked decidedly mischievous, and it became easier to understand the friendship between this quiet, gentle fellow and Armand de Boisbaston, as well as Eloise's attraction to him.

Adelaide reached for her goblet and took a sip, all the while wondering what impish impulse had suggested that she talk about her heart. "You must have been happy to see him out of captivity and safely returned to England."

"Indeed, I was," Randall answered as he proceeded to tear a piece of bread into tiny bits. "His steward stripped the estate to raise Armand's ransom, and I gave what I could. The abbot of the monastery near his family's estate, remembering his kindness to them, and even though we used to steal their apples when we were boys—well, Armand would steal them and I would eat them," he confessed, "gave all they could spare, as well. After I had the money, I went to the castle where he was being held. I truly believe I arrived not an hour too soon. Another day, and I think Armand would have died in that cell." Randall shivered. "If hell isn't fire and brimstone, I think it will be like that cold, dank, dark place."

Adelaide shivered, too. "He's fortunate to have such a good friend."

"We've been good friends since boyhood, my lady," Randall replied, his shy smile lighting the grim mood that had descended upon them. "He was my protector, and I his tutor. Armand was no scholar when it came to Latin and Greek, and his arithmetic was worse."

"Did his father intend him for the church?" she asked, although she simply couldn't imagine Armand being a priest. Or celibate.

"He was to be the best nobleman in the land, like his older brother, Simon. Bayard, too. His father expected them to be the best at everything. Knights can be more than soldiers, my lady, and Armand's father intended them to be high in the king's counsels, and to travel on royal business."

"Some fathers, whether they intend it or not, force

their sons to compete for honor or favor," Adelaide noted, although she and her sisters had had no such burden. Her father had thought all three of his daughters useless, except to trade as brides.

Randall nodded. "Armand's father favored Simon, and Bayard's mother spoiled her son. Armand grew up practically on his own, my lady, but he loved Bayard too much to begrudge him his mother's preference, and he admired Simon too much to be bitter."

Although Armand hadn't succumbed to resentment or jealousy, what a love-starved childhood he must have had! At least she'd had her mother's love and devotion before she died.

She could guess what Randall would think of *her* when he heard that the betrothal had been broken, and it was painful knowing she would lose this young man's good opinion.

"What have you been saying to Randall to make him look so serious?" Armand asked, interrupting her thoughts. "Should I be jealous?"

"Not unless I should envy Eloise," she said in reply, then instantly regretted her hasty words when she saw a sparkle of amusement come to his eyes.

His hand covered hers, strong and warm, the sensation filling her heart with an intense pleasure that she'd never experienced before, except when he kissed her.

"She's a very charming young lady," he replied,

leaning closer, "and I can see why you like her, but she's not nearly as fascinating as you."

This was surely part of the ruse, too, and she mustn't forget that, no matter how exciting his expression, his words or the touch of his hand. And she should take advantage of this moment. "I need to speak with you in private."

His brow furrowed for the briefest of moments before he caressed her cheek, that gentle motion sending another thrill of excitement through her that she tried not to notice. "I was thinking the same thing, beloved."

Had he heard the conspirator, too, or perhaps learned something of importance?

"I'm weary of spending my days in the castle, and tomorrow promises to be fair and sunny," he said. "I'm sure the earl's steward won't begrudge us the use of two horses—or four, if Randall and Lady Eloise will join us?"

Why did he want Eloise and Randall to come with them?

Because it would stave off some of the worst of the gossip, and since they were supposedly betrothed, Eloise and Randall wouldn't look askance if they sought a few moments alone, her logical mind supplied.

Their company should also prevent Armand from taking advantage of the situation, if he were so tempted.

Or if she were, her conscience suggested.

It would probably be best not to ride out with him at all. "Sooner would be better."

"As delightful as the thought of being alone with you in a dark corner may be," he quietly replied, "considering the exciting speed of our courtship and my willingness to humiliate myself for your love, I fear we'll be too closely watched tonight. It would be too risky—unless you think it's worth it?"

Since she didn't know who she'd heard the second time, either, and because the conspirators apparently felt secure enough to linger in Ludgershall, she decided it wasn't urgent—especially when she recalled the thrill of dangerous excitement that filled her when he spoke of being alone in a dark corner.

"Tomorrow will do," she said, hoping that wasn't a mistake. "Perhaps we could go to Pickpit Hill. They say the druids built it, and I haven't yet seen it."

And she would stay on horseback, where there would be no possibility of touching. Or kissing.

She realized the master of the hall had silenced the musicians, and that everyone's attention was on them.

"Lord Armand," the king called out, "I say *again,* can you tear yourself away from Lady Adelaide to play chess?"

"With pleasure, sire," Armand said before he took her hand and raised it to his lips, pressing his warm, soft mouth upon the back of it. "After all, I will have many evenings to be with the lady when she's my wife."

A few excited whispers started among the women, as well as chuckles from the men, and giggles from the younger ladies.

"What are young people coming to these days?" Lady Ethel demanded. "Such a vulgar display!"

Adelaide didn't think his kiss was vulgar, but it *was* disconcerting. "My lord," she whispered through clenched teeth. "You are making us a spectacle."

"Am I?" he murmured as he let go, regarding her with devilish amusement in his eyes. "It was merely a slight demonstration of my love, my lady."

He leaned close again and dropped his voice to a whisper. "Just think what I might do if we were really betrothed."

Leaving her with that disquieting thought, he strolled toward the dais as if this hall were his own.

FRANCIS SCOWLED as he watched Armand slaver over Adelaide's hand.

"Come now, Francis, why so grim?" Lord Richard drawled as he slid onto the bench beside him. He adjusted the heavily embroidered cuff of his scarlet silk tunic over his white linen shirt. "The lady's made her choice, and what of that? In time, Armand will be back in Normandy trying to reclaim the king's lost lands and she'll be left at home. With any luck, next time Armand won't come back."

"Sweet heaven, my lord, how heartless you sound," Lady Hildegard said from her place nearby.

"Do I?" Lord Richard queried, turning to her and raising a quizzical brow. "I would say practical."

"And are we to be practical in matters of love, my lord?"

"If we're wise, my lady."

Frowning, Hildegard wondered if she should set her sights on another man as she reached for her wine.

"I WOULDN'T BELIEVE IT if I hadn't seen it myself," Sir Alfred slurred as he handed a small pouch of silver to Charles de Bergendie. "A proud man like that swearing his oath a second time."

"I'd never humiliate myself that way," Sir Edmond declared, looking at them with all the confidence of youth.

"Oh, come now, why not?" Charles asked. "What harm to repeat it when a woman like that is the reward?"

"She's already given him her favors," Alfred said.

"So rumor has it," Charles returned. "Perhaps she hasn't, after all."

The group of young knights all looked at the lady as her betrothed sauntered toward the dais, each of them contemplating what it would be like to make love with her, and especially to be the first.

"De Boisbaston's a lucky bastard," Alfred muttered as he reached for more wine.

"I wouldn't say that," Charles said as he watched Armand take his seat across the chessboard from the king.

CHAPTER ELEVEN

ARMAND GASPED as the cold water hit his face the next morning. Leaning against the washstand, he breathed deeply. Randall had already gone to mass and to break the fast some time ago. He'd moaned in response to Randall's query, drawn the covers back over his aching head and gone back to sleep.

He should have left the soldiers long before he did. He'd realized by the time they'd finished the first wineskin that none of the soldiers bedding down in the hall were the conspirators; they were mostly Welshmen, with that distinctive lilt to their voices. A couple had been from Gascony, and one or two from the north. The rest, like Godwin, were natives of Wiltshire he recognized from visiting here before.

God's teeth, what a night! First the humiliation of swearing his fealty again, then the exquisite torment of sitting beside Adelaide as they dined, knowing that their betrothal was a sham, yet stirred by desire every time he glanced at her.

The challenge to play chess with the king had actually come as a relief. John was a clever, experienced player, so he'd had to play close attention to the game. John had eventually won, which put him in an expansive mood. For a moment, he'd even dared to hope John would offer to return the crucifix, which he'd toyed with throughout the game.

He hadn't, of course. Instead, he'd slyly noted that Lady Adelaide had apparently retired without bidding him good night. "I never took her for a modest woman, but perhaps your demonstrations of affection are too much for her."

"Perhaps," he'd replied with a smile, letting the king make of that what he would as John called for his wife and took himself to bed.

He'd felt no reason to smile the few times he'd caught sight of Adelaide talking with other courtiers during the game. It was necessary if they were to find the conspirators, and they weren't really going to be married, yet he'd still been jealous.

Which was utterly ridiculous. She was *nothing* like the woman he wanted to marry, even if she was beautiful. She was far too arrogant, too sure of her own ideas. Her worth. Her value.

Yet when he kissed her, he forgot everything except the desire she inspired, her intelligence, her courage, her warranted pride, until she made it very clear that whatever her kiss seemed to imply, she was with him only out of necessity.

He threw back his head and shook the hair out of his face, then brushed it back with his fingers. He didn't relish a jolting ride on horseback with Adelaide this morning, but it was obvious she had something to tell him, as he had to tell her about John's order regarding her sisters.

He went to the bed, grabbed the shirt that lay upon it and, drawing it over his head, went to the window. It was a fine summer's day, perfect for riding. Maybe that would help clear his head, and he should welcome being away from the court, especially the king.

In the yard below, servants bustled about their morning business. Smoke billowed from the louvered opening in the roof of the kitchen. A few soldiers on their way to relieve their comrades at the gates or on the wall walk meandered across the cobblestones, some still carrying the remainder of a loaf of coarse brown bread, others wiping their lips or jesting with a comrade.

He hadn't met every soldier in Ludgershall, so it was still possible the assassins were among them. He had suspected a soldier might be involved because they were trained to kill and had experience of it. A man who'd never ended the life of another might balk when the time came, no matter how right or just he believed his cause. He'd seen it in battle before. His squire, poor young Albert, had thrown up and nearly passed out the first time he'd seen a man die a bloody death.

He wouldn't rule out servants or the clergy, either. As he'd told Adelaide, one could put on the appropriate garments and claim to be anything. He could probably pass for a priest if he wanted to, thanks to Randall's help with Latin and Greek.

Or perhaps not, he thought when he remembered the lust Adelaide inspired. God save him, he'd felt desire for a beautiful woman before, but those former attractions seemed like minor yearnings compared to the strength of the physical longing Adelaide aroused.

What was it about her that stirred him so? he wondered as he tucked his shirt into his breeches and put on his leather tunic. Had it been the way they'd met? He had nearly laughed aloud at the sight of the well-dressed noblewoman at the mercy of a little bundle of fur, until he realized she was in real pain.

Then he'd been stunned to find himself looking into the grateful eyes of an astonishingly beautiful woman. He'd immediately felt like a ragged beggar, an impoverished nobody…until she smiled. Then he'd felt as proud as the day he'd been knighted.

It had been weeks since he'd felt proud of himself.

He buckled his swordbelt around his waist. Did *that* explain the depth of his feelings for this woman, that she had made him feel proud and worthy again? And was it pride or desire that warmed him when he saw how differently she acted toward other men?

He sat on the cot and reached for his boot. He shoved his foot inside and encountered something jammed in the toe. Mystified, he pulled his foot out and reached into the boot, to find a leather bag.

Full of coins.

He dumped the contents onto the cot, where it formed a clinking pile of gold, silver and copper, and stared at it for a long moment. Was it possible…?

He began to count and his suspicions were quickly confirmed. The leather bag held two hundred and eight-four marks. His missing money.

The thief must have returned it, for anyone else would have had no need for subterfuge. But why? And how was he going to explain this to Adelaide, who'd given away her crucifix and written to her sister for the full amount of Bayard's ransom?

He ran his hand through his hair and tried to decide what to do.

Perhaps he need not tell Adelaide about the restored money. After all, he couldn't get her crucifix back from the king, and she'd already written to her sister for the money for the ransom.

Later, he could simply say that he'd had a sudden windfall of some sort, or that Bayard's ransom had been reduced, or some other…lie.

THERE WERE few things Adelaide enjoyed more than riding, especially when it took her away from the court, and on a day as fine as this. Overhead, puffy white clouds like something God imagined simply for His own pleasure dotted the sky. A hawk wheeled slowly, its wings spread wide. The air was fresh with the scent of dew-damp foliage and wildflowers, moist ground and the faraway hint of wood smoke from the charcoal burners in the forest, the smell like a whisper on the breeze. Behind a hawthorn hedge she could see a farmer's cottage made of wattle and daub and heard geese squawking, as well as hens clucking and a woman calling to them as she scattered their food.

Armand rode silently beside her, and for that silence, she was grateful, although later she must tell him about that voice in the hall last night. For the moment, she would take a little time to appreciate being away from the whispers, the gossip and the attempts to curry favor, to be where she didn't have to weigh every word as she usually did—something she wished Armand had done.

Eloise and Randall were a short distance behind them, chatting merrily away. Adelaide hoped this was a sign that they would one day marry. She wanted Eloise to be happy, and Eloise dearly wanted to be a wife and mother. Randall was a good man, and would likely give her that happiness.

To her, however, marriage was still something to be avoided, even if she was beginning to realize that all men might not be selfish beasts concerned only with their own pleasures and worldly success. Nevertheless, she didn't want to bind herself to any man for life, to give him power over her body and her future, to have him make all the decisions whether they affected her or not.

Farther back rode their two guards, for the steward, Walter de Chevron, had insisted that they take an escort. She had noted the easy camaraderie the guards shared with Armand, despite the difference in rank. Yet although Armand laughed and joked with them as they mounted and prepared to ride out, the soldiers' responses were as respectful as they were amiable. It seemed Armand de Boisbaston had the ability to inspire both respect and affection, like Gillian, who could joke with the servants but never had to tell them to do a thing twice.

Was that because he, like Gillian, was a middle child? Was that some compensation for being neither the powerful eldest nor the indulged youngest?

As the eldest, she'd always had to be responsible. She must lead, first and foremost, without expecting affection in return.

She slid her companion another glance as they passed a stand of ash and oak, gazing at his long, manelike hair. Looking at him, it was easy to see how the Greeks could have imagined a creature that was half man, half horse.

Armand caught her watching him, and his smile seemed to reach out and caress her. "A lovely day, my lady. It's been a long time since I was able to enjoy such a fine day with so beautiful a companion."

A little trill of delight danced through her body at his words, but she reminded herself that she had more important business than indulging in flirtation, even if it had to look that way.

For that reason—and that reason only—they should get farther from the others.

She kicked her heels into her mare's sides, sending the startled beast into a gallop along the road. Chunks of mud flew up from the horse's hooves, and the trees went past in a blur. Nonetheless, she could hear Armand behind her in hot pursuit.

Her blood raced as the excitement of the chase seized her, regardless of its cause. Ahead, she could make out the domed shape of Pickpit Hill. Her mare's flanks churned beneath her as she urged the horse on. Wanting to get there first. Needing to win.

The hood of her cloak fell back, and she could feel the wind in her face. A thick, fallen branch from an oak tree lay half across the road. Rather than steer her horse around it, she let the mare leap, landing with a jarring thud but not slowing her pace for an instant.

Armand's horse was right behind her—until it balked at the branch. She knew it had because she could hear him cursing.

She drew her mare to a panting, snorting halt and turned to look at Armand and the gelding the steward had let him borrow. It was stepping around the branch as warily as if it thought it was a snake.

"It seems, my lord, that my mare has the courage of a stallion," she said with a laugh, "while the earl's gelding is as nervous as a novice."

Armand was obviously none too pleased with his mount, or her observation. "This is what comes of borrowing a horse," he grumbled. "I think my own poor nag would at least have tried."

Adelaide stroked her mare's neck. "Well, don't be too troubled, my lord. I could tell it was not the rider but the horse."

He nodded as he slipped from the saddle. "I assume this race had another motive than simply proving to me that you ride very well. You have something to tell me, my lady?"

He stood beside her horse and raised his arms, silently offering to help her dismount.

Which would mean holding her in what was almost an embrace.

"Yes, I do," she said, ignoring his stance. "Last night, before the ceremony—"

"Forgive me for interrupting, but I think this is hardly how two lovers would converse, and Randall and Eloise will be upon us soon. You'll also be able to speak more quietly if we're close together, and we're nearly at the hill. We can take that path." A nod of his head indicated a narrow way through some blackthorn and wych elm leading to the smooth mound just beyond.

He was unfortunately right.

"Since you have more experience of how lovers should behave, I'll bow to your knowledge," she reluctantly replied. "However, I can dismount by myself."

"As you wish."

She threw her leg and skirts over the saddle and

spoke the moment she was on the ground. "When I was waiting for you to swear your oath in the hall last night, I heard one of the conspirators behind me. But when I turned to see who it was, I found myself facing Hildegard and I couldn't see beyond her. The crowd was moving about so, I never did discover who it was."

"Could it have been a servant?"

"They weren't mingling with the courtiers at the time."

Armand took hold of her horse's reins along with his own and started walking toward the hill. "I spent several hours in the company of the castle guard last night, and they're mostly Welsh or men of Ludgershall. There are other soldiers belonging to the nobles staying here, but I didn't hear anyone who sounded like the conspirators, although I may have missed some who were on guard."

"Surely it couldn't have been soldiers we overheard," she said, falling into step beside him, taking care to avoid the muddy patches on the ground. "Their voices and accents marked the conspirators as educated men."

"Not every foot soldier or guard is an ignorant peasant. Some may be younger sons of nobles or merchants who've fallen on difficult times, either through their own weaknesses or a change in the family fortune. And a soldier is trained to kill, my lady. Such a man's conscience may trouble him very little, and his desire for money could be great."

"I hadn't thought of that," she admitted. "I thought perhaps it was more likely to be someone playing the part of a clerk or a clergyman, for they're educated men. But when I was with the king's clerks the other day, I didn't recognize any voices there, either."

"At least we seem to be narrowing the field a bit."

"A little," she agreed. "As long as there's the possibility that the conspirators are still here, we'll have to keep searching. Did you send a message to the earl?"

"Yes, although it had to be vague. Still, he's a cautious man by nature, and well able to defend himself, so I have confidence he'll be safe. The archbishop, though…that was a little trickier. I've asked Randall in a general sort of way about his friends in Canterbury, and I've hinted that it might be a good idea to suggest to them that in these dangerous times, the archbishop take special care. More than that I feared might be too risky. Nevertheless, I pray to God we find the traitors soon."

They reached the bottom of the mound supposedly created by druids and looked up at the smooth, grassy surface dotted with patches of white campion and yellow bedstraw.

Adelaide's mind wandered to visions of primitive festivities, with bonfires and singing and dancing by the light of the full moon, and men half-naked, long hair to their shoulders…

"So Hildegard confronted you in the hall, did she?"

Startled out of her reverie, she discovered a little

glimmer of amusement in her companion's dark eyes. "What did she want?" he asked.

"She doesn't approve of our betrothal. Well, to be more precise, she doesn't approve of *me*."

"Randall says she's as good as betrothed to Lord Richard."

"Eloise doesn't think so." She couldn't resist adding, "Your arrival seems to have caused some disruption in the court."

The amusement disappeared from Armand's face as he looped the horses' reins over the low branch of an elm. "The only person I want to upset is the king."

"You can't help being handsome," she said.

"Any more than you can help being beautiful," he replied as he turned toward her, speaking in that deep, low tone that made her heartbeat flutter. "I gather your sisters are beautiful, too."

Her brow furrowed as she wondered what had brought Gillian and Lizette to his mind.

She could come up with one reason he might think of Gillian, at least. "Gillian will send the money as soon as she's able," she assured him. "I believe it may be here as early as the day after tomorrow."

Instead of looking relieved, he frowned. "As pleased as I am to hear that, I wasn't thinking about the money. John's ordered me to invite your sisters to our wedding."

Adelaide clasped her hands tightly and fought back her dismay. "Of course. Now that I'm spoken for, he wants to offer them as prizes and rewards instead.

"He'll try to seduce them, too," she added, her voice full of disgust. "Thank God there'll be no wedding, so they won't have to come and I can stay at court to protect their welfare."

"You mean keep them safe from the king or other lustful knaves?"

She decided the time had come to make her purpose at court clear to him, to have him understand what she was really doing there—something she hadn't even explained to Eloise. "I haven't come to court simply to enjoy myself, my lord, or because the king commands it. I'm here to keep us from being married off at the king's pleasure, for as long as I possibly can. While I do that, Gillian runs the estate."

His frown deepened. "And Lizette?"

"Lizette does what she likes, for she'd have it no other way. Fortunately, that means staying away from the king. If she ever did come to court, she'd probably tell John right to his face exactly what she thinks of him and wind up executed for treason."

Armand plucked a long piece of grass, which he wound around his powerful fingers. "I hope your sisters appreciate what you're doing for them. Or do you have other goals at court that make your task more pleasurable?"

To speak of pleasure was to take this conversation where she didn't want to go, so she replied with pert insolence, "Why, I have the pleasure of meeting handsome men like you, my lord, and leading them on a merry chase."

He did not smile in return. "And what will you do, I wonder, when you're finally caught?"

"That day will never come, for I am very swift."

"And clever, too, without a doubt. But love can trip even the fastest, most determined racers, like Atalanta and the apples."

They heard the sound of approaching hoofbeats, and Randall calling out their names.

"Here!" Armand shouted back. He turned to her with a look that made her blush. "I fear, my lady, that we don't look much like lovers at the moment."

She began to back away. "Don't lovers ever talk to one another? We could be enjoying a pleasant conversation."

"It's possible," he replied as he reached out to cup her shoulders and pull her toward him. "But this would be more likely."

CHAPTER TWELVE

ELOISE HARDLY KNEW where to look when they came upon Adelaide and Lord Armand kissing passionately at the bottom of Pickpit Hill. To be sure, they were betrothed, but it was still embarrassing catching them at such an intimate moment. Randall obviously shared her discomfort, for he was blushing, too. The two soldiers, however, chortled and grinned and nudged each other as if they were delighted.

When even that didn't announce their presence to Adelaide and Armand, Randall loudly cleared his throat and they finally moved apart. Adelaide turned bright red, but Lord Armand didn't appear the least bit disconcerted.

"Forgive us for such disgraceful behavior," Lord Armand said with jovial good humour. "All the blame belongs to me, of course. I find I can't restrain myself with I'm with my beautiful bride-to-be."

Adelaide looked away, yet it didn't seem from any maidenly modesty. Instead, she looked...peeved! But surely she didn't expect anyone to be shocked that they'd been kissing. Not when they were betrothed.

To be sure, it was disconcerting to find them thus, but no one here would rush to judgment.

"Did you know they used to think druids were buried here?" Randall said, speaking matter-of-factly as he walked forward. "Nobody's ever found any gold or other things, though, so perhaps they built it to put an altar on, or some such thing. There must have been quite a bit of heathen worship around this part of the country. Consider Stonehenge, for instance."

As he carried on and led them up the hill, Eloise tried to pay attention, for Randall knew a great deal of interesting things about druids and the past. She also enjoyed the sound of his voice, and the shy way he'd glance at her, as if he really cared about what she thought and was talking mainly to her.

Nevertheless, she was still troubled by Adelaide and her less-than-joyous countenance. To be sure, Lord Armand was not to *her* taste. He was too much altogether, and she didn't want to be married to a bold warrior who would always be off fighting wars for the king, or otherwise doing his knightly duty. She would prefer a husband who stayed close to home.

She could understand why other women would want Lord Armand, though. He was handsome, and he was confident without being arrogant, unlike most of the men at court who were arrogant for no reason other than their rank. He'd also suffered, and unjustly, too. Many a woman would want to offer him comfort if she could.

So why was Adelaide upset?

Perhaps because they'd been interrupted, and she'd wanted more...time...with her betrothed.

Her dread assuaged by that conclusion, Eloise returned her attention to Randall. He was animated and excited, saying something about sunrise at Stonehenge during the summer solstice.

Randall could be passionate, too, she didn't doubt, and happy would be the woman who stirred that fire within him.

Two DAYS LATER, Lord Richard looked up from a letter supposedly from a tailor in London.

"Marcus hasn't yet found a chance to do what we sent him to do," he said to Oliver. His voice was different—stronger, sterner, deeper— and so was his stance, the foppish courtier replaced by a determined rebel.

Oliver leaned back against the wall of the man's chamber. "Aren't you the one always counselling patience? Better he should be cautious than get caught. Any word from Wales?"

Richard shook his head as he rolled up the parchment and shoved it back into his tunic. "No, not yet. I hear Armand sent the earl a message."

Oliver nodded, but he didn't look the least concerned. "Asking for money. I read it myself before the messenger left." His lips curved into a smile. "It seems the messenger has some debts, so was glad of a few extra coins."

"Your initiative continues to amaze me."

"All in a good cause, my lord. This country will be better off when John and his supporters are dead."

Richard raised a brow. "And Lady Adelaide a widow?"

Oliver merely smiled.

"Francis still has his eye on her, you know."

"He may look all he likes, but he'll never have her."

"Given her apparent affection for Lord Armand, she may not want *you,* either."

Still Oliver smiled. "We shall see, my lord."

As RICHARD was discussing the latest news from Marcus, Armand was trying not to slip on slick grass wet from two day's rain and to parry the downward stroke of Sir Charles's broadsword.

Both men were stripped to the waist, wearing only breeches and boots, as they exercised in the outer ward, watched by Sir Edmond, Lord Richard, Sir Alfred and several other male courtiers.

Armand raised his sword to block another blow. He felt the jarring hit all the way up his arm, through his shoulder and halfway down his back. His arms were still damnably weak, and his knee hurt like the devil was jabbing it with his pitchfork. He should never have climbed Pickpit Hill.

He lifted his arm to swing again, but he couldn't get it high enough. Charles easily evaded the blow, and when Armand's own momentum threw him off balance, Charles connected with Armand's blade, making him stumble and fall to the ground, landing hard on his aching knee.

Armand held up his left arm, upon which he wore a small round shield. "Enough," he said, panting more from the pain than from loss of breath. "I yield."

Charles smiled with proud satisfaction as he reached down to help his opponent to his feet. "You gave me a good fight."

"A year ago, I would have given you a better one," Armand replied, feeling sore, weak and old as he regarded his youthful companions. Charles and the others, including the silent, Irish Sir Oliver who stood watching impassively, were a good three years younger than he.

He could easily come to hate Sir Oliver, he thought as he remembered how the Irishman had danced with Adelaide again last night.

This ruse was getting to be as hard to bear as his imprisonment. It was a whole different kind of hell acting the tender lover while knowing that their lively conversations in the garden or in the hall were only performances to her. In spite of his determination to act just the same, he felt like a desperate, lovestruck fool trying to win a reluctant maid who had a bevy of admirers dancing attendance upon her.

"My father says you were the best he ever saw in a melee, after William Marshal," Sir Charles said.

"I heard you were better," Lord Richard drawled. He'd declined a practice fight, saying he would prefer to observe and learn. Armand thought it more likely he didn't want to get his clothes dirty, or feared the embarrassment of being beaten by an older man.

Armand shook his head as he walked over to join them, trying not to grimace with pain or limp, although his knee was giving him agony. "There's no one better than the Earl of Pembroke, and I'm flattered to be considered second-best to him."

Sir Alfred held out his wineskin, but Armand shook his head. "Not for me this early in the day, and when I'm so parched. Water is better."

He lifted a jug of fresh, cold well water that he'd brought for this very purpose and drank deeply. The cool and refreshing water ran down his chin and over his sweat-streaked chest.

He set down the jug and wiped his lips with the back of his hand. "If I drank wine like that now, I'd be drunk, and that's no way to be when you're at the king's court. The ladies don't like it."

Alfred glanced at his wineskin and put it down on the bench beside him.

"I've just got to ask you, my lord," Sir Edmond de Sansuren said as Armand reached for his shirt lying on the bench and put it on. "Why do you wear your hair so long? Doesn't it interfere with your eyesight when you're fighting?"

"It wasn't this long the last time I was engaged in

battle. Then it was cut like yours. However, there aren't any body servants in a dungeon."

The young men exchanged looks.

"You've been free for some time now," Lord Richard noted, speaking for them all.

"I have, but I don't intend to cut my hair until my brother is freed. It's my reminder that he's still imprisoned and suffering until I can pay his ransom."

He declined to mention that he also wished to remind the king of Bayard's captivity and his own suffering.

Sir Oliver was the only one who looked less than impressed.

"You don't approve?" Armand asked him, determined to hear what that young man had to say. He looked strong and ruthless enough to kill without compunction.

"I was wondering what your betrothed thinks about it," Oliver replied.

He sounded vaguely familiar, but not like one of the men in the garden.

Perhaps he was, and Armand's memory was at fault. The more time that passed before they found the conspirators, the harder it was going to be to be sure they'd found the right men. He would hate to accuse a man unjustly.

"She's never complained about it," he said in answer to Oliver's question before he turned his lips up in a smile every bit as proudly satisfied as Charles's had been. "In fact, she quite likes it."

Charles and Alfred laughed, Lord Richard looked pensive, and Edmond and his brother, Roger, grinned. Sir Oliver, not surprisingly, did not look pleased.

"Clearly there was a positive side to being imprisoned," Charles said, still grinning.

Armand hastened to set him straight. "There is no positive side to being chained for days and given only brackish water to drink and a bowl of mush every few days to eat. There is no positive side to being in the dark for weeks, and watching helplessly as your companions die."

"It's too bad John's such a beast," the sixteen-year-old Roger declared. "If he hadn't murdered Arthur and starved the men of Corfe, you wouldn't have had to suffer as you did. The French would have been more chivalrous.

"Come, you know I'm right!" Roger exclaimed when the other men said nothing. "Even before he killed Arthur he sent his henchmen to castrate and blind the boy to prevent him from being king. Thank God Sir Hubert prevented it. If only he could have prevented the king from murdering his nephew with his bare hands and throwing the poor lad's body into the river. And now John's got Arthur's sister locked up in Bristol. I wouldn't be surprised if he never lets her out!"

"Be quiet, Roger. You're talking treason," Edmond warned.

"I'm telling the honest truth, and you all know it," Roger retorted. "Isn't that right, Lord Armand? If John hadn't murdered his nephew and let those men at Corfe starve to death, you would have been treated with more respect and courtesy, as a knight should."

Armand twisted the hilt of his sheathed sword between his hands, the point digging into the ground, as if he would grind it into John if he could. "Nobody knows what happened to Arthur, and it's said the men of Corfe preferred to starve rather than take their chances with John. They were either very brave, or very foolish, depending on your point of view."

"What's *your* opinion?" Charles asked.

"I think life is not something to be lightly thrown away, but I was not in their situation," he answered honestly. "It's not for me to judge their actions."

"Then you believe the king is worthy of our respect and allegiance?" Oliver queried.

"I *know* the king is my liege lord, and that I've sworn to be loyal to him, and so I will be," Armand replied. "Does that mean I must approve of all he does? To do that would make me little better than his dog, or a slave."

"Well said, my lord," remarked a woman behind him.

At the sound of Adelaide's voice, Armand immediately got to his feet.

She walked toward them with her usual grace, clad in a woollen gown of a rich red. Her girdle accentuated the graceful sensuality of her walk, and her white silk veil fluttered around her beautiful face.

Out of the corner of his eye, he saw the younger men surreptitiously brush and adjust their clothes.

She had that effect on him, too, making him very aware that he was sweaty and dishevelled, and clad only in a loose, open-necked shirt, dirty breeches and muddy boots. His tunic still lay on the bench and he could barely resist the urge to grab it and tug it on.

In spite of his regret about his attire, he put a smile on his face and said, "Good day, my lady."

She smiled brilliantly back, making his heart leap with pleasure and filling him with pride, even if their betrothal was bogus.

"Forgive me if I'm interrupting," she said in her most dulcet tones.

The young men simultaneously claimed that she was most welcome—with the notable exception of Sir Oliver, who said nothing at all.

She lowered her eyes as if she was the most bashful maiden in England. "Would you gentlemen mind if I took my betrothed away from you?"

"Whether they mind or not, I'm tired and ready to do nothing more rigorous than stare at my beautiful bride," Armand said, grabbing his tunic from the bench and leading her away.

"You don't look very tired," she noted as they walked toward the castle gate.

"Your presence has invigorated me."

Her lips turned down in a displeased frown. "You don't have to act the besotted lover when we're alone."

"Then what do you want, my lady? I don't think it was to pretend that you couldn't pass the morning without seeing me again."

Godwin and Bert, once again on guard, greeted them with a grin and a nod, and let them pass without a challenge.

"The king's servant came to see me while I was sewing," she said quietly as they walked around a cart full of baskets of fish and eels, and he had to strain to hear her in the crowded, noisy yard. "John wants to know when the wedding ceremony will be. He expects it to be as soon as possible. He leaves for Salisbury in three days, and he's *generously* allowing us to take up to a fortnight to summon my sisters there, so we can be married in Salisbury Cathedral."

They came alongside the garden gate. A few of the serving women were at the well, drawing water and surreptitiously watching them.

Armand grinned a devilish grin, and before Adelaide could stop him or say a word in protest, he grabbed her around the waist and hustled her into the garden, closing the gate behind them.

She struggled to calm herself and *think,* although she'd found it difficult to think coherently ever since she'd seen Armand sprawled on the bench, his long, muscular legs stretched out in front of him, his damp shirt clinging to his sweat-soaked body, with the neck open to reveal a broad expanse of muscular chest. "What do you think you're doing?" she demanded.

"We're supposed to be lovers, my lady," he reminded her as he stepped back a pace.

For the past two days, as the rain had fallen and kept all within Ludgershall, Armand had played the passionate, devoted lover to perfection—too much so. It was becoming more and more difficult to remember that their betrothal was merely a ploy, and she shouldn't fall in love with him, no matter how much she was beginning to admire him, or how he looked at her with those dark, smoldering eyes that played havoc with her self-control.

Because even if she fell in love with him, she could never marry him, or any other man. She had given her word.

"As a matter of fact, my lord," she announced. "I was going to suggest that it's time we began to sow the seeds of our broken betrothal. That way, when we make that announcement, people will think back and say they could see it coming. Hildegard will enjoy that especially."

Armand ran his hand through his dishevelled hair. "I see. Perhaps I should flirt with the ladies in the hall tonight, then."

"That's a fine idea," Adelaide replied, telling herself it was.

"While you continue flirting with the men."

"If I've been flirting, my lord, it was because it was necessary."

"You seemed to enjoy it."

She tilted to her head to study him, wondering if he was genuinely upset or not. "You know why I did that—or is this a rehearsal for quarrels to come?"

They heard women's voices, including the queen's, and Hildegard's giggle. Armand made a face as sour as Adelaide had ever seen, then drew her into the nearest alcove. Standing close beside him, acutely aware of his proximity, she could hear his heartbeat— or was that her own pounding in her ears?

"What is that I see?" the queen called out. "The hem of a lady's skirt, I think. Who is there?"

Adelaide realized she had no choice but to reply. "It is I, Your Majesty," she said, stepping onto the path.

Richly attired in a deep blue, silk-brocade gown lined with emerald sarcenet, with sapphires sparkling at her neck and more jewels on her fingers, the queen ran a measuring gaze over Adelaide. Behind Isabel stood Hildegard and various other ladies of the court, including Jane, who blushed as if she'd been caught doing something immoral.

"Hiding in the garden, my lady?" the queen queried. "Why? Is somebody after you? Or are you up to something you shouldn't be?"

"I was—"

She gasped when Armand's arms came around her waist and he pulled her back against him.

"Forgive us, Your Majesty. We sought a few moments alone."

"Have you not been alone together enough?"

Adelaide blushed, while Armand said, "Can two people in love ever be alone enough?"

Hildegard sniffed disdainfully, while some of the other ladies sighed wistfully and Adelaide tried not to notice the sensation of Armand's arms around her.

"Perhaps they may be when they are tempted to sin," Isabel replied. "I think, Lord Armand, that you should leave your betrothed and wash and change into something more befitting one of the king's noblemen. Don't you agree, Lady Adelaide?"

Adelaide nodded as Armand released her. "Yes, Your Majesty. He's really quite unkempt. If only I could convince him to cut his hair, I would be a happy woman indeed."

She sensed Armand's displeasure, but told herself this was also necessary.

"Is this so, my lord?" Isabel asked. "You refuse her request to cut your hair?"

"I've vowed not to cut my hair until my brother is free. Although I can't satisfy my beloved in that, Your Majesty, I hope to please her in other ways."

His deep voice was so full of unspoken promise, Adelaide hardly knew where to look.

"That seems an odd vow," Hildegard said. "I thought perhaps you'd come to believe yourself another Samson."

She turned her mocking eyes onto Adelaide. "That would make you Delilah."

"Only if I cut off his hair without his permission," she said. "I have no intention of doing that."

"Thank God," Lady Jane murmured, then blushed bright red when she realized she'd spoken aloud.

"What's that?" her mother demanded. "What did you say?"

"She was paying me a compliment," Armand said to Lady Ethel, who regarded him as if he'd cursed her.

He turned back to the queen. "If Your Majesty will excuse me, I shall leave you ladies to discuss biblical comparisons while I go and make myself more presentable."

"Yes, do, my lord," the queen commanded.

Before he left, Armand smiled at Adelaide in a way that would make any woman envious of her good fortune. "Adieu, beloved."

"Adieu, my lord," she answered in return.

ADELAIDE GOT AWAY from the queen and the other ladies as quickly as she could. She fetched her sewing and went to the hall. She didn't want to be alone, to brood about the situation in which she was embroiled. Eloise would find her there, and so would the messenger from Averette, should he arrive. Unfortunately, several of the male courtiers were lounging in the large chamber, too, discussing the various merits of hawks and hounds.

Eloise arrived almost at once, giggling as she sat beside Adelaide, who had set up her embroidery frame near an arched window to take advantage of the light.

"It's all over the court about you and Lord Armand being together in the garden again," she whispered. "Really, Adelaide, I thought you'd be more careful."

"I seem to have little choice," she truthfully replied as she pushed her needle through the taut linen. "I lose all sense of discretion when I'm with Armand."

Eloise's smile drifted away, replaced with genuine concern. "I also heard you told the other ladies that you want Armand to cut his hair. That's not what you told me."

"It's attractive, but it's out of place at court," she lied. "I fear other courtiers won't take him seriously if he continues to look like a barbarian."

"Oh, I hadn't thought of that," Eloise said with a little frown. "You're probably right. It would be a pity, though. It suits him somehow." She gave Adelaide a rueful smile. "We're obviously not the only ones who think so. Marguerite tells me Hildegard's nearly mad with jealousy. And I gather Lord Richard's made it clear he has no intention of marrying her. Sir Oliver's been telling him about an Irish heiress of great wealth and beauty whose father hopes to make an advantageous marriage with an English lord."

Adelaide glanced up from the pattern of holly

leaves she was working on to look at the group of men across the hall. "Perhaps Oliver has designs on Hildegard himself."

"I haven't seen any particular sign of interest on his part," Eloise said. "I've also heard that he's rarely slept alone since he's been here, and not just with serving wenches, either."

Eloise suddenly blushed and sucked in her breath. "Oh, sweet heaven, he's coming this way!"

CHAPTER THIRTEEN

ADELAIDE would have preferred to get up and leave before Oliver reached them, but she was hemmed in by her embroidery frame and the basket containing threads, needles and a small cutting knife.

Then she realized that Sir Oliver's attention could be another excuse for breaking the betrothal with Armand.

"Good day, ladies," Sir Oliver said, arriving at her side. "I was summoned by your bright eyes."

This was the first time she'd heard Oliver speak when there wasn't a lot of other noise either from courtiers talking or minstrels playing. There was a familiar quality to his voice, yet she was nevertheless quite certain he wasn't one of the conspirators they'd over-heard.

"What a lovely thing to say," she replied with an innocuous, if amiable smile.

Eloise shifted uneasily as she nodded a greeting. There was a confused, wary look on her face as she regarded Adelaide, but her dismay couldn't be helped.

"I've been thinking how little I know about Ireland," Adelaide said to Oliver. "Since the king has a keen interest in that part of his realm, perhaps I should find out more about it."

"What would you like to know?" Oliver asked, laying a hand on the back of her chair.

That seemed an impertinent familiarity, but she ignored her discomfort. "I've heard the people there are quite barbaric."

Oliver shook his head. "They have their tribal loyalties and can be quite fierce about it, but their monasteries are full of learned men. And they can tell stories like no one else. That's an art in which even the poorest and most humble excel."

The door to the hall opened, and Armand came striding into the chamber, followed by Randall FitzOsbourne. Armand had washed and put on a clean shirt, tunic and breeches, and combed his hair.

Adelaide felt that same jolt of excitement she always did when she laid eyes on him, as she had the first time and the last. He stirred her desire as no man ever had—as she'd believed no man ever could.

That made him more dangerous than any man, at least to her peace of mind.

Meanwhile, Armand's eyes narrowed and his lips pressed together. Because of the situation with John, or the loss of his money, or because she was talking to Oliver?

"Good day, my lady, Lady Eloise, Sir Oliver," he said when he joined them, and with a distinct chill in his voice.

"Sir Oliver has just been telling us about Ireland," Adelaide said.

Armand raised a haughty brow. "Has he now?"

Oliver's dark eyes flashed with answering challenge. "Is there a reason I shouldn't?"

"No, no reason," Armand said, his eyes hostile in spite of his smile as he reached out and took Adelaide's hand. As though she belonged to him.

It wasn't difficult for Adelaide to appear displeased about that.

A little look of triumph appeared in Sir Oliver's brown eyes as he bowed and stepped back. "Since I don't want to cause any trouble for the happy couple, I'll take my leave. If there's anything more you wish to know about Ireland, my lady, just ask me and I'll do my best to answer," he said before sauntering back to Lord Richard and the others.

"There was no need for you to be so rude!" Adelaide whispered to Armand, albeit loudly enough for Eloise and Randall to hear.

"I wasn't rude," Armand replied, as sulky as a petulant child.

If he was feigning that reaction, he was doing a very good job. "You were hardly friendly," she said sharply.

"You were being friendly enough for both of us."

"I was being *polite*," she replied. "And I wanted to learn something about Ireland—or would you prefer that your wife be an ignorant ninny?"

"I would prefer that my future wife not flirt with every man at court."

"I wasn't flirting—was I, Eloise?"

Eloise squirmed with discomfort. Adelaide hated to do this to her, but there was no help for it. Eloise couldn't know the truth about the betrothal, or the ending of it. "*Was* I, Eloise?" she repeated.

Eloise came to the defense of her friend. "She really wasn't. You should apologize, my lord."

Adelaide was as taken aback by her friend's unexpected demand as Armand, while Randall stared at Eloise with outright awe.

"Apologize?" Armand muttered after a moment's silence.

"Yes," Eloise replied. "What you said was insulting and completely unjustified. You should be ashamed of yourself."

At that, Armand became the very image of contrition. Kneeling beside Adelaide's chair, he took her hand in his and looked up into her eyes with apparently genuine remorse. "Eloise is right and I was terribly wrong. I'm a jealous fool. Forgive me, beloved?"

Adelaide knew he was only playing a part, but a woman would have to be made of ice to be immune to his heartfelt plea, and she was not. "Of course... beloved."

Eloise sighed with satisfaction, and Randall looked relieved. Then Armand placed his hands upon

Adelaide's cheeks and, regardless of the presence of the others, brought her close for a kiss.

A tender, gentle, forgiveness-seeking kiss. A light touch of his lips upon hers that made her heart yearn for something she had long believed would only give her pain.

He broke the kiss and looked into her eyes. "I'll apologize again when we're alone," he whispered as he rose.

God help her! She didn't dare risk being alone with him again. Not tonight, and not ever. She was a weak mortal, after all, and the temptation he offered was almost more than she could resist.

Almost.

LATER THAT EVENING, after the ladies had retired, Armand walked slowly up the steps toward his bedchamber. Torches flickered in their sconces, and the light of a full moon shone through the windows.

Despite saying he would apologize to Adelaide again when they were alone, he'd managed to avoid being solely in her company. She was too tempting, and he was finding it more and more difficult to remember that their love was supposed to be a lie.

She, however, seemed to have no difficulty with that, or with setting the stage for the end of their betrothal. Her flirtation with the Irishman had certainly seemed genuine....

Unfortunately, his jealousy wasn't completely

feigned. When he'd seen Adelaide smiling and talking with that Irishman, he'd wanted to throttle the man for his presumption.

That reaction had to be some last, unquenchable bastion of primitive male pride, because he didn't love Adelaide—which was good. Even if the quarrel in the hall had been intended only for show, it was uncomfortably like the arguments between his father and his stepmother, forcibly reminding him that he wanted a pliant, quiet, amiable wife—a bride completely different from Lady Adelaide D'Averette.

He could still admire and respect her, of course, but he must and would subdue any other feelings she aroused.

He passed the stairwell that led to a different set of apartments—the ones where Adelaide had her chamber, he knew—when a flurry of hasty footsteps on the stairs made him halt.

A woman rounded the curve, one hand on the railing carved into the stones. She came to a halt, bending over with the effort to catch her breath.

"Oh, praise God!" Lady Jane cried when she saw him, her face white in the darkness. "Please, help me!"

Armand was beside her in an instant, supporting her as best he could. "What is it? What's happened?"

"It's Mama. She fell from her bed and her breathing's strange."

"We should summon a ser—"

"Yes, yes, but first we must get her back into bed. She's lying on that cold stone floor!"

Lady Jane was nearly hysterical. Better, perhaps, to do as she asked first, then summon a servant. "Very well."

Jane took his hand and, holding up her skirts with the other, practically pulled him up the stairs.

She looked cautiously into the corridor before leaving the stairwell, which struck him as odd, and it occurred to him that something might be wrong—and it might have nothing to do with her mother. "My lady—"

"My lord, please!" she hissed, opening the door to the nearest chamber and tugging him inside.

The light of a single sputtering candle, set in a holder on a small wooden table, did *not* reveal an elderly woman lying on the floor. He heard no sounds of distress from the other side of the bed, either. The room was empty, except for its furnishings and the feminine articles scattered on the top of the table.

Fearing a trap, Armand unsheathed his sword and turned as Jane closed the door and shot the bolt home. Then she braced herself against the door as if invaders were upon them.

"Why have you brought me here?" he demanded.

"Why…why have you drawn your sword?" she cried when she saw the weapon in his hand.

Still concerned this was a trap, he didn't lower his blade. "Where's your mother?"

"S-safe in her bed," Jane stammered. She started toward him, an anxious yet intense look in her blue eyes. "Please, put up your sword, my lord. You aren't in any danger."

Armand did not sheath his blade as he stood his ground. "I ask you again, my lady, why have you brought me here?"

She clasped her hands in a pleading gesture. "I want you to make love to me!"

He felt as if he'd taken a heavy blow on the head. "What?"

She kept coming toward him while he backed away. "No man has ever asked to marry me, or tried to seduce me, not even the king. I'm nearly twenty-five years old, and I want to know what it's like to make love, even just once."

He held up his hand to silence her, as well as keep her distance, as he sidled toward the door. "My lady," he said, trying to be patient and sympathetic despite her outrageous request, "I'm flattered you want me to be your lover, but I've pledged my troth to Lady Adelaide."

"Men break their promises all the time."

"*I* don't."

"No one need ever know. It can be our secret."

"*I* will know I've broken faith with Adelaide."

"You're not married yet," Jane pleaded, watching him like a starving man eyeing a banquet.

"As good as," he retorted as he reached the door.

She ran to bar the way. "So you *have* made love with her!"

"As good as," he repeated. "Now let me leave, my lady, and we'll forget this ever happened."

She suddenly turned her back to him and, laying her head against the door, began to sob. "I might as well be diseased—or *dead!*"

God save him, what a predicament! He wished Adelaide were here. A woman would surely know what to say to comfort Jane. "I'm sure there's still cause for you to hope that—"

"Oh, you're a *fool!*" she cried, pushing away from the door and facing him, her nose red and her eyes brimming with tears. "I know the truth, and so does every woman here. I'm going to grow old without ever having a husband or children. All *I* have to look forward to is taking care of my mother until God is pleased to take her and then it will be the convent for me until I die. Imagine having such a future spread before you—how would you like it? Wouldn't you want to know love—passionate love—just once?"

"Lady Jane," he said gently, for he did understand despair, "I had death in my future not so long ago. But I also had hope and so must you. You have friends here and—"

"Friends? You think the ladies here are my *friends?* They pretend to be to my face, but I know they laugh at me behind my back. Oh, what a silly creature! Oh, poor old Lady Jane!" She began to sob again, her breaths coming in great gasps, a drip of mucus dangling from her nose.

"My lady, please," he implored. "Don't cry. You do have friends here. Lady Adelaide—"

"Will have you whenever she likes after you're married," Jane replied through her tears. "Beautiful women get whatever they want. The rest of us have to take what we can get, and be grateful—but I can't get *anyone!*"

She wiped her nose with the long cuff of her gown and looked at him beseechingly. "I know you need money for your brother's ransom."

Sweet heaven! "My lady," he said, trying not to sound angry or indignant, although he was both, "I hope you don't expect me sell my body to save my brother."

"Oh, no! Oh, merciful Mary!" she wailed. "I was only offering to help you if you would help me!"

"I cannot. I *will* not."

With an anguish sob, Jane wrenched open the door and fled the chamber.

Armand took a moment to calm himself, but only a moment. He had no idea whose chamber this was, but he was sure he didn't want to be discovered here. He had enough to trouble him without that. As for Lady Jane, surely she wouldn't want anyone else to know of this confrontation.

After ensuring that no one was in the corridor, he crept into the hall.

A door banged against the wall and then a body

hurled itself against him, sending him crashing to the floor and knocking the wind from his lungs.

"Thief! Blackguard! Bastard!" a woman cried as she jumped on him, beating him with her clenched fists.

Armand caught a glimpse of an enraged face through the mass of long, dishevelled dark hair and grabbed her arms to make her stop. *"Adelaide?"*

She stopped hitting him. "Armand?"

"Yes."

"What are you doing here?"

"Getting pummelled," he grimly replied, trying not to notice the sensation of her nearly naked body on top of his as she straddled him. She was clad only in a thin linen shift that did little to hide her shapely form, and her hair fell about her in unbound waves of disarray.

She scrambled off him and got to her feet.

The moonlight made her shift nearly transparent, and God help him, he couldn't look away. The sight of her was nearly enough to make him forget the excruciating pain in his knee, or to wonder what had caused her to attack him.

As he rose, she crossed her arms—more from anger and the chill of the corridor than from the realization that she might as well be nude, he thought. "What's afoot, my lady?"

"There was someone in my chamber," she answered. "I was trying to catch him, but he got away."

Any thought of desire or anything other than the danger she'd been in fled Armand's mind as other chamber doors along the corridor opened and the frightened faces of ladies and their maids, who often slept on pallets by the doors of their mistresses' chambers, appeared in the doorways.

Clutching a bedrobe about her, Eloise hurried toward them, an obviously terrified maidservant trailing behind her. "Adelaide!" she cried in alarm. "Are you hurt? Were you attacked?"

She'd posed the very questions Armand was about to ask, while he also wondered where Adelaide's maid had gone. Perhaps she'd been warned, or paid to leave.

"Whoever it was, he didn't touch me," Adelaide answered. "I'm unharmed."

She did seem well and even quite composed, but he could see the little quiver of her lip when she spoke. If she wasn't about to swoon or collapse in a frightened heap, she wasn't as unmoved as she pretended.

She was a brave woman, and one capable of as much self-possession as he'd ever seen a man exhibit. Perhaps it was a mistake to think he could guess what was going on in that shrewd mind of hers.

"What's happening, Jane?" Lady Ethel's querulous voice demanded from the farthest chamber. Jane's pale face quickly retreated from the doorway, and it was just as swiftly closed.

At nearly the same time, the steward and three foot soldiers arrived at the top of the stairs. De Chevron wore an open shirt and breeches, and his feet were bare. The soldiers, who'd probably been on watch, were mail-clad and had their swords drawn.

"What's amiss, my lord?" de Chevron asked, looking at Armand and averting his gaze from the stunning presence of Adelaide.

"There was someone in my chamber," Adelaide said, her voice still firm, although she flushed and wrapped her arms more tightly about herself, perhaps finally realizing how scantily attired she was.

"I'll wager there was," one of the soldiers muttered under his breath.

Armand glared at the man. "Do you have any particular knowledge of a thief loose in Ludgershall Castle?" he demanded, his voice as cold as the North Wind.

The man flushed and mumbled, "No, my lord."

"Then keep your observations to yourself," the steward snapped.

"I didn't see who it was," Adelaide continued, addressing Armand and the steward, and ignoring the soldiers.

"Where's your maidservant?" Armand asked. "She left you alone and unattended?"

"The lady would have no maid in her chamber," de Chevron hastened to say, no doubt fearing this lack would reflect poorly on him, or his master.

"He's quite right," Adelaide confirmed. "While my father lived, I shared a very small chamber with my sisters, and since his death, I prefer to be alone in my chamber at night. During the day, Walter has ensured I have a maidservant as I require."

It was an odd arrangement, and obviously one with some risk attached, but he could well believe that the lady would be so insistent that de Chevron would have no choice but to acquiesce to her request.

"Might I suggest everyone else retire and leave this matter to me and my men?" the steward proposed.

"An excellent idea," Armand seconded.

Despite the apparent eagerness of her maid to go back to their chamber, Eloise hesitated. "Adelaide, would you like me to—?"

"I'm quite all right, and I'm sure that I'll be safe now," she assured her friend. "Please, go back to bed."

Eloise nodded and did as Adelaide requested, while her maid fairly ran to their room.

Adelaide raised herself on her toes and reached for a torch from one of the sconces in a way that made her shift tighten across her breasts. Then she marched back to her chamber, followed by de Chevron and his subdued men—and Armand, trying to rid his mind of the vision of her nearly naked body.

De Chevron ordered the soldiers to remain outside before he and Armand entered the room, now illuminated by the torch Adelaide held in her trembling hand.

Both men stared at the disarray. Someone had opened Adelaide's clothes chest and tossed all her garments, veils, shifts and stockings around the room. Her fur-lined cloak lay slashed to pieces upon the floor. Her gowns had been deliberately torn, too.

Armand went to Adelaide, standing stiff and motionless in the midst of the destruction and chaos. He could see the shock beneath her stoic expression, the whiteness of her cheeks, and the dismay deep in her eyes.

He spied her bedrobe lying on the foot of her bed. It had apparently escaped the massacre, and he hurried to put it around her slender shoulders.

"Here, let me take that," he said softly, lifting the torch from her trembling hand and handing it to the dumbfounded steward. "Come, sit down."

He led her to the bed and made her sit. When he saw her slippers peeking out from beneath the bed, he knelt to put them on.

Her feet were frigid and he rubbed them a moment to warm them. "As long as it was only your clothes," he said. "If you'd been hurt…"

If she'd been hurt, he wouldn't have rested until he found the culprit. And that lout would rue the day he'd been born.

"You have no idea who did this, my lady?" the steward asked.

"I woke—I think when that bottle of perfume was

broken—and realized someone was in my chamber. It was too dark to see clearly, but I saw…a person…so I got out of bed and gave chase."

"You should have called for help," Armand said, appalled as he imagined what might have happened if the miscreant had turned and attacked instead of fleeing.

"I didn't think of that," Adelaide admitted. "I saw someone in my room and just…" she shrugged her shoulders "…went after him."

"That was a very dangerous thing to do. You should have summoned the guard."

Armand spoke sternly to hide his dismay and the overwhelming concern he felt for her safety. It was nearly as strong as his fears for Bayard.

No, he suddenly realized with a sense of undeniable conviction, he cared about her even more. Bayard, after all, was a trained warrior. No matter how courageous she was, Adelaide was still only a woman.

"If it happens again, I shall attempt to recall your sage advice, my lord," she said with more than a hint of annoyance.

He hadn't meant to wound her pride.

He would say no more about what she should have done. After all, he probably would have given chase, too.

"Then it was a man you saw?" de Chevron asked.

"I *think* it was a man wearing a cloak. It could have been a woman," Adelaide replied.

"Can you tell if anything is missing?"

Adelaide got to her feet, resolve in every feature. "I'll be happy to take an inventory. I assume you'll start a search for unlawful intruders, and have all the guards informed, as well."

How could he not admire and respect such a woman? How could he not care about her fate?

"I'll start a search immediately," the steward said, heading for the door. "The sentries were alerted when I called for the soldiers, so if it was a thief, he'll still be here and we'll catch him. I'll also post a guard outside your door, my lady. No one will disturb you again."

"No, they won't," Armand said, "because I intend to stay with my lady."

Adelaide was obviously not pleased by his announcement. "A guard outside my door will be ample protection," she said firmly.

No matter how capable she was, or how brave, he simply would not risk any harm coming to her. "I'm not leaving you alone."

"My lord, I appreciate your concern for your betrothed, but that would not be… appropriate," the steward said. "My men will keep her safe."

"I mean no criticism of you or your men, Walter, but at least for tonight, I'm staying here," Armand said, making it clear he would not willingly go.

Adelaide turned away as if embarrassed, but not before he caught the look of fury in her eyes. There would be harsh words from her when they were alone, but he didn't care. She could rail at him all she liked, as long as she was safe.

"As you wish, my lord," Walter de Chevron said as he went to the door. "I'll still post a guard outside."

"Thank you," Armand said.

Adelaide also nodded her thanks, but the moment the door closed behind the steward, any gratitude disappeared from her features. She glared at Armand as if *he'd* been the intruder.

"Spare me your tirade, my lady," he said with grim resolve. "I'm *not* leaving you alone in this chamber tonight."

CHAPTER FOURTEEN

"AM I HURT?" she demanded. "Am I sobbing in terror?"

He gestured at the disarray around them. "Are you safe? Have you no enemies? Has it not occurred to you that you might be in grave danger?"

"Whoever it was, he ruined my clothes and left me alone."

"This time."

"I hardly think anyone would be fool enough to try to harm me with a guard outside my door."

"I'm not taking any chances," Armand adamantly replied.

"Oh, so you will rule me? I remind you, sir, you are not my husband and never will be."

"Need I remind *you* that there's a guard outside the door? Lower your voice, my lady, and remember that we're supposed to be in love. How devoted and concerned a lover would I be if I left you alone after this distressing event? As far as the court is concerned, we've already made love at least once and are as good as married, so I will act the part of your dutiful husband, as you should act the dutiful, loving bride."

"You go too far with this ruse," she said through clenched teeth, her hands balling into fists.

"I go as far as I see necessary, my lady."

"Oh, yes, as *you* see fit!" she retorted, wrapping her bedrobe more tightly about her. "Well, understand this, *beloved*. I will not allow any man to control me. I survived my father's tyranny, and I won't bend my knee before another man."

"God's wounds, my lady, am I asking for your surrender?" he demanded, throwing up his hands in frustration. "I assure you, I'm not—only that you do your duty, as I must do mine, even if it means being betrothed to a woman who's not the sort of wife I want, humiliating myself before the king who betrayed me, and risking my brother's life. You might as well save your breath and stop trying to make me do otherwise."

"Doing your duty doesn't mean you have to stay in my chamber."

"I believe it does."

She sat on the bed and, suddenly, her shoulders slumped as if she were overwhelmed with fatigue. "Very well, my lord. Stay. I have no more heart to argue with you tonight."

She must really be exhausted, and perhaps this destruction of her garments was more upsetting to her than he'd assumed.

His frustration and annoyance began to dwindle and the urge to comfort her slipped into its place.

Unfortunately, he could just imagine how she'd react to that.

"Do you think this has something to do with the conspiracy?" she asked. "Do you suppose the traitors know we're aware of their plot and this is some kind of warning?"

"It could be," he replied, leaning back against her dressing table and deliberately keeping his distance. "But if it is a warning, it's a poor one. It's much too vague, for one thing. I think it's more likely an act of spite or jealousy. I've known this sort of sabotage before, in a garrison where one soldier seems to be favored over another. The one not so favored takes out his anger on the other by destroying his weapons or armor. Since your clothing was ruined, this strikes me as more the act of a woman—perhaps Hildegard."

"Yes, that could be," Adelaide agreed as she rose and began to pick up her clothes. "I can see Hildegard doing something like this."

She paused and glanced at him when he started to help. "You don't have to do that," she said as she reached out to take one of her shifts from him.

"I don't mind lending a hand," he said, refusing to relinquish her soft white garment. "Since we're not really betrothed and thus unlikely to do anything people would expect a betrothed couple to do when spending the night in a bedchamber together, I might as well help you."

Unlikely to do anything a betrothed couple would do in a bedchamber? Adelaide's throat went dry and her hands began to tremble again as she gathered up more of her clothes. "So you're staying here to protect me from Hildegard or another woman?" she said, trying to sound amused.

"Unlike most men," he replied as he continued to help her pick up her clothes, folding them and making a pile on the bed, "I don't believe women are incapable of violence. If you'd had a weapon in your hand tonight, I would no doubt be dead."

"I can't disagree," she said, "yet I think I can protect myself against another woman."

"If you were equally armed, I don't doubt it. But anyone can be defeated by a better-armed opponent."

"You believe Hildegard capable of murder?"

"I'm not sure she would have the will when it came time to actually do the deed," he answered. He gestured around the room. "Something like this, though...most certainly. Where is Hildegard's chamber?"

She remembered where he'd been when she knocked him down. "It's the one you were coming out of," she said slowly, turning toward him and wondering what exactly he'd been doing there.

"I wasn't enjoying a clandestine encounter with that harpy, if that's what you're thinking," he said as he bent down to pick up the remains of her cloak.

"It would be nothing to me if you were," she said a little too sharply. "After all, we're going to have to break the betrothal sometime, and if people think you've also been sleeping with Hildegard—"

"They'll think I'm the same sort of lascivious cad my father was," he retorted, his hands gripping her cloak as if he wanted to tear it anew. "That is not something I want."

He tossed the remains of her cloak onto the bed. "As a matter of fact, I was on my way to my chamber when Lady Jane sought my help. She told me her mother had fallen from her bed. I suggested summoning a servant, but she claimed she wanted to get her mother up from the floor first. She was so upset, I agreed, only to discover when I got to the chamber that her mother wasn't there. I feared it might be a trap—and it was," he finished in an angry mutter as he bent down to retrieve another torn garment.

Adelaide stared at him, nearly as dumbfounded as when she'd first seen her chamber in the torchlight.

"A trap! Is Jane involved in the conspiracy?" That was difficult to believe…

"No."

His words were a relief, and yet… "Then what sort of a trap was it?"

"That's not important. I wasn't in any danger. I left the chamber and you knocked me to the ground."

He was purposefully avoiding her gaze. And was he *blushing*?

Why would he be embarrassed…? He was a very attractive man, and Jane a woman. "Did she kiss you?"

That made him look at her. Or rather, glare at her. "No!"

"But she tried?" Adelaide prompted. She could understand why a woman would want to do that. None better, perhaps.

"Did I say she did anything of that sort?"

The more he prevaricated, the more certain she was that she had guessed aright. "Then she had another reason to be alone with you? Perhaps she had some Greek or Latin that required translating?"

"What happened in that chamber is between Lady Jane and me, and no business of yours!" he growled, snatching up another garment and tossing it onto the bed without even trying to fold it.

"Of course you don't have to tell me if you don't want to," she said as she reached for a torn veil, "although I can certainly understand why Jane would be tempted. You're a very attractive man."

He glanced at her sharply. "You find this amusing?"

"No. Sad, rather. Poor Jane."

He closed the lid of her chest and sat on it. "She said she feared she was never going to marry and she wanted to experience love at least once. With me."

"I hope you weren't too angry with her."

He jumped up and began to pace like a caged beast. "I tried to be kind, in spite of being made to feel like some sort of male harlot."

He was truly disturbed by what had happened,

which said more plainly than any words that he was no lustful scoundrel.

"She made you feel like a thing, not a person," Adelaide said softly. "And now you know how *I* feel every day of my life."

He stopped pacing. "Every day?"

"Every day that I'm at court," she affirmed.

He regarded her with new understanding in his dark eyes, a sympathy she unexpectedly found more disconcerting than his anger. "I suppose it can't be easy being a knight, either," she said, walking toward the window where the nearly full moon shone in the night sky. "To go where the king commands and do as he orders, especially when the king is a man like John."

"No, it's not," he agreed, following her. "There were many times in Marchant it would have been easy to surrender, had my oath and my honor not forbade it."

"You saved many innocent lives by surrendering when you did," she said, upset to hear the self-condemnation in his voice, and very aware that he was close behind her. "If you hadn't surrendered, many more people would have died. And you paid a heavy price when you did."

"Not as great as some," he murmured.

She turned to face him. "Your squire's death was not your fault," she whispered, wanting to comfort him. Needing to.

"You know?"

"Yes, I know." She reached out to lay her hand on his arm. "You did everything you could. You mustn't blame yourself."

Although his mouth became a grim, hard line, remorse and anguish filled his gold-flecked eyes. "He didn't deserve such a death. None of my men did."

"Because you were abandoned by the king who should have done all in his power to save you. It was not your fault, Armand."

He bowed his head and covered her hand with his, that simple gesture more tender, more full of meaning, more thrilling than a kiss.

But perhaps he would kiss her, too, and she would not be sorry…

He didn't kiss her. Instead, he said, "I have something to tell you, Adelaide. I found the ransom money that was stolen from me in my boot."

She stared at him with shocked dismay. "You got your money back after taking the one thing of value I possessed?"

"I *was* robbed," he insisted, his hands stiff at his sides. "The money was returned to my chamber and put in my boot. Why, I don't know. A guilty conscience? The thief feared he was going to be caught? Whatever the reason, I give you my word of honor as a knight and a de Boisbaston that I did not have it when I gave your crucifix to the king."

She made her way to the bed and sat heavily.

"But why would a thief, having taken your money, give it back?"

"That's what I've been asking myself since I found it in my boot."

"It could be he wants to make trouble between *us,*" she suggested.

"That could be—and he nearly succeeded."

"You must admit it's very strange."

He sighed and nodded. "It seems as if nothing but strange things have happened since I came to Ludgershall." He smiled then, a small, wry, self-deprecating smile. "Things must have been rather dull before."

"I wouldn't say that," she replied, wrapping her arms around herself as she thought of all the times she'd felt poised on a knife edge when bandying words with the king or other courtiers.

"I suppose it was vain of me to say that. It can't be easy for you here." His brow furrowed as he studied her. "You must be exhausted. You should go to bed and try to sleep."

"If I do that, where will you be, my lord?"

He dragged the stool over to the wall opposite her bed and sat, then leaned back, so that his back was against the wall and the front two legs of the stool were off the floor. He crossed his arms over his broad chest. "Right here."

That couldn't be comfortable; the stone wall would be chilly against his back, at the very least.

"I spent three months in a dungeon sleeping on

fetid straw, so you need have no concerns about my comfort."

In spite of his hearty words, she moved aside the pile of clothes on her bed and pulled the coverlet from it to take to him.

"I thank you, but I don't need it," he said with a smile.

"There are plenty of other coverings on my bed. I'll be warm enough without it."

He took the coverlet with a nod and a look in his brown eyes that warmed her more than any bedding could. "Thank you, my lady. But if you get cold, you must tell me."

And he would...what?

Give her back the coverlet, obviously, she thought, silently reproaching herself for impure thoughts as she hurried back to her bed. She quickly shrugged off her bedrobe and slipped beneath the sheets, leaving the pile of clothes right where it was.

Yet in spite of the late hour, sleep would not come. She was still too agitated by what had happened, and distracted by Armand's presence. She kept straining to hear if he moved. She wondered if he could really sleep in such a position, or if he'd only told her that to assuage her doubts about his comfort.

He shifted a few times, and on each occasion, she held her breath. She wasn't afraid that he would hurt her, or force himself upon her.

She was afraid of her own weakness.

When she was near Armand, when he was acting

kindly, when he was apparently as different from her brutal father as it was possible for a man to be, she found him almost irresistibly attractive. At those times it was easy to forget her vow and why she'd made it. Instead she kept recalling that she'd never promised to be celibate.

She sighed and turned onto her side. Finally, in the east, the dawn began to break. She could hear the early-morning songbirds. They soon gave way to the noises the servants made as their workday began, and the changing of the guard.

She looked away from the window to the wall opposite—and encountered Armand's steadfast gaze.

"Too upset to sleep, my lady?" he asked quietly, shifting his weight forward so that the stool rested on all four legs.

"I'm not used to having a man in my bedchamber."

That brought an amused smile to his face. "Nor I to sitting on a stool in the presence of a woman to whom I'm supposedly betrothed."

"No, I suppose not."

She started to get out of bed, and he rose and handed her the bedrobe. His gaze flicked to her breasts, and her nipples visible beneath the thin fabric in the early-morning light.

Sweet heaven! She might as well be naked! She abruptly turned her back to him as she put on her bedrobe and reached around to lift her hair from beneath it. The maid would likely be here soon—

His hands slipped through the curtain of her hair and brushed the nape of her neck as he lifted it. While she stood as stiff as a plank, he let her hair slip through his fingers.

"It's softer than velvet," he murmured.

Her whole body reacted as if he'd caressed her with his hands.

She stepped away and faced him, wrapping the robe about her as if it were her armor. "You flatter as well as Francis."

When she saw the injured look in his eyes, she immediately, and earnestly, regretted her impetuous words.

"There's no need to insult me," he said, moving away.

"You caught me off guard," she admitted. "I've never let *any* man do anything like that. You…upset me."

Regarding her steadily, he gently took hold of her shoulders. "Is that the *only* way I make you feel, my lady?"

She couldn't meet his earnest gaze, couldn't prevent the blush that colored her cheeks and warmed her body. Couldn't answer.

"I think not," he whispered as he brought her close and bent his head to kiss her.

Stop him! her mind cried. *This is wrong. It will only cause you more trouble. Heartache or dishonor and a broken vow. Stop now, while you can!*

But she was helpless to deny the desire welling up inside her. As always it arose strong and hot and potent, and this time, she was powerless to subdue it.

Her need overthrew her inner protests. Here, now, the only thing that seemed important was this man and his kiss, her desire and need and longing that yearned to be fulfilled. The future was unimportant. The present was all in all.

With a low moan, she surrendered to the heated sensations aroused by his lips upon hers. His mouth slid over hers, tasting and teasing, while her arms glided around his narrow waist and her hands splayed against his muscular back.

His hands were in her unbound hair before they slid to her buttocks and pressed her closer. Her nipples tightened, and her nether lips began to swell and soften as if in silent invitation when she felt his hardened shaft against her.

He gathered her in his arms and carried her to the bed, laying her upon it. She reached up for him and, capturing his mouth with hers, pulled him down beside her, her clothes tumbling unheeded to the floor.

He stroked her body while their tongues entwined. Then, as her arms went around his neck to hold him closer, his fingertips lightly, delicately, brushed over her breast and the taut tip of her nipple. Her thin shift provided only the flimsiest of barriers, little more than nothing as he teased her nipple with the pad of his thumb, and when his knee gently nudged apart her legs, she eagerly lifted her hips to push her body against his thigh.

His lips began to meander down the column of her

neck toward her collarbone, and he planted a host of kisses there as he moved lower. Meanwhile, he bunched the skirt of her shift in his hand, so that her leg was bare nearly to the top of her thigh. That achieved, he began to caress her limb, beginning below her knee.

It seemed a tender torture as his hand slowly progressed higher and then higher still, until he arrived at her hip.

That tickled and she bucked—and in the next moment, his lips were crushing hers with more ardent need. She was completely aware of his body against hers, her breasts against his chest. Then she felt the heel of his hand against her *there*—a gentle, yet inexorable pressure.

Moaning, she arched and held him tight, bringing her body more into contact with his. Still he stroked with his hand against her naked, moist mound. Then he slipped a finger inside.

As the tension burst in throbbing waves of incredible power, she let out a cry, the primal sound loud in the stillness.

The door to the chamber opened.

With a gasp, Adelaide twisted away and sat up as Eloise came bustling into the room, a grass-green gown over her arm.

CHAPTER FIFTEEN

"I'm NOT at all surprised you're still abed, Adelaide," Eloise said as she went to the stool and laid the gown upon it before turning toward the bed. "To wake up and find a man—"

She let out a shocked gasp, then backed toward the door, her face as red as wine. "I'm so sorry! I didn't know...didn't expect... I just brought... I thought you answered my knock and I..."

She fumbled with the latch for a moment, then ran out of the chamber, the door banging shut behind her.

Armand, too, sat up. "That was unfortunate."

To her chagrin, Adelaide realized he was trying not to laugh.

"Unfortunate?" she snapped as she started snatching up her clothes and putting them on the bed. "It was considerably more than that."

He rose and put his hand on her arm to make her stop. "There's no need to be upset, Adelaide. We *are* betrothed."

"For now," she said, twisting out of his grasp. She

went to her dressing table, grabbed her comb and raked it through her disheveled hair.

Of course she was upset. He wasn't exactly free of frustration himself. Nevertheless, he meant what he said. He would do what was necessary to make things right. He knew she valued honor as much as any man. So did he. And he was not like his father.

"All will be well, Adelaide. I give you my word as a knight of the realm that I'll marry you."

He was completely sincere. He wanted Adelaide D'Averette for his wife as much as he wanted Bayard to be free. He wanted to take her home to Boisbaston, where she would be his chatelaine and they would raise a family of fine sons and beautiful daughters.

To his surprise and dismay, she frowned as she forcefully laid her comb back on the table. "I thank you for the offer, my lord, but this betrothal was meant to be a ruse, and so it will stay."

"But—"

"I will not marry you, Armand."

At her harsh response, his heart seemed to shatter, even as he struggled to make sense of her refusal. Her kisses, her embraces, her passion this morning, all had contrived to make him think her feelings for him went far beyond their ruse.

Obviously, he was wrong.

Beneath the pain of that realization lay another bitter wound that reopened like a festering sore—that he was incapable of winning another's affection, as he hadn't been important to his father, or worth his stepmother's notice, except to be criticized.

Then the pride that had sustained him in his youth and childhood, the knowledge that Bayard loved him, and Randall liked him, arose to seal the wound. "Forgive me for thinking that being my wife was not the worst fate in the world."

Her tone softened and so did the look in her eyes as she addressed him. "I don't think that at all. I simply meant what I said. I won't marry you."

Her words did not assuage his bitterness. "Instead you would have me be like every other lecher who's tried to seduce you, except that I nearly succeeded where so many others have failed."

"I know you're not like that. You're better than many a man at court."

Her words brought him no comfort, only more pain and confusion. "Yet not good enough for you."

"My decision has nothing to do with you."

In some ways, that was worse. "Is that supposed to comfort me?"

She clasped her hands and looked at him with genuine regret. "I won't marry you because I can't marry *anyone,* Armand. I made a solemn promise I would never marry."

He stared at her, dumbfounded. "Who forced you to do such a thing?"

"No one *forced* me," she replied. "I made the

pledge of my own free will, and as you value your word, so do I."

She kept her gaze on his face, hating herself for hurting him, sorry for what she must do, wishing she could have spared them both, yet willing him to accept that as he would not forswear his oath to the king who'd abandoned him, neither would she break her promise to her sisters.

Or she would be nothing but a weak and fickle woman after all, and her sworn word worth less than dust.

"After my father died, when my sisters and I finally had a little freedom, we wanted to stay free, or as free as any woman can be," she explained. "We swore we would never subject ourselves to husbands, and we made a solemn pact that we would never marry."

She squared her shoulders, as determined as he had ever been. "I will not—I *cannot*—break that promise. Not even for you."

He had never felt so helpless, not even in his chains.

For as he looked at Adelaide's resolute face and recalled her courage, strength and fortutide, he realized those qualities he admired so much would work against him in this. She was no weak-willed, capricious female of the sort who gave all women a reputation as silly, foolish, indecisive creatures. She would never break a vow.

She would never marry him.

"If you've given your word, you must keep it," he said.

Then he left the room without another word, or even a glance in her direction.

WHEN HE WAS GONE, Adelaide sat on the bed and stared, unseeing, at the closed door. This was what must be, she told herself. Like her sisters, she had given her word, and her honor demanded she keep it, even if she was no longer certain that marriage would be slavery. She had been so sure no man would ever see her as worthy of the respect he would show another of his sex. She had believed she would never, ever, meet a man with whom she would wish to spend the rest of her life.

She'd been wrong. So very, very wrong…

Another rap sounded on her door, softer and more cautious. A maidservant, probably.

She didn't want to see anyone. She wanted to be alone. She wanted to weep. Like a weak and foolish girl.

She swiped at the tears that had already fallen on her cheeks and reminded herself that she was Lady Adelaide D'Averette. She had stood firm before her brute of a father to protect her mother and her sisters, and she would just as resolutely accept the consequences of her promise now.

"Enter!" she called out, determined to act as if

nothing was wrong, and to continue the ruse of the betrothal until she could find out who was plotting to murder the earl and archbishop.

It wasn't a maidservant who peered into her chamber. It was Eloise.

"Please, come in," Adelaide said, all too aware of the last time she'd seen Eloise. Blushing, she quickly took refuge in washing her face.

"I'm so sorry, Adelaide, truly!" her friend said meekly as she ventured into the chamber. "I was so concerned you'd have nothing to wear and I wanted to give you that gown."

"I appreciate your thoughtfulness," Adelaide replied as she wiped the cool water from her face. "I might be able to manage with my own gowns and shifts, though. There are a few that need only to be mended to be wearable."

"Oh, but I have more than I can wear, and so do several other ladies. Look."

Adelaide glanced over her shoulder, to see Eloise with her arms full of clothing. She hurried to take some from Eloise and put them on the bed, while Eloise laid the rest of her burden there.

"Marvelous, isn't it?" Eloise said. "You're more popular than you know."

Adelaide gazed in wonder at the variety of gowns, shifts, stockings and veils.

"More than one lady said she was sure it was Hildegard's doing. Of course, Hildegard's denying she had anything to do with it, but nobody believes her. Even Lady Mary sent three shifts. They're likely to be too short for you, but they're better than nothing. And Lady Wilhemina's provided seven gowns."

"I'm surprised those two have been so generous," Adelaide said, running her hand over the green gown. "I always thought they valued Hildegard's friendship more than mine."

"Until now, perhaps. Hildegard's made it very clear that she's considering any help to you a personal affront. I wonder if that's why Lady Jane was acting so peculiar. She didn't say anything at all, or even look at me."

"Perhaps she didn't want to upset her mother," Adelaide said, although she could guess why Jane had behaved that way. Jane was surely upset about what had happened with Armand last night. She probably thought Armand had told her—Adelaide—all about it, and was afraid they'd tell others.

"I know her mother has very strict notions of propriety," Eloise said, "but I always thought Jane was a little more forgiving. After all, you and Armand *are* betrothed. Unfortunately, it seems she's not."

However Lady Jane was behaving, Adelaide wanted Eloise to know at least part of the truth.

"We didn't make love."

Eloise eyes widened. "You didn't? But I saw…that is…" She fell awkwardly silent and began to needlessly straighten one of the gowns until she changed the subject. "Do you think Hildegard ruined your clothes?"

"I wish I knew," Adelaide replied, relieved not to be talking about what had—or had not—happened with Armand last night. "I know it wasn't you, or Jane…"

The moment she said Jane's name and saw the change in Eloise's expression, she wanted to bite her tongue and call her words back. But she couldn't. "Jane was talking to Armand when my clothes were being destroyed," she explained.

"Oh?" Eloise replied, a host of questions implied in that sound.

It was not for her to tell of Jane's desperate loneliness and what she'd tried to do. "I don't think I should say anything more."

The light of curiosity went out of Eloise's eyes, replaced with a hurt it pained Adelaide to see.

"If you don't want to tell me…" she murmured.

"It was between Armand and Jane, so I don't think I should."

"Of course. I understand. Armand must share your confidences now, not me."

Adelaide didn't want this sham betrothal to cost her Eloise's friendship, but she really didn't think it was her place to describe what had happened between Jane and Armand.

"I'll leave you to dress," Eloise said, moving toward the door. "I'm sure a maidservant will be along soon. Or would you rather rest?"

In truth, Adelaide wanted to snuggle back under the covers and be by herself, away from Armand and everyone else, but if she kept to her chamber, what would that say to Hildegard, or whoever had ruined her clothes? That she could be undone by such a cowardly act?

"Thank you, Eloise, but I'll go to the hall and I'd take it as a great favor if you'd stay and help me dress. I'd rather have your company than one of the maids. And then we can go to the hall together, if you don't mind being seen with me."

To Adelaide's relief, Eloise smiled. "Of course I don't mind being seen with you. You're my friend, and it's not as if you've done anything truly disgraceful."

Not yet, Adelaide's desire whispered.

Not ever, her resolve retorted.

HEAD BOWED, Armand strode into the chamber he shared with Randall. His friend stood in the middle of the room, as tense as if he'd been waiting for hours and his expression—

"Bayard!" Armand gasped, his legs nearly giving way. "Is he dead?"

"No, no! I've had no such news," Randall said quickly.

As Armand sank onto his cot, he thought of another reason Randall might look like that. "Is William Marshal dead?"

Frowning with puzzlement, Randall shook his head.

"No, although I have had news of him, and it's not good."

That would explain Randall's anxious demeanor and Armand feared his warning had come too late. "Is he ill?"

Randall's sandy brows contracted even more as he sat on the bed opposite. "He's quite well, as far as I know. His return from Wales is going to be delayed. That wasn't what's troubling me. Walter de Chevron told me about the intruder in Adelaide's chamber last night."

Of course. "It's disturbing, but she wasn't harmed, thank God."

"He also told me you insisted on staying in her chamber."

"Yes, I did. I wasn't willing to take any chances with her safety."

Randall's gaze faltered. "I trust you're planning to have the wedding soon. By now all the court will have heard about last night, and, well, surely I don't have to tell you what they'll be saying."

Armand got to his feet and started to pace, just as he had in Adelaide's chamber and that small cell.

Adelaide knew what people would be saying about them, but she still wouldn't marry him. And after they had identified the traitors, or, he supposed, after a length of time if they didn't, she'd declare their betrothal ended, regardless of the consequences.

He came to a halt and clasped his hands behind

his back, his left hand holding his right clenched in a fist. "Actually, I'm having second thoughts about marrying her."

Randall stared at Armand as if he couldn't comprehend what he was hearing.

He probably couldn't, and although Armand was pleased to recognize that as a compliment to his honor, he now had to make his friend believe he could be dishonourable and break a promise. "I don't deny she's an attractive woman. Clever, too. But she's much too inclined to tell me what to do. You can guess how much I enjoy that."

Randall's expression hardened, more stern than Armand had ever seen. "But you spent the night in her chamber."

So he had. So he'd insisted—another decision gone awry. "Yes, I did—to protect her. But whatever the gossips of the court are saying, I never made love with her. Lady Adelaide is still a virgin."

Randall's eyes widened for an instant; then his stern indignation returned. "Whether she's a virgin or not doesn't matter. You spent the night in her chamber, and unless you marry her, her reputation will be destroyed."

"She's a beautiful woman," Armand countered. "She'll easily find another husband who won't be bothered by the rumors, especially when I make it known I didn't take her maidenhead."

Randall regarded him with blatant disbelief.

"Whether you did or not, would you really consider breaking the betrothal?"

God's wounds, why couldn't Randall just accept what he was saying? "You know what it was like when my stepmother was alive. I want peace in my household, and I'm beginning to fear that might not be possible with Lady Adelaide for my wife."

"Doesn't your betrothal agreement, your promise to marry her, mean anything to you?" Randall asked incredulously. "Are you forgetting this is exactly the sort of thing your father did—promise marriage only to dishonor and then abandon his conquest?"

"I'm not like my father," Armand growled, grinding his fist into the palm of his hand. "I haven't made love with Adelaide."

"But you did promise to marry her. God's holy heart, Armand, I've been defending you since Marchant, but I'm beginning to wonder if I really know you."

"I won't be bound in a miserable marriage," Armand insisted, and that, at least, was true.

Randall limped toward the door. He paused on the threshold and looked back, his visage cold and harsh. "I thought you were a man of honor, Armand, but if you won't marry Lady Adelaide, you are indeed your father's son."

As Randall slammed the door behind him, a fog of sorrow, dismay and despair crept over Armand. He sat on his cot, buried his face in his hands and wished he'd never come to Ludgershall.

ALTHOUGH SHE had the comforting presence of Eloise beside her, Adelaide mentally girded her loins as she crossed the threshold of the hall that morning.

Mercifully, Francis and Oliver weren't present. Neither was Lord Richard or the de Sansurens; unfortunately, Hildegard was, and many of the other ladies were regarding Adelaide with frank curiosity as they whispered behind their hands.

"Shameless hussy!" Lady Ethel muttered loudly from her seat on a bench by one of the pillars. "Don't go near her, Jane. I don't want you tainted."

"Yes, Mama," Jane replied from her place beside her mother. She didn't even glance at Adelaide, and although Adelaide had an explanation for why Jane would act that way, it hurt nonetheless.

"Well, if it isn't the *honorable* Lady Adelaide," Hildegard declared, marching toward her.

"I *am* an honorable lady," Adelaide replied.

"Everybody's heard that Lord Armand spent the night in your bedchamber. Do you expect us to believe that he never laid a hand on you the entire time?" Hildegard demanded.

"Lord Armand stayed in my chamber to ensure that I wasn't attacked. As for what happened when we were alone, Armand de Boisbaston is the most honorable, chivalrous nobleman at court, so it naturally follows that since we aren't yet wed, I am still a virgin. Sadly, the same cannot be said of all unmarried women at court."

She smiled at Hildegard with equal disdain.

"Armand wasn't the only one not in his rightful chamber last night, was he, Hildegard? I don't recall seeing your inquisitive face at the door of your chamber after the intruder fled my room."

Hildegard lifted her pointed chin. "I was asleep."

"You must sleep very soundly."

"At least I sleep alone!"

"That's not what I've heard, although perhaps you're alone by the time you sleep."

Hildegard flushed and her hands balled into fists. "How dare you say such things to me, you...you *slut!*"

Adelaide took one step forward. Hildegard stumbled back, as if she feared Adelaide would strike her. But Adelaide never resorted to slaps or blows. To do that would be to react like her tempestuous father.

Instead, she used her voice, stern and cold. "If you're wise, Hildegard, you'll never insult me again. And if you're the person who crept into my bedchamber like a thief and ruined my clothes, you should flee the court. Armand will have the perpetrator of that act punished—and so will *I*."

As the two women stared at each other, a slight commotion heralded the entrance of the queen with her usual coterie of maids and ladies-in-waiting. One maid hurried forward to plump up the cushion on the smaller of the two chairs on the dais, while another carried the train of the queen's heavy gown of bright blue damask.

When she had taken her seat, Isabel gestured for

Adelaide to approach. "I heard what happened last night," she said in her little-girl voice. "What a terrible thing! And in one of William Marshal's castles, too. I swear there is nowhere safe in England!"

"It was more like the work of a petulant child than an outlaw," Adelaide replied as she bowed to the queen. "Or perhaps a jealous woman."

She heard Hildegard's sharp intake of breath, but felt no guilt. It was quite possible Hildegard had destroyed her clothes, and even if she hadn't, she deserved some discomfort for the cruel things she'd said to Eloise.

"You weren't hurt, I hope?" the queen inquired.

"No. Only my clothing was touched."

The queen ran her eyes over Adelaide's gown. "That one was spared?" she asked, her tone implying that it was too bad an ugly gown was saved while other, prettier garments were ruined.

"Lady Eloise has generously given it to me. She's as kind-hearted as you, Your Majesty."

The queen smiled, as Adelaide had expected she would. Isabel liked to be flattered, and whether it was sincere or not didn't seem to matter a whit. Or perhaps Isabel was incapable of comprehending that not all flattery was genuine.

"While I appreciate Lady Eloise's generosity, I suggest you get yourself some gowns that fit you better," Isabel replied. "That one is too tight."

"Yes, Your Majesty, I'll repair what I can and have some new gowns made as quickly as possible."

The queen folded her petite hands in her lap. "I'm told a messenger has arrived from Averette."

Adelaide's heart leapt.

"If he brings your dowry, I hope Lord Armand will allow you to use some of the money for suitable garments."

If the messenger had brought the dowry, she could give it to Armand and he could free his brother.

In Normandy.

Which meant he would leave Ludgershall, and her.

She had known that day would come. She had been aware that this situation, this betrothal, was temporary and doomed to end.

Her vow had made it so.

"We heard something else about last night that leads us to assume the wedding between you and Lord Armand should take place very soon," the queen continued.

In spite of her distress, Adelaide met Isabel's gaze steadily.

"Nothing would make me happier," she said before she bowed and began to back away. "If you'll excuse me, Your Majesty, I really should find the messenger from Averette."

After the queen inclined her head, Adelaide headed for the double outer doors, giving Eloise a brief nod of farewell as she passed.

She hurried across the courtyard toward the stables where she expected to find the messenger, and tried not to think about Armand leaving. Instead, she thought about how happy he would be when his brother was free. How his eyes would light with joy, and she envisioned the smile that would bloom upon his face.

She was passing by the alley between the armory and the stable when a hand reached out and grabbed her.

CHAPTER SIXTEEN

"WHERE ARE you off to, my proud and haughty Lady Adelaide?" Francis demanded as he pulled her into the narrow space. "Meeting your lover in the stable this time?"

Still holding her arm tightly, he raised his voice to a feminine pitch. "I like to spend time with horses. They soothe me." His voice returned to sardonic mockery. "I'm *sure* you get soothed in the stables."

"Have you forgotten what happened the last time you waylaid me, Sir Francis?" Adelaide charged as she tried to pull her arm free of his grasp. "Are you, perchance, keen to lose your life?"

"Do you think I'm afraid of Armand?" he scornfully replied. "He isn't the mighty warrior you seem to think he is, and one day I'll prove it. Then his lovely widow will be left all alone. I can wait for you, my lady. I'm a patient fellow—although I do occasionally give in to a fit of temper."

He smiled and dared to touch her face. "You slumber so peacefully, like an angel. It was very difficult not to climb in beside you last night, my dear, but as I said, I can wait."

"It was *you*, you childish cur!" she cried, fairly shaking with rage as she jabbed his chest with her finger. "You destroyed my clothes!"

Francis moved closer, his breath hot on her face. "I admit nothing, except that you're beautiful and tempting, and you damn well know it, teasing men and toying with us at your whim. Baiting us and then withdrawing, cold as ice after heating our blood. My God, Eve and Delilah and Jezebel were nothing compared to you. But one day, my lady, and willingly or not, you'll come to my bed, and on that day, *my lady*, I'll remember every word, every insult, every scornful look, and you'll pay for each and every one."

"That will *never* happen," she retorted. "I would rather die than share your bed. And *you'll* pay for what you did last night."

"You think so? I don't. Even if you can somehow prove I ruined your clothes, remember that I have friends, my lady—powerful friends. If you or Armand accuse me, you'll be hurting yourselves, as well as that braggart half brother of his he thinks is so wonderful."

Not wanting to hear another word, Adelaide pushed past Francis. He grabbed her arm again and shoved her hard against the wall. "Act the honorable lady all you like, Adelaide, you're no better than a whore—and one day, I'm going to treat you like a whore."

She shoved him away with all her strength. "Armand will *kill* you!"

Francis laughed as she ran into the yard. "He can try—if he doesn't care about his brother."

Adelaide stopped and slowly wheeled around to face him. "What do you mean?"

Francis leaned back against the stone wall, his arms crossed and smirking satisfaction on his features. "I mean, my lady, that I have friends in Normandy, too, so you and Armand had best take care how you treat me."

He sounded like a spoiled child. And had he forgotten where they were? "Your threats don't frighten me, Francis, nor will they affect Armand. He has friends, too, including the Earl of Pembroke."

With that, she turned on her heel and hurried out of the alley, ready to seek out Armand and tell him what she'd learned, until she saw the man at the door of the stable. The middle-aged soldier's name was Thomas, and he was a trusted member of the garrison of Averette.

The messenger from Gillian, no doubt.

Joy, despair, relief and worry coursed through her as she rushed toward him. She glanced back over her shoulder once, to see a scowling Francis slink away, then hurried on toward Thomas, and what he had brought her.

"ANOTHER ALE, my lord?" Bessy asked Armand as he sat in her tavern. She stood beside his table, a pitcher of her finest brew in one hand, her other hand on her ample hip, and a smile on her face.

He nodded, holding out his mug. He was nowhere near drunk; he didn't want to be, but he didn't want to be in the castle, either, where Adelaide would be.

Or Randall. God help him, Randall had left him as if he carried the plague, and with good reason, believing what he did.

"Thank you for the other day, my lord," Bessy said as she poured the golden beverage. "I've decided to send Moll off to stay with her grandmother for a while."

"That's wise," Armand agreed. "I'd keep her there until the king moves on."

Bessy nodded and went off to tend to another customer—a prosperous merchant, judging by his fine woolen garments, wide embossed belt and soft leather boots—while Armand took a drink of ale.

He was on his third mug of the excellent brew when the outer door opened and Lord Richard d'Artage sauntered into the tavern, followed by Sir Edmond and his brother, Sir Charles and that damned, dark-haired Irishman.

"Jesus, Mary and Joseph, if it isn't Armand de Boisbaston!" Sir Oliver declared, approaching his table while Bessy headed for the kitchen door and, Armand noted, the stout cudgel leaning against the wall.

"What are you doing here, my lord, all by yourself

and away from your lovely betrothed?" the Irishman asked. "Have you come here to recover? Did she wear you out?"

Even through his anger, Armand had that nagging feeling that he'd heard Sir Oliver's voice before, although unfortunately not in the garden. It would have given him a measure of satisfaction if he could prove this insolent fellow a traitor. "I remind you, sir, that you're speaking of a lady and my future wife."

Oliver bowed. "I meant no disrespect to the lady," he said with a roguish grin that did nothing to assuage Armand's anger. "She's as lovely a lass as ever I've seen. I hope she knows what she's doing marrying you."

Armand got to his feet, prepared to challenge the Irishman then and there.

At the same time, Bessy gasped and dropped her jug, but not because of them. King John had appeared in the door of the tavern.

As the scent of the spilled ale added another smell to the already pungent aromas, the king strolled into the low-ceiling room, looking about him as if he'd never been in such a place before, although he most certainly had.

"Good day to you, Lord Armand," he said. "I must say I didn't expect to find *you* here. I hope your charming lady eventually had a peaceful slumber, in spite of all the excitement. I've heard several ladies were too upset to sleep, but then, they no doubt felt less protected."

Clearly John had heard about last night—all about it.

"It was most distressing, sire," Armand replied as Bessy gathered up the pieces of the jug and sidled toward the large cask of ale. "So much so, I insisted on staying in Lady Adelaide's bedchamber. I thought my presence would comfort her, as well as prevent the perpetrator from returning."

The king's low, lascivious chuckle was one of the most disgusting sounds Armand had ever heard. "I'll wager you comforted her, all right. Not that I blame you. She's one of the most beautiful women I've ever seen."

"Despite what you might have been told, sire, I have not yet had the pleasure of making love with my bride."

The king made no secret of his scepticism. "You spent hours in your betrothed's bedchamber and didn't take her?"

"No, Your Majesty."

As the other men exchanged either awed or blatantly skeptical looks, the king smiled. "So, the lady keeps even you at bay."

"The vows have not yet been exchanged before the chapel door, Your Majesty, and she's a woman who values honor as much as I do. However, I'm sure she'll be worth the wait, and no man will ever have a more trustworthy wife."

The king's smile dwindled. "I'm beginning to

think I should have asked for more before I agreed to your betrothal."

Armand stiffened and the atmosphere in the tavern grew tense. Every man there knew John was capable of rescinding his permission and demanding more money. Nevertheless, Armand said, "Your permission has already been granted."

John laughed. Cruelly. Heartlessly. "No need to look like I've just announced your execution, my lord. I have no intention of rescinding my permission, although I could. I was merely making an observation. Yet here you are and she is back at the castle without you. Well, there's no reason for you to coddle her, I suppose. I daresay Marshal will be most distressed when he hears what happened. He takes such things to heart, poor fellow."

"He is a very fine man, Your Majesty."

"I never said he wasn't," John replied as he sat on one of the cleaner benches. "He's proud, of course, as all great knights are, but there's no one I trust more than Marshal. As long as I have him on my side, my rule is safe."

It sounded as if the king genuinely appreciated the earl's support, although that gratitude could spring from selfishness, too. John might well be aware that without the finest knight in Europe to stand by him, his reign would be short-lived. If that were so, John would surely not be part of the plot to kill Marshal and the archbishop.

"Ah, here is the lady herself and likely looking for you, my lord," the king said, nodding at the door leading to the yard.

Adelaide stood on the threshold, as poised as a queen, lovely and welcome as freedom, as bright and delightful as the first flowers of spring, even though she wore a dark woollen gown that didn't fit properly.

Wondering what had brought her there, certain it must be important, Armand bowed to the king. "If you'll excuse me, Your Majesty."

The king nodded and turned his attention to Bessy. As Armand went to the door, the other knights slid onto benches, except for Oliver, who watched them leave with an inscrutable expression on his bearded face.

"WHAT IS IT?" Armand asked Adelaide as he took her arm and led her away from the king's *routiers* who waited in the yard. He spotted Godwin, who'd returned after delivering his message to the earl, near the king's horses.

He was relieved Adelaide hadn't come to the village alone, especially after what had happened last night, yet he didn't want Godwin to hear their conversation. Whatever had compelled Adelaide to seek him out here must be important and thus best discussed in private.

"I believe Bessy would welcome your company," he said to the soldier, who nodded gratefully and hurried into the tavern.

Armand and Adelaide continued toward the banks

of the small river that ran beside the village, through a grove of ash, withy-alder and rowan trees, away from the busy main road.

"What is it, my lady?" he asked when he was sure they couldn't be overheard.

"The messenger from my sister has arrived."

Judging by her serious demeanor, Gillian had not sent the money she'd requested.

Loath to have his hopes dashed, he said nothing more as they came to a halt behind a stand of willow trees, where they were screened from both the road and the tavern.

As Adelaide took his hands in hers, a smile brightened her face, and his heart began to beat again.

"Gillian couldn't send five hundred marks," she said with a touch of regret, "but she sent just over four hundred. Since the stolen money's been returned to you, that will be more than enough to ransom your brother."

"Oh, thank God," Armand murmured, unthinkingly pulling her into his embrace and holding her close. He hadn't been this happy and relieved since the door to his cell had opened and he'd seen Randall standing there.

Adelaide gently extricated herself from his embrace. "I'm sorry if I gave you any cause to worry. I would have told you sooner if the king and those others hadn't been at the tavern."

She looked away, for once not boldly meeting his gaze. "You'll want to take the money to Normandy as soon as possible, I suppose."

"Yes," he replied, realizing he should leave at once. Leave *her*—to rescue Bayard.

But the problem of the conspiracy would remain, and she might be in danger. "We still don't know who's plotting against the earl and archbishop."

"I'll continue to try to find out who it was," she replied with her usual confidence.

Of course she would. "I'll return to court right after I free Bayard."

"That may not be wise," she said. She moved back and leaned against the trunk of a large tree, its branches falling around them like a curtain. "It might be better if you stayed away from John and the court. John will surely not be pleased when we break the betrothal, even if he's already made a profit by it. He'll be less likely to take out his anger on me after I remind him he can still use me for his own gain."

"But he might." Armand could imagine a score of ways John would have his vengeance on a woman, if he so chose.

On the other hand, Adelaide's beauty and title, and hence her value, as well as her own abilities to manipulate the king, should offer her some protection. Perhaps the worse she need fear was being wed against her will…although for her, that would likely seem little better than death.

It would be a torment for him, too, knowing that she'd been given to another, and as easily as another man bestowed a robe or other gift.

"What if the king won't give you permission to go back to Normandy?" she asked, breaking into his thoughts.

"I don't plan to ask for John's permission. Otherwise I'll be risking his refusal."

"It might be best to leave at once," she agreed. "I can tell John where you're gone afterward." She lowered her head, then glanced up at him, as bashful as the most shy of maidens. "You'll go today, then?"

It was as if they were in the stable again, the day of their meeting, and some of the charm of those first moments together seemed to weave itself around them again.

"Not today," he said quietly. "It will be dark soon. Tomorrow."

She nodded. "Tomorrow." She gave him a wistful smile that broke his heart. "You'll be able to cut your hair."

"Would you like me to cut it?"

"What difference does my opinion make?" she asked, turning away and plucking a leaf that she twirled between her thumb and forefinger.

"I'd like to know."

"Very well," she said, dropping the leaf that fluttered to the ground. "I like your hair the way it is."

God help him, what was he doing, staying here like this? He should be rushing back to Normandy, or preparing to.

Yet in spite of his desire to free Bayard, there was

another equally strong desire holding him back. Once he left Ludgershall, it would be the end of…whatever he shared with Adelaide.

Then she looked at him directly, and he saw something that thrilled him to his soul, and broke his heart anew—a longing and despair, a soul-deep yearning that matched his own and the sorrow of loss he knew all too well.

Drawn by that look, and the need to be with her, to take her hands in his, to touch and kiss her, he pulled her into his arms and captured her lips with his.

She clung to him and returned his kiss as if she believed this was their final farewell.

If only she hadn't made that vow, he would never leave her.

He deepened the kiss, angling his body so that she was more fully against him, feeling the length of her slender, womanly body against his. It was a dangerous indulgence, but one he could not deny.

He gently pushed his tongue against her lips, entreating her to part them. She did, moaning softly when his tongue slipped into her mouth. The sound enflamed him further and he brought his hand around to cup her soft, warm breast that fit so perfectly into the palm of his hand. Her nipple puckered and tightened, growing taut beneath his touch. Still kissing her deeply, he kneaded gently, sensing her increasing excitement.

She drew back and for a moment, he feared he'd gone too far, until she spoke, her voice husky with desire. "My vow was not to marry. There was nothing in it about being celibate. Come to my bedchamber tonight, Armand. Please."

He could scarcely believe what he was hearing. It was as if he were having a vision, or dreaming in the daytime.

"I mean what I say, Armand. I want to be with you." She gave him a shy, yet determined, smile that could only belong to Adelaide. "Like Jane, I would have one night of passion. Of love."

She did care for him. She must, or she would never give herself to him, or speak of love. And just as suddenly, Armand knew that he loved Adelaide D'Averette. Now, as he was on the point of leaving, of finally rescuing his brother, he knew the full depth of his feelings—even as he knew he couldn't take what she offered.

"I won't love you and then abandon you," he said, tempted nearly beyond all reckoning, yet strong in his resolve to be an honorable man. "That's something my father would do, and I will not be like him."

"This is not the same," she replied. "You won't be seducing and callously abandoning me. It is my request that you love me, and mine that we not marry. You'll be going to save your brother, as you should. You need feel no guilt."

Honor and passion, desire and determination, warred within him. "What if you get with child?"

She smiled, although there was sorrow in her eyes, too. "It would be a gift."

She was thinking with her heart; he must answer with his head. "It would be a bastard."

The desire dwindled from her eyes, replaced with a hint of the shrewdness that belonged to the woman who'd so successfully navigated her way through the dangerous waters of John's court.

"Many a respected nobleman is a bastard—William Longespee, King Henry's bastard, for one. Illegitimacy need not be a stain if you acknowledge the child."

"And I would. No child of mine, legitimate or not, will ever be cast out, or turned away, forced from the gates as if the child should be ashamed of being born. But natural children of kings are treated with respect because of their fathers. The same may not be true for any child of ours."

She spoke without hesitation. "Do you think I would let any child of mine be mocked and belittled?"

She lifted his hand and pressed a kiss upon his calloused palm, then held it against her warm, soft cheek. "Have no fear for the child's fate, Armand. Our babe will be well cared for at Averette, and I will have my sisters to help me, or to take my place, should anything befall me."

She meant if she died.

If she died, so would his heart.

"I would want to see my child from time to time," he said, his voice rough with suppressed emotion. And her. He would want to see her, too. Be with her, if only to see her face and hear her voice.

"Of course. You'll always be welcome at Averette."
Finally her gaze faltered. "Even if you marry another."

Oh, God! Oh, sweet blessed Savior! How could he
ever do that? How could he pledge his troth to another
woman, loving Adelaide as he did?

He couldn't. He felt as if he, too, had made a vow
never to marry. "And when I return? When we've
found the conspirators and saved John's reign? What
then, Adelaide? What then for us?"

"Oh, Armand, please, don't ask me such questions." She clasped her hands, her eyes pleading.
"Please, just come to me tonight."

He had not the strength to refuse or to question her
anymore. His desire was too strong, his need to be
with her just once, even if that meant he could never
truly love another woman, too overwhelming.

"Yes," he whispered as he took her in his arms, and
kissed her. "I'll come to you tonight."

CHAPTER SEVENTEEN

AFTER RETURNING from the village, Adelaide hurried to her chamber to dress for dinner. She wanted to look her best for Armand tonight. She would have the maid dress her hair around her head like a coronet, with a crimson ribbon entwined in the braids. Beneath her lovely gown, she would wear her finest, softest shift that had escaped the attack upon her clothes. She would smile and laugh and tease him a little. She would make this night one to remember. She would say nothing of Francis, and what he'd done and the threats he'd made. Not tonight.

As she passed by the chamber Lady Jane shared with her mother, the door opened and Jane appeared with one of her mother's many shawls over her arm. "Adelaide!" she cried, coming to an abrupt halt, her eyes wide with surprise, and a blush creeping up her face.

"Jane," Adelaide replied somewhat warily. She wouldn't have been surprised if Jane had brushed past her without a word.

"I'm sorry about your clothes," Jane said with

every appearance of sincerity. "I think you were very courageous to chase after that intruder. I'd surely have swooned."

"It was very frightening," Adelaide agreed, wondering if Jane was being more friendly because she didn't think Armand had told her what had happened between them.

"You're so beautiful and brave and clever, it's no wonder Lord Armand wants to marry you." Jane tried to smile, but her face crumpled. She dropped the shawl and covered her face with her hands. "While I'm so old and ugly and foolish!"

"Hush, Jane, hush," Adelaide said, using the same tone she did when she comforted her sisters. She picked up the shawl, put her arm around the weeping Jane and gently shepherded her back into her chamber.

The smell of Lady Ethel's many potions and ointments filled the small room. To one side of the chamber was a large bed encumbered with heavy curtains and thick coverings; another, smaller trundle bed was beside it, and Adelaide was sure that wasn't used by a maid but by the long-suffering Jane.

"Oh, Adelaide, I'm so ashamed!" she sobbed. "You're being so kind to me when I wanted to…tried to…"

"It's all right, Jane. I know. I made Armand tell me why he was in the corridor after I knocked him down outside Hildegard's door."

Jane lowered her hands, revealing a mottled face

and puffy eyes. "Oh, no! I hope you didn't think he'd been with *her!*"

"I didn't, but I did wonder what he was doing there," Adelaide replied as she tossed the shawl on the bed, then poured some cold water into the basin on the washing table. She dipped a square of linen into it and after wringing it out, gestured for Jane to sit on the stool. Then she handed her the cool, damp linen to wash her tear-streaked face.

"Armand's a very attractive man and it must be difficult and lonely for you caring for your mother," Adelaide said as she took back the cloth.

"You're not…you're not angry?" Jane asked with a sniffle.

"No," Adelaide assured her. "I understand loneliness. I miss my sisters and my home very much."

"At least you have Armand."

For now. For tonight. But never to marry.

She forced her attention back to Jane. "Your life is far from over and you may yet marry. There are plenty of people who admire your patient devotion to your mother, and I'm hopeful that one day, a perceptive man will admire you, too."

"An old man who needs a nursemaid, perhaps," Jane said bitterly, glancing at the multitude of jars and clay vessels on the table beside her. "What joy in that for me? What passion? You may understand loneliness, but how can a beautiful woman like you really appreciate what my life is like?"

"My beauty is no great gift," Adelaide replied. "It makes me the prey of every man at court, including the king. I'm like an object on display, a thing for them to possess, not a person to be cherished."

"I've never considered that," Jane mused aloud as she pushed one of the clay vessels away from the edge of the table. "Still, it's better than not being wanted at all." She got to her feet. "I should go." Picking up the shawl, she sighed and said, "Mama will be wondering what's taking me so long."

She started toward the door, then turned and looked back at Adelaide, who was following her. "I'm going to miss you when you're married and gone from court."

Adelaide didn't answer, and as they went their separate ways, she regretted that she hadn't spent more time with Jane. She could have helped her with her mother, perhaps, and given her some time without that constant, querulous companion. Perhaps she could invite Jane to Averette soon, if Lady Ethel would give her leave to go.

Jane couldn't really comprehend her life, either, though, or appreciate why Adelaide envied her—not for having to take care of the demanding Lady Ethel, but because the lascivious courtiers left her alone.

But would she really have liked being ignored, Adelaide wondered as she reached the door to her chamber, or being patronized or made a figure of fun, as Jane so often was?

She entered her chamber, to find one of the maids

diligently repairing the lovely crimson gown she usually wore with an embroidered bliaut. Thus attired, she felt the equal of any queen.

She would wear those garments tonight, for Armand.

And after tonight, she might never see him again.

IN SPITE OF her resolve to be cheerful and entertaining, it wasn't easy for Adelaide to feign a light and happy heart as she sat beside Armand during the evening meal. She was too conscious of Armand's impending departure to enjoy herself, especially when Armand sliced off the choicest bits of meat from the roasted beef and venison and ham for her, whispering endearments and touching her hand, acting just as a lover should.

Looking at her just as a lover should look, too, with desire and yearning, and she could scarcely contain the urge to demand that he go to bed with her at once.

As tense as she was, Armand seemed relaxed, and the other courtiers were positively giddy, because the king and queen weren't in the hall. The official explanation was that the king was slightly indisposed and the queen was tending to him. Everyone surmised that the king's indisposition was one that required not rest in bed, but a different sort of ministration from the queen.

Even Hildegard seemed a livelier, happy person as she flirted with Sir Charles and Sir Edmond. Only

Lady Ethel was regrettably unchanged, keeping her daughter busy while constantly complaining.

Eloise and Randall were happy, too. Eloise sat to Adelaide's right, with Randall beside her, all their previous reticence gone. They talked and laughed, conversing in a way that gave her hope their future together would be a blissful one.

While she remained alone.

Eloise turned to Adelaide when they rose to allow the servants to take down the tables for dancing. "Randall told me Armand's leaving for Normandy in the morning."

"Gillian has sent my dowry, so naturally he wants to free his brother as soon as he can," Adelaide replied.

"I'm sure he'll come back to you quickly," Eloise said, her expression sympathetic as she tried to comfort her friend, completely unaware that Adelaide wasn't sure what would be worse—to have Armand return and perhaps court another, or stay away.

She had so little time to be with him! To have him all to herself. To love him.

If he did return to court, could she not be his mistress? Wouldn't being in Armand's arms be worth the shame? She wouldn't be breaking her vow then...

Yet surely the day would come when a man of honor like Armand would want an honorable union, and she couldn't give him that. Wouldn't it be even more difficult to part with him then?

As soon as the floor was cleared and the minstrels in place, Randall asked Eloise to join him in the dance. When they went to take their places, Armand turned to Adelaide with that smile he seemed to save for her alone.

"Would you like to dance, my lady?" he asked, his voice low and husky, making her feel as if he'd embraced her.

"I'd rather be alone with you," she whispered, no longer willing to wait, as her hand sought his.

"You would rather we retire?" he asked, his tone teasing while his eyes smoldered with desire.

"Wouldn't you?" she countered just as cheekily.

His smile alone was enough to make her tremble with anticipation. "Actually, I would."

They started for the door, until Armand caught sight of Francis, who was slouched on a bench, his back against the wall and a goblet of wine in his hands.

"Go on to your chamber, Adelaide," Armand said. "I want to have a few words with Francis before I leave Ludgershall."

Adelaide didn't want this night ruined by any dealings with Francis. "Leave him, Armand. He's not worth the trouble."

"I will only be a moment."

She saw the stern resolve in her beloved's face, heard it in his voice, yet still she said, "And in that moment, what will you do but raise more enmity between you? He has powerful friends, Armand, who can do great harm to you and your brother with a stroke of a quill and a few words in the king's ear while you're off fighting John's battles. Leave him, Armand."

Frowning, Armand moved back into the shadows cast by one of the thick tapestries depicting a lady's garden. "He's said something to you, hasn't he? What, and when?"

She had no choice but to follow him, unless she wanted those nearby to hear this conversation. "It doesn't matter."

"Tell me," he insisted.

She reached up to stroke his cheek. "Is it that important?"

"If he threatened you, it is *very* important, and I won't leave this hall until you tell me what he said."

She realized she had no choice unless she wanted to argue. "He confessed that he ruined my clothes, and when I told him he would regret that, he threatened you, and your brother, too."

"That damned—!"

"Nevermind," Adelaide said softly, gazing up at Armand and willing him to heed her. "Come with me."

He shook his head. "Not just yet. Now more than ever I have to speak with Francis before I go." He gave her the ghost of a smile. "I won't threaten him directly, but I won't leave Ludgershall without making him understand that if he harms you or Bayard, he will regret it."

"I can look after myself."

Armand's expression softened. "Bayard would say the same, so let me do this for my sake, Adelaide—my peace of mind. I promise I won't be long." He smiled. "I have no wish to linger in his company when you're waiting for me."

She didn't try to stop him anymore. Instead, she nodded her agreement and left him.

AS HIS BEAUTIFUL Adelaide continued out of the hall, Armand strode toward Francis. He would rather draw his weapon and challenge that disgusting coward here and now, but Adelaide was waiting and he didn't want their last night together marred by violence.

Francis scrambled to his feet when he saw Armand approaching. Other nobles who were not dancing, including Sir Charles and the avidly curious Hildegard, noticed the long-haired noblemen's determined march and sidled closer.

Armand was very aware that he had an audience; so was Francis, and the onlookers seemed to give him confidence.

Well, why not? Francis could safely assume Armand wouldn't try to kill him in the hall of Ludgershall.

"What do you want?" Francis demanded as Armand came to a halt.

"Merely to take my leave of you before I go to Normandy to pay my brother's ransom and bring him home," Armand said with a smile, as if they were the best of friends.

Francis frowned. "Does the king know you're departing Ludgershall?"

"Would you have me interrupt him?" Armand inquired with the same amiability. "I don't think he would welcome me tonight, do you?"

Charles stifled a guffaw, and several others laughed, too.

Armand paid no heed to their audience. "Before I go, Francis, I'd like to apologize to you for my disgraceful show of temper the other day. Alas, I have yet to learn to govern my rage, as all chivalrous, honorable men should, especially where Lady Adelaide is concerned. Why, I would have killed you as soon as look at you when you accosted Lady Adelaide by the wall. Thank God I didn't—but I may wind up taking off someone's head for even a perceived insult to my lady. That would be a terrible thing, would it not?"

Francis regarded him warily, but said not a word.

"And thus you have my apology, and my sincere promise that I shall attempt to moderate my temper in the future."

"Good," Francis muttered, a scowl darkening his features.

Armand clapped a hand on Francis's shoulder with so much force, the man's knees nearly buckled, but it was the look in Armand's eyes that really made him weak.

"I trust there won't be any cause for misunderstanding, whether I am here or not," Armand said. "Randall writes a good letter, you know."

He stepped back and raised an interrogative brow. "So do we understand each other, my friend?"

Rubbing his shoulder, Francis nodded.

"Excellent!" Armand cried with every appearance of bonhomie before he turned on his heel and strode from the hall.

ADELAIDE OPENED the door to her chamber and discovered that Armand was already here, standing by the window with his back to her. He'd lit a rushlight and its weak flame flickered in the darkness.

How had he managed to get there ahead of her? Had he decided not to speak to Francis after all, and come up the other stairs? "Armand?"

The man turned.

"Sir Oliver!" Adelaide gasped. "What are you doing here? Get out!"

He was beside her and holding the door closed before she could even turn around. "No need to flee or call for help, my lady," he said, his Irish accent more pronounced than usual. "I mean you no harm. I know Armand would slice me open from chin to crotch if I hurt you."

In spite of his assurances, she cautiously backed away.

"I've brought you something that I couldn't give you anywhere else," Oliver announced.

He held up a necklace that sparkled in the feeble light. A gold and green cross on a golden chain.

"Mama's crucifix!" she gasped in disbelief, reaching for it. "How did you get it?"

He held it just out of her reach. "It's better if you don't ask too many questions, my lady. Just accept it as my gift and be grateful."

Her eyes narrowed as he continued to hold it away from her. "How grateful do you expect me to be?"

He barked a laugh and shook his head. "Lord preserve me, you've been too long at court. I don't expect anything in return except your thanks."

She held out her hand, palm up. "Then give that to me and I'll thank you."

Again, he shook his head. "Not yet. Not here. There may be a search if the king realizes it's missing, although I doubt he'll notice since he has finer jewels to wear. But if he does, you won't want to have it found in your chamber or around your lovely neck. I'm going to bury it at the base of a tree about ten miles from here in Chute Forest. You can retrieve it later, when it's safer.

"Just follow the road east from here and when you enter the forest, you'll see a tree that's been struck by lightning. I wouldn't be so daft as to pick that one—too obvious by half. From there, you look north, and you'll see a little runt of an elm, with an oak beside it. It'll be at the base of the oak on the west side."

"Thank you," she said, wondering if he would really do that, "but I still don't understand why—"

"I don't have much time," Oliver interrupted, glancing out the window, "and there's more I have to tell you. I know about the conspiracy to kill the earl and the archbishop."

"What conspiracy?" she asked, determined to get some answers before she revealed what she knew.

He grinned. "You're a sly one, my lady, but no more sly than me. I know about this conspiracy because I'm in on it, too—or so the others think. I realized the day I arrived at court that something was brewing and made it my business to find out what. It was easy to play the discontented, ambitious nobleman, and soon enough I learned what was afoot. Richard's the man behind it, although it wouldn't surprise me to discover he acts on orders from another."

"Richard? But he's a vain fop!"

"He's no more a fop than I am, and he's no fool, either. Don't underestimate him—that's what he wants. He's sent a fellow named Marcus to poison the archbishop. Marcus won't succeed because I gave him a potion that will only put the man to sleep.

"Francis is traitor, too, but I don't think you need to worry too much about him. Can't keep his mouth shut, for one thing. I'd keep my eye on Sir Alfred more than him. He's drunk half the time, but the other half loathes the king for seducing his sister."

Adelaide had heard that sad story. Alfred's sister had died giving birth to the king's bastard.

Oliver crossed to the window. "And now, my lady, I've got to go."

For the first time she noticed the grappling hook and rope coiled at the base of the window, which explained how he'd gained entrance.

"I'd appreciate it if you would free the hook and toss it down to me when I reach the ground. They don't come cheap."

"Wait!" she cried softly, following him to the window. "Why are you telling me all this? Why did you steal my crucifix from the king and why are you giving it back to me?"

He answered as he affixed the hook to the sill and tossed the rope outside. "Because you're a brave, valiant woman and John's a bad, wicked man." He straddled the sill. "Farewell, my lady."

"Thank you!" she said fervently, suddenly certain he would do as he said. She couldn't explain why she had such faith in him, but she did nonetheless.

"What the hell," he muttered, and before she could stop him, he tugged her close and kissed her.

She was so startled, she didn't hear the door open, or the latch fall into place as it closed.

CHAPTER EIGHTEEN

"*WHAT THE DEVIL—?*"

Adelaide whirled around. Armand stood in front of the closed door, drawing his sword, rage twisting his features.

Like her father in a fury, raising his hand to hit.

"It's not what you think!" she cried, pushing away from Oliver and hurrying toward Armand.

He barely glanced at her, all his attention, and his wrath, focused on the Irishman who climbed back into the room.

"I should kill you here and now for attempting to assault my lady," Armand growled, "but that would be too quick a death for such as you, even if you didn't succeed."

Adelaide rushed to Armand before he alerted the guards. "That isn't why he came here. He knows who the conspirators are."

His sword still raised, Armand looked down at her. "How does he know that?"

"Because I'm one of them—or so *they* think," Oliver declared, planting his feet. "More fools them.

And there's no need to get your breeches in a bunch, my lord. I wasn't assaulting your bride, although you have to admit she's a devilishly attractive woman. You can't blame me for stealing a kiss."

"I can and I do."

"He's got valuable information, Armand, about the conspiracy," Adelaide said, intervening before they came to blows. "Richard's the leader."

"Richard?" Armand repeated, still sceptical as he regarded Oliver the way he would a bedbug. "That's impossible."

"Why?" Oliver challenged. "Because he plays the fop, the same way you're pretending your bethrothal is real?"

"What makes you think that?" Armand retorted.

A roguish gleam came to Oliver's brown eyes. "No need to try to deny it. I'm good at sneaking about and discovering secrets, and you've no need to worry. I haven't told anybody else. I can keep a secret, as well as find them out."

"He also gave the archbishop's assassin a harmless potion instead of poison," Adelaide said, hoping Armand would put up his sword, at least.

"*You* gave it to him?" Armand repeated.

"Aye, I did. I don't want the whole country at war over who sits on a throne. War's a game for knights, but it's hell for peasants."

"Since when does an Irish nobleman care about peasants?"

"Who said I was an Irish nobleman?"

As Adelaide and Armand stared at Oliver, equally dumbfounded by his pronouncement, he grinned, although his eyes were not jovial. "Look closely, my lord. Granted it's been years, but we *have* met before."

Adelaide's gaze flew from Armand to the Irishman and back again, while Armand's brow furrowed with concentration. Had they truly met before? Where, and when? In a nobleman's hall? In battle? In Normandy? It couldn't be recently—

"I'm your brother."

"What?" she gasped, while Armand turned as pale as bleached linen.

"My only living brother's in Normandy," he said, his voice low and wary, and there was doubt deep in his brown eyes.

Eyes that were like Oliver's, and so was Armand's straight nose, and his lips, and perhaps the line of his jaw, although Oliver's was hidden by his beard.

That would explain why Oliver's voice seemed so familiar...

"Your only living *illegitimate* brother," Oliver said, not taking his gaze from Armand's face. "My mother brought me to our father's castle when I was eight years old, to beg him for money and food before we starved. I saw you hiding in the hall behind a screen, while you heard him call my mother a whore. She hadn't been until our father seduced her with a host of promises he didn't keep and left her with child. Tell me, brother o' mine, did you watch him whip us out the gates, too?"

"That was *you?*" Armand asked, truly shaken, telling her he had indeed witnessed such a scene.

No wonder he had so quickly agreed to acknowledge any child she bore out of wedlock and said that no child of his would be turned away....

The Irishman lifted his tunic and shirt, exposing several long scars on his muscular back. "This is all our father ever gave to me. You got the best of everything, while I, also our father's son, got nothing but these marks."

"You think it was any easier growing up under that brute's rule?"

"At least you knew you'd eat every night. You didn't watch your mother die of cold and starvation."

"I watched my mother die after my father pushed her down the stairs. I had to listen to my father curse and belittle my stepmother, while she denounced him for a lecher and adulterer. I lived in the midst of their hatred for years. And that dungeon in Normandy was no heaven on earth."

"All right," the Irishman grudgingly admitted, leaning against the windowsill as if this was his chamber. "We both suffered because of that lout."

And so they had, Adelaide thought, at least as much as she had suffered from her father's neglect and rage and bitterness.

She went to Armand and took hold of his hand. "Now you both are free." As she was.

"And you're a knight, as well," she said to Oliver.

"Me, a knight? Don't be daft," the Irishman scoffed. "I'm a thief. It's taken me years to learn to speak like English nobles instead of an Irish peasant. You'd be surprised how easy it is to gain entry to wealthy homes when you sound like a knight. Once in, it's easy out again with jewels and the plate."

Armand put his hand to his forehead. "God's blood," he murmured as he sat on the bed. "You're an impostor *and* a thief?"

"Aye," the Irishman said without a jot of shame. "The real Sir Oliver de Leslille got drunk in a village in Cornwall where I happened to be. He fell and cracked open his head, and who was I to ignore a chance to go to court? Right now he's enjoying his recovery in Cornwall. I left him with a woman who could be counted on to take good care of a rich man's son."

"And you came to the king's court only to steal?"

"O' course. The traitors and their plans just came my way, so to speak. But alas, I've found the king's jewels to be too well guarded, even for me. I've decided to seek out easier pickings."

"Yet you got my crucifix back for me," Adelaide noted.

Oliver—or whatever his name was—actually blushed, while Armand looked even more stunned. "What?"

"He got it back for me," she explained. "He's going to hide it in Chute Forest until it's safe for me to retrieve it."

"Is that true?" Armand asked, obviously not willing to believe him.

Oliver bristled. "Just because a man's a thief doesn't mean he's completely without honor—the same way those that claim to be honorable can be worse than thieves, and one little necklace wasn't so difficult, not when one of the queen's maidservants considers you a very handsome fellow."

Adelaide found that easy to believe.

"Oh, hell, might as well make a clean breast of it," Oliver muttered. He squared his broad shoulders. "I was some bitter and wanted a little revenge, so I stole your money from your chamber, too, Armand."

"What kind of thief keeps stealing and giving his booty back?" Armand demanded.

Adelaide knew what Armand was really asking—was Oliver truly just a thief, or was he some other kind of criminal?

Oliver guessed his half brother's meaning, too. "Jesus, Mary and Joseph, is it so surprising the son of a whore would turn out to be a thief? Or that he'd try to rob the richest? As for the kind of thief I am, I'm the best—except for a pesky conscience that won't let me rob a man I'm proud to call brother, or a valiant, good woman who shouldn't have to give something she values to a man like John."

Before they could reply, he tugged his forelock with mocking humility. "And now that you know all my secrets, it's time for me to go, and glad I am to be leaving. At least thieves don't yammer about honor and honesty while lying through their teeth."

Once more Armand's brother straddled the windowsill. "Richard and those others fear you and your brother more than you think, Armand. And let Francis know you're on to him. That coward'll betray every one of the traitors if he thinks it'll save his miserable life."

Oliver gave Adelaide a roguish grin that made him look more like his brother. "I don't suppose you'd care to leave this honorable dolt and come away with me, my lady? I can't promise you much except adventure, excitement and me, o' course."

She didn't think he was serious, but she was when she answered. "I'm grateful for your help and for getting back my mother's crucifix, but no, I won't go with you."

"Ah, well, worth the asking," he replied as he climbed out the window.

"You never told us your real name," Adelaide cried as she ran to the window and looked down. Sheathing his sword, Armand joined her and watched as the Irishman held tight to the straining rope, his feet against the outer wall.

"Better not to know," he replied, smiling up at her. "Better not to meet again, either, my lady, or I might come all over evil and take you away with me."

With that, he began to lower himself down the wall.

Together Adelaide and Armand watched him descend as nimbly as an insect. After ensuring that the sentries on the wall walk weren't watching, she freed the hook and threw it down to him.

"We've just abetted a thief," Armand muttered as his illegitimate half brother gathered up the hook and rope and, after a brief salute, disappeared into the shadows.

"He may be a thief, but he's also your brother, and a good man, I think. I believe he was telling the truth about Richard. Perhaps there *is* a sharper mind in Richard's head than he lets on."

Armand slumped back against the wall beside the window. "God's wounds, I don't know what to believe anymore. How do we even know he's really my half brother? Those scars aren't proof. They only mean he was beaten once. He could have been anybody."

"How many people know about that boy and his mother coming to your father's castle?"

"Servants and soldiers saw them."

"Then how do you explain the fact that he looks like you? Granted not enough that it's obvious you're related, but you have the same coloring, the same chin, the same lips. And his voice is like yours, too. That's why he sounded so familiar."

"I know. You're right." Armand sighed. "And his mother wouldn't be the first or only ignorant girl my father seduced and abandoned."

Hearing the pain in Armand's voice, Adelaide took his hand and led him to the bed, where she sat and drew him down beside her. "He's given us a way to stop the conspiracy—through Francis. He likely will betray his cohorts if he thinks he's in danger."

Armand nodded. "I'll come back to court as quickly as I can after I ransom Bayard and we can accuse Francis then."

He put his arm around her and she leaned her head on his broad shoulder. How wonderful it would be if she could always lean on him, to feel his comforting strength and know that she need not stand alone against the world to protect her sisters.

But thus it was, and she would protect Armand, too, if she could. Armand would endanger himself if he accused Francis directly, so while he was in Normandy rescuing his brother, she would work against de Farnby. She would plant seeds of doubt and distrust in John's mind, and those of other barons, too, while reminding them of the honor and worth of Armand de Boisbaston.

She wouldn't tell Armand any of this before he left, though. He would protest and try to stop her, and she didn't want that. Nor did she want to waste any more time tonight on treason and conspiracies. All she wanted to do was be with Armand.

She lifted her head and wrapped her arms about his neck. Armand smiled, and the worry left his features as his eyes darkened and filled with an intent that set her own heart beating with anticipation.

"Well, my lady," he said softly, in that low, husky rasp that was seduction itself. "Here we are, alone."

"Here we are indeed," she whispered.

"Do you truly want to make love without marriage?" he asked gently, tenderly, and she knew that if she said no, he would not protest, or try to change her mind.

And for that, she loved him even more.

"Yes, Armand, with *you,* and more than I've ever wanted anything," she said, sure of her decision. Feeling no shame, no fear, no guilt, only love and certainty. "Please, Armand, love me."

As he pulled her close and kissed her, she wrapped her arms about him, embracing him with fervent need and desire. Eagerly responding, Armand deepened the kiss. She parted her lips in silent invitation and welcome, a welcome he accepted while his hands meandered over her back. He tugged the veil from her head and, still kissing her, released her hair so that it fell about her shoulders and down her back in a tumble of thick, silken waves.

Breaking the kiss, he trailed his lips down her neck as she arched her back, her hands grabbing his tunic to hold him.

"Make love with me, Armand," she whispered.

"I will."

"Now!" she insisted, a new urgency in her voice, born of passion and desire deferred.

With that same urgency, she sought the knot of the lacing of his shirt beneath his tunic.

"Let me do that," he said, his gaze holding hers as he untied the knot and loosened the laces.

When she slipped her hand inside to caress his naked flesh, he smiled that incredibly seductive smile and asked, "What next, my lady? Tonight, I am yours to command."

Warmth threaded through her body as she realized he meant what he said. Tonight, he would do whatever she asked. She would have a freedom such as she'd never hoped to have. And she would use it to delight them both.

She got off the bed and, taking hold of his hands, pulled him to his feet. "Take off your tunic," she ordered, her voice low and full of invitation.

He raised his tunic and slowly pulled it over his head, then dropped it on the floor beside him.

"Now your shirt," she said, moving back so that his whole body was in her sight.

When he'd done that and stood half-naked before her, his magnificent torso exposed to her admiring eyes, she whispered, "Now your boots."

He leaned over, his shoulder-length hair hiding his face, and removed first one, then the other, letting them hit the floor with dull thuds. Still bent down, he raised his eyes and provocatively murmured, "Breeches, my lady?"

She swallowed hard and nodded, then watched as he put his swordbelt and sheathed sword on her clothes chest, then peeled off his woollen breeches and tossed them aside.

When he stood before her totally, unabashedly

naked, the evidence that he was aroused was impossible to miss.

"What would you like next, my lady?" he whispered, sounding like the very embodiment of passion.

"My laces," she whispered, turning and presenting her back to him. "Untie my laces."

"With pleasure," he replied.

He stood behind her and his long, deft fingers made short work of the knot. When he had untied it, he lightly brushed the back of her neck with his lips.

Although that made her shiver with delight, she said, "I didn't give you leave to kiss me, did I? I thought I was in command tonight."

"As you wish, my lady," he said, his deep voice sending new thrills along her body. "I shall try to exert some self-control."

"Until I give you leave to lose it," she seductively replied, pulling down her gown and wiggling a little to get it lower. Her actions exposed her white linen shift, a garment so much washed, the fabric was thin and soft against her skin, like the brush of his fingertips.

"If you continue to move like that, my lady, I won't be able to restrain myself for long."

Holding her gown to her breasts, she turned to face him. "Then I shall stand perfectly still and let you finish undressing me."

His eyes flared with desire as he approached, and, with gentle, loving hands, he took hold of the neck of her gown. He eased it over her breasts, down her waist and over her hips as if he were unwrapping a precious object.

She stayed as still as she could, although she trembled with excitement when she stood before him clad only in her shift.

He slowly surveyed her from the crown of her head to the toes of her slippers. When he raised his eyes again to her face, she was taken aback to see pain in his eyes. "You are so beautiful, Adelaide. And strong and good. I respect your vow and why you made it, but how I wish you could be my wife!"

"I wish I had never made that promise, either," she replied, meaning it with all her heart. "If I hadn't, I would do all I could to be worthy of you."

"You are—you are more than worthy. It is I—"

She put her fingers against his lips. "You are more than worthy, my lord—a man of honor, deserving of the utmost admiration and respect. Your willingness to abide by my vow is the greatest proof of that, even though it means we cannot marry."

She untied the drawstring of her shift. "But we are here together now, and I want nothing more than to spend the night in your arms."

Little by little, regarding him steadily, she pulled her shift first from one shoulder, then the other. And then down to her waist.

She eased her shift below her hips and took it off. Lastly she kicked off her slippers, so she stood before him naked, covered only by the curtain of her unbound hair.

"Let us be husband and wife tonight in one way, at least," she whispered when he made no move to touch her or come any closer. "Love me, Armand."

"I do," he said, admitting the deep truth of his heart. "I love you, Adelaide."

She held out her arms to him.

If this was all he could have of her, if being her lover was the only form of happiness they could share, he would take it.

He swept her up into his arms and carried her to her bed, joining her there, kissing and caressing her, whispering a lifetime of tender words as he stroked and touched and licked and sucked and gave full liberty to his desire. She returned his kiss with fervent need, while her hands worked their feminine magic on his heated skin. Yet she did more than kiss. With the instinct of a woman who seeks to give as much pleasure as she receives, she slid her lips away from his, to taste the skin of his jaw and his neck, where they lingered on his throbbing pulse. Then to his shoulder, and from there, she found his taut nipple.

She sucked it into her mouth, the sensation nearly sending him over the edge of ecstasy right then. He gritted his teeth, holding off while he positioned himself, raising himself on his hands as he prepared to enter her.

And she prepared to receive him. Never had she

felt such passion, such need, such desire. She wanted him with every fibre of her being, as she loved him with every fibre of her being.

That hunger must be sated. Now. At once.

She must be more than ready. There would still be pain, and blood. She didn't care. He had suffered far worse than that. He still suffered, and she could give him ease.

He was wonderful. Noble. Good. Handsome. Virile. Not perfect, though. Impulsive. Stubborn. Proud. Yet if she had not made that vow, and despite her childhood, she would marry him in a heartbeat and believe herself blessed.

Shifting her hips slightly, she sought to encourage him with her body and then with softly spoken words as she reached for his shaft and placed him at the entrance.

He pushed inside, past the thin membrane as it tore. She gasped at the sharp pain and he raised himself a little. "Adelaide?" he asked, a host of queries in his concerned expression.

To answer, she raised her legs and locked them around his thighs, pulling him closer and ignoring the lingering little agony. "My decision," she said, willing him to believe she was sincere. "My choice."

He lowered his head, almost as if he were at prayer, and then, with a low moan, buried his face in the side of her neck. Breathing hard, he thrust again, and it was as if her maidenhead had never existed. Her body had accepted him, taken him into itself and welcomed him.

There was no pain, no discomfort, as he undulated and pressed his lips to the throbbing pulse of her neck. He murmured her name, and it was as if all the praise he could ever heap upon her were contained in that one word.

The tension, the need, began to build within her. Her body moved in unison with his, rising and falling as if they were in a boat on a gentle tide.

Then, not so gentle. His breathing grew more ragged, the tendons in his neck more strained, his thrusts more powerful. She responded in kind, with primitive, wild passion, letting him take her where he would.

And never had she felt more liberated.

Sensations flooded her body, her mind, as if she and Armand were one being, seeking and striving for the same release, that same completion. The feel of his hot skin. The strength of his muscles. The scent of his flesh.

She clung to him, panting, anxious, yearning.

He was harder yet, and stronger, and more powerful, his body crashing into hers with fierce compulsion—until he groaned loudly in her ear. At nearly that same moment, the tension within her snapped, and they were like two wild untamed creatures, arching and gasping and riding out the wave of their desire as its ultimate release overcame them and sent them to the more peaceful shore.

To rest in each other's arms, sated, together and complete.

A LITTLE LATER that night, Richard waited for Francis in the shadow of the hut in the garden.

"What the devil did Armand want with you?" Richard demanded as his fellow conspirator joined him.

Francis recalled the hostility lurking in Armand's eyes. He'd been certain that bitch had told Armand he'd been the intruder who'd destroyed her clothes, but why, then, hadn't Armand accused him?

Maybe Armand didn't know, and only suspected. Perhaps Adelaide realized she was responsible for what he'd done. She should, because she was, that hypocritical whore.

There was no need for Richard to know these things, however. After all, it didn't directly affect their plans. "He wanted to apologize for his anger toward me before he leaves for Normandy."

"He's got the money then," Richard said. "I'd heard a messenger had arrived from Averette. I'm surprised John's letting him go. I didn't think he'd want both the de Boisbastons back in England."

"John doesn't know. Armand said he wouldn't interrupt the king."

Richard's frown deepened. "Yet he wanted to apologize to a man who's made no secret of his lust for his bride-to-be before he left?"

Francis lifted his chin. "Why not? It's a mistake to be my enemy."

Instead of agreeing, Richard regarded Francis with outright disdain. "Are you mad? Armand de Boisbaston may not be rich, but he still has powerful friends—at least as powerful as yours. No, the man's up to something—or suspects *we* are."

Francis's courage ebbed, for that would explain Armand's behavior better than any feeling of remorse or fear.

If Armand suspected them, he must put some distance between himself and his fellow conspirators. "I think it's time I went north to try to persuade more of the barons there to join our cause."

"You're more useful here," Richard replied, "especially if Armand is leaving. The young queen likes you, or at least finds you amusing. For now, that means you can do more good by staying at court. And don't tell me you've given up all hope of wooing the fair Adelaide?"

"The fair Adelaide is no longer worth the trouble." Especially if the de Boisbastons planned to accuse him of treason.

"I should think taming her after the way she's treated you would be very satisfying. Besides, there's the chance that Armand will meet his doom in

Normandy when the king invades again, as he surely will. Armand's estate would then go to his widow."

Adelaide *and* Armand's estate—it was tempting, but still… "Or Armand may live. And if he frees Bayard, that's another loyal knight to fight for John."

Yet there must be a way to get what he wanted. What he deserved for flattering and fawning over that hog of a king and his insipid little queen. After all, that was why he'd joined Richard and the others in the first place.

"Wouldn't it be better to rid ourselves of both the de Boisbastons now?" he suggested. "Destroy Armand before he gets to France so Bayard continues to rot in Normandy?"

Richard adjusted the cuff of his silken tunic as he considered the suggestion. "I believe you may be right, Francis. Indeed, I think you are."

AS SHE NESTLED against Armand, Adelaide tried to hold back her tears. Tears were a weakness. A woman's foolishness. She had known that he must leave. She had accepted it. Making love should make no difference. She had given herself freely, and freely they would part.

Yet now it was even more of a torment to imagine him wed to another, to think of another woman sharing the bliss she had found in his arms. It was a torture to think that she had experienced the joy of joining as husband and wife with Armand only to lose him.

The tears threatened to fall, and she blinked them

back. Armand mustn't see them. He mustn't believe she felt any remorse or disappointment for what they'd done. This was as she'd told him it must be. No legal binding contract. Nothing to force her to do as he commanded, to be his property.

With a sigh, Armand lifted a strand of her hair and rubbed it between his fingers. "I've been longing to touch your hair from the first time I saw you."

She closed her eyes and, fearing her voice would tremble with sorrow, didn't trust herself to answer.

He nodded at the open window, where she could see the first faint streaks of dawn. "It's getting late."

She subdued her sadness. That could wait until he was gone. Then she could cry. And weep. And rage. "I know."

"I ought to go."

He was right, yet she clung to him tighter. "Yes."

He kissed her tenderly, and when he looked at her, there was fierce determination, as well as love in his dark eyes. "I'm going to come back to you, Adelaide," he vowed. "Whether you marry me or not, we'll be together. I love you too much to let you go. I don't care what John or anyone—"

A heavy fist hammered on the door and a rough voice called out, "Armand de Boisbaston, open in the name of the king! You are under arrest for high treason!"

CHAPTER NINETEEN

"TREASON?" Adelaide gasped, clutching the sheet over her breasts as she swiftly sat up.

Armand was already out of the bed and tugging on his breeches. "Stay here," he ordered as a fist continued to pound on the door.

She would not cower in the bed like a coward. She scrambled out from beneath the covers and quickly retrieved her shift from the floor.

The harsh voice of Falkes de Bréauté once more demanded entry. "Open in the name of the king!"

"A moment to dress!" Armand shouted in reply.

The door burst open and John's *routiers,* led by de Bréauté, crowded into the room. Adelaide hastily grabbed the sheet from the bed to wrap around her still-naked body. Half-dressed, his feet bare, Armand held his shirt in his hands, and yet he was like a coiled snake or crouching cat, ready to strike.

Adelaide frantically looked for Armand's sword and spotted it on the chest, but before either one of them could reach it, one of the *routiers* grabbed it.

She stepped in front of Armand in case he was

tempted to attack regardless of his defenceless state. "How dare you?" she demanded of de Bréauté. "Have you no shame?"

The *routiers* laughed, while Falkes drew his sword. "Lord Armand de Boisbaston, you're under arrest by order of the king. I am to escort you to the dungeon. If you don't come quietly I also have orders to kill you." His gaze flicked to Adelaide. "Or anyone else who interferes with the king's command." He addressed the *routiers*. "Bind him, men, and take him away."

"No!" Adelaide cried as two *routiers* rushed forward to grab Armand's arms and hold him.

And then Lord Richard d'Artage, dressed in his usual finery, well-groomed and coifed despite the early hour, strolled into the chamber. He contemptuously surveyed Adelaide and her lover. "So, the mighty and honorable Lord Armand de Boisbaston is nothing but a traitor, after all."

Adelaide's whole body quaked with rage and dismay as she glared at Richard. "You're the traitor! You're conspiring against the king! We heard you!"

"Did you indeed?" Richard remarked, apparently not a whit disturbed. "Then why haven't you gone to the king and accused me?"

"We had no proof."

"How unfortunate."

"I'm a loyal servant of the king," Armand declared as the *routiers* began to pull him toward the door. "I've sworn an oath—twice."

"And broken it, apparently," Richard said.

"We know you're plotting against the king," Adelaide charged. "You and de Farnby and others besides. We know you plan to kill Marshal and the archbishop. But you're the one who's going to die a traitor's death!"

Richard dropped his foppish mask and revealed the vicious, ambitious brute beneath. "I don't believe you, or you would have already gone to the king."

He ran another scornful gaze over her body, and the sheet that shielded her nakedness. "Be grateful you aren't charged, as well, my lady. Be *very* grateful, because we know Armand isn't alone in his plotting. His brother, allegedly imprisoned, is really enjoying the hospitality of the Duc d'Ormande and conspiring with Philip of France against John, his lawful sovereign. This talk of a ransom is merely an attempt to blind us to his treasonous activities."

"That's a damn lie!" Armand shouted, his face red with fury, the gold flecks in his eyes like little tongues of flame. Yet even as he denied the charge, there was a touch of hope in Armand's voice and Adelaide guessed why. This meant that Bayard was almost certainly still alive.

Richard flinched but stood his ground. "Whatever Bayard's doing in the duke's castle, he's not in the dungeon. He's been seen strolling along the wall walk with the Duc d'Ormonde's pretty young bride."

"That can't be!" Armand retorted. "My brother's

no traitor and he isn't plotting with Philip. Even if he's not imprisoned as I was—and I pray God he's not— I'm sure the need to pay a ransom for his freedom is genuine. He may have the liberty of the castle without being able to leave."

"I won't waste any more time talking with a traitor," Richard said to Falkes. "Take him away."

"Find Randall," Armand called back to her as the *routiers,* followed by de Bréauté, frogmarched him out of the room. "Tell him what's happened."

"I will!" Adelaide cried.

As their footfalls echoed in the corridor, she turned on Richard, loathing him as she'd never hated anyone, not even her father. "You stinking, traitorous cur! You'll rot in hell for this—after you've been executed for treason!"

Richard gestured for the remaining *routiers* to go, and as they obeyed, a shiver of fear ran down Adelaide's back.

Nevertheless, she held her head high. She would *never* show this lout fear. She would summon all her courage, strength and resolve, for Armand's sake.

So she did not flinch or otherwise show any sign of dread, and she spoke with cool deliberation when they were alone. "I believe I must congratulate you, Richard. You attacked first and so have won the preliminary battle. It's a pity such a clever man as you, however, is ultimately doomed to defeat."

Richard laughed softly and reached out to grab

hold of the end of the sheet wrapped around her body. "It's a pity such a lovely, intelligent woman has allied herself with a traitor."

"That would be true if I'd ever been so foolish as to ally myself with you, or Francis or Oliver," she said, guessing what he was about to do. Even so, and although she tightened her grip on the sheet, she didn't make any extraordinary effort to hold it. If she did, he would believe he could intimidate her.

"Speaking of Sir Oliver, have you seen him this morning?" she asked, as if they were chatting in the hall surrounded by courtiers. "I have it in my mind that he's run away."

Richard's eyes narrowed slightly.

"Nor do I have any idea why you were so stupid as to ever include Francis in your plans," she continued. "He will never be faithful to anyone. The only person he thinks of is himself—rather like Oliver. Now *there's* a clever fellow for you. He realized he had thrown in his lot with dolts, and has wisely departed."

"You're spouting nonsense," Richard returned.

Despite his bravado, she caught the tremor of fear in his voice. Unfortunately, her triumph was short-lived, for he suddenly tugged hard. The sheet snapped from her body, and Richard laughed when she stood naked before him.

No doubt he expected her to shriek and cry and attempt to cover herself. She wouldn't give him that satisfaction, either. Covered only by her long, dark hair, she stood before him boldly, as if she were garbed in the raiment of a queen. "Such a brave fellow you are, Richard, to use shame and embarrassment as your weapons. Sadly for you, I'm not ashamed of my body, just as I'm not ashamed of anything I've done— as you should be."

Richard drew his sword.

"Will you kill the king's ward, Richard?" she asked, still not backing away. "What excuse would you give when they find my naked, bloody body? That I, unclothed and unarmed, attacked you first? Or will everyone assume— especially the women—that you tried to rape me and when I resisted, you killed me? What do you think will happen to you then?"

"You whore!" he cried, raising his sword. But the fear in his voice betrayed him, and she knew he would not strike.

"I'm not a whore," she said, "and everyone at court knows that. If I were, I would have been in John's bed weeks ago. Or Francis's. Or maybe even yours, if I were desperate enough."

"Bitch!" He gave her a back-handed blow so hard, she fell to the floor, landing on her hands and knees. She covered her head, expecting more, memories of her father's fists and curses rushing through her.

Instead, with an oath, Richard marched from the room, slamming the door behind him.

For a moment, Adelaide drew in deep, ragged breaths as she fought the sick feeling in her belly and summoned her courage, certain of what she had to do.

She would find Randall and tell him what happened, then go to John. She would tell the king the truth—who the real conspirators were and what they planned to do. John must learn the truth. She would make him believe her.

She got to her feet and found her shift. As she pulled it on, a soft knock sounded on the door. In the next moment, a distraught Eloise ran into her chamber, followed by an equally and obviously upset Randall, holding a rusty sword in his hand.

"Oh, Adelaide!" Eloise cried softly as she hurried to embrace her friend.

"Is it true?" Randall demanded, gripping his sword so hard, his knuckles were white. "Is it true that Armand's been arrested for treason?"

"Yes—accused by the men who are really plotting against the king," she replied, her determination to save Armand invigorating her. "We found out about their conspiracy and were trying to get proof, but the king's enemies have moved against us first."

Eloise and Randall exchanged surprised and dismayed looks, as well they might.

"We didn't tell you because we feared that might put you in danger," Adelaide explained. "Help me with my gown, Eloise, while I tell you what we've learned, and how."

As Eloise did as she asked, Adelaide told them everything, beginning with what had happened in the garden.

The one thing she left out was that the betrothal was a ruse, necessary only to allow her and Armand to meet with a minimum of speculation. She simply couldn't bring herself to reveal that lie, because now she wished it wasn't. Now, when he was in such grave danger, when he had been willing to honor her vow, she was willing to break it. In spite of everything, and because of everything, becoming Armand de Boisbaston's wife was more important than her promise.

"I must go to the king," she finished. "I have to tell him who the real traitors are."

"Let me go with you," Randall said.

"I'm going, too," Eloise declared. "The king will surely listen to the three of us."

As comforted as Adelaide was by their heartfelt offer of assistance, she said, "I think it's best if you don't. Revealing that you know about the conspiracy could still put you in danger."

Eloise took hold of Adelaide's cold hands in hers and met her friend's gaze steadily. "We're your friends."

"And that may be enough for us to be condemned as traitors anyway," Randall reasoned, "so we're going." Neither his tone nor his expression would permit dissent.

Obviously she, no doubt like many others, had been wrong to think Randall FitzOsbourne lacking in either determination or fortitude. A glance at Eloise proved she was equally resolute.

"We are blessed to have such friends," Adelaide said with sincere gratitude. "Come."

No one said anything more as they left her chamber and hurried toward the king's quarters. John must be there; it was too early for him to be anywhere else.

When they reached the corridor near the king's chamber, Falkes de Bréauté, with several *routiers* behind him, blocked their path.

"Move aside!" Adelaide commanded.

The mercenary only smirked. "Why the hurry, my lady?"

"Let us pass," Randall ordered, "or by God, you'll regret it!"

Eloise—the formerly, mild, meek Eloise—defiantly seconded him. "Yes, let us pass."

"The charges against Armand de Boisbaston are false," Adelaide declared, "although there *is* a conspiracy against the king. We know who's leading it, and if you don't let us see John, you could be putting him in danger."

Falkes licked his lips. "No doubt the king'd be happy to see *you* in his bedchamber, my lady, but I don't think he'd want you to *talk*."

"You'd better let her pass, de Bréauté," Randall said through clenched teeth. "It could be your life if you don't."

"When did you grow so bold, cripple?" de Bréauté sneered as his *routiers* snickered behind him.

"When I decided to save the king," Randall retorted.

"If John's overthrown," Adelaide said, "where will that leave you, Falkes? Provided you survive the rebellion, of course."

De Bréauté hesitated, and she saw doubt appear in his dung-brown eyes.

"Lady Adelaide alone, then," he muttered, lowering his sword.

Adelaide nodded her agreement and silenced Eloise and Randall's protests with a look. "I'll make John see the true danger he faces."

She lowered her voice and spoke so that only they could hear. "In the meantime, find Godwin. We must get a message to the Earl of Pembroke. He'll believe Armand's innocent."

They both nodded and turned to leave, while Adelaide again faced Falkes and raised an imperious, questioning brow.

Without another word, he led her toward the king's chamber, where he rapped on the door with the hilt of his sword.

A harried-looking middle-aged body servant cautiously opened it. "What do you—?"

He didn't get to finish his question, because Adelaide pushed her way past him and into the sumptuous chamber.

The king sat at a table covered with bottles, jars and

small casks that likely contained jewels. He held a mirror in one hand and a comb in the other. Frowning, he turned toward her. "Who dares to—?"

He smiled, lizardlike, when he saw her. "Oh, it's you, Lady Adelaide. I would call this a charming surprise, except no doubt you've come about your duplicitous betrothed. Have no fear—you aren't tainted by his treason."

"Your Majesty, I—"

"Go to the queen and tell her I shall be delayed at mass," John interrupted, waving a plump, dismissive hand at the servant. "Then wait in the antechamber. This lady and I will discuss this matter in private."

Adelaide clasped her hands together as the door shut behind the servant. She wasn't afraid for her own sake. She was afraid the king wouldn't believe her.

"Majesty," she began, "you have to know Armand is innocent of this charge. He is your loyal, faithful servant who has sworn his fealty to you twice."

"What I *know*," the king said as he turned back to his mirror, "is that a king is never safe. He can never trust anyone—not his father, not his mother, not a sister or brother or loyal retainer. A king is always alone and must always be alert for traitors and betrayal."

Adelaide approached his ebony chair. "Sire, you *do* face danger, but not from Armand. He and I overheard men plotting to kill the Earl of Pembroke and the Archbishop of Canterbury. Their plan is to cut those trustworthy props from beneath you, to make you

weaker and to sow the seeds of discontent and rebellion. We were going to tell you about the plot as soon
as we were sure who was involved, but we only discovered their identity last night. Sire, the traitors in
your court are Lord Richard and Francis, and perhaps
Sir Alfred, too."

The king's brows rose. "And it was just last night
you learned of this?"

"We learned of the conspiracy before, when we
overheard the traitors talking," she explained, cursing
herself for preventing Armand from going to the king
that very day, even if they didn't yet know who was
involved in the plot. "But we didn't see who it was,
and their voices were muffled. We wanted to be sure
before we made any accusations. In the meantime,
Armand warned the archbishop and the earl."

The king rose and strode over to a table covered
with scrolls beneath a shuttered window. "Lord
Richard, whom you charge with being a traitor,
brought me a letter this morning from one of my loyal
knights in Normandy. Here—read it yourself, if you
can."

He grabbed one of the scrolls and threw it at her.
She put her hands to protect her face as the parchment
flew past her and landed on the floor.

"Bayard de Boisbaston is *not* being held for ransom," the king declared, his voice rising with anger.
"He's enjoying the *hospitality* of the Duc d'Ormonde,
one of Philip's most loyal noblemen. He's free to go

at any time, if he so chooses, and he does *not*. He's thrown his lot in with Philip, that slimy little French eel, when he should have been loyal to *me!*" John shouted, smacking himself on the chest.

"That would be damning evidence, sire," she agreed, trying to remain calm despite the king's rage, "if it's genuine. It may not be. Even if that is the truth, Armand isn't a traitor. *He* hasn't betrayed you, or broken his oath, and he never will. He's as loyal to you as the Earl of Pembroke."

John's lip curled with scorn as he settled his bulk back into the delicate chair, which miraculously didn't break. "By the teeth of God, my lady, you're a bold one! You remind me of my mother, and that's no compliment, I assure you."

"Majesty, please, listen," she pleaded, softening her tone in the hope that would help. "It's not Armand you should fear. It's Lord Richard. He's the one planning to overthrow your rule, with Francis's help."

"Lord Richard and Sir Francis?" John scoffed. "Hardly a dangerous pair. Richard thinks more about his hair than politics, and Francis only cares about getting women into his bed. They haven't got the intelligence or ambition to plot treason."

"They do, Your Majesty," she insisted. "Richard's vanity is his disguise—his way to make you think he's harmless. And Francis *is* ambitious, and as treacherous as a snake. He'll follow whoever promises him the greater reward."

John's eyes narrowed as he steepled his fingers and looked at her over the tips. "I find it very interesting, my lady, that you're accusing the very men who denounced your betrothed."

"Richard and Francis must have realized we had discovered their plot and moved to protect themselves by accusing Armand first. I tell you, Majesty, they plan treason and rebellion against you."

The king twisted one of the many rings glittering on his chubby fingers. "What proof have you of these accusations?"

"Our word," she said as hope began to kindle at the king's change of manner. "Surely the word of Lord Armand de Boisbaston is worth a good deal. And so is mine, for it isn't lightly given."

"So I am to take *your* accusations on faith alone? That is all you can offer in Lord Armand's defence?"

"Yes, Your Majesty. You've arrested the wrong man."

The king rose. "Unfortunately, my lady, even if I believed you, I can't make judgments without evidence. Otherwise, I could be accused of playing favorites."

Adelaide ground her teeth in frustration. John "played favorites" among his courtiers all the time, just as his father and mother had favored one child over another, to the detriment of Europe. "Armand de Boisbaston would give his own life in your service. He already very nearly has."

"Although he hates me." John smiled when he saw the dismay she could not hide. "Come, my dear, I'm not a fool. It's obvious every time he looks at me."

"Even if that's so, he will never break his oath of loyalty to you. He would rather die."

A speculative gleam appeared in to the king's eyes. "If he's willing to risk his life to prove his loyalty, no doubt he'd be eager to do so to prove his innocence."

She realized at once what John was thinking, for he was a great proponent of trials by combat. Some claimed he was interested in justice, others that he merely enjoyed a bloody spectacle. Whatever the reason, John would likely agree to such a contest, and surely Armand would win. Not only was he a proven warrior, he was innocent, so God would give him the victory. "I'm sure he would be willing to prove it in any manner you decide, sire."

The speculation in John's eyes became greed as he folded his arms across his chest. "If I'm to preside over a trial by combat, my progress to Salisbury will have to be delayed."

She knew where he was headed with this, too. John accepted bribes for nearly everything. "Naturally Armand and I would be eager to recompense you for the inconvenience of such a delay."

"Even to five hundred marks?"

The whole of Bayard de Boisbaston's ransom. Yet what other choice did she have when Armand's life was at stake? "Yes, sire."

"He won't be able to ransom his brother, whom he

seems to hold so dear," the king pointed out, smiling with vindictive pleasure.

"If Armand is defeated, he stands convicted of treason, and Bayard de Boisbaston stands convicted with him. In that case, the ransom would be forfeit to the crown anyway, along with the rest of their estate."

"A most excellent point," the king concurred as he sauntered toward her. "You make a fine advocate, my lady. But perhaps that is not enough. I wonder what *you'd* be willing to do to see your betrothed set free?"

All her life Adelaide had railed against her fate being in a man's hands. Now, she held Armand's in hers.

What was she prepared to do for him?

Anything. Whatever John wanted, it was worth enduring for Armand's sake.

She faced the king squarely. "I'm willing to do whatever you deem necessary, Your Majesty."

John began to circle her. She stood motionless, as if she were trapped in a snare, willing herself not to flee.

"You have played a good game, my lady," John said, "setting my courtiers against each other in a bid to gain your favor. By God's teeth, you've even danced *me* a merry jig with your come-hither looks and coy deferments.

"Those days are at an end at last."

CHAPTER TWENTY

JOHN PULLED her into a suffocating embrace. His fat arms held her against his belly and she fought not to gag as his mouth, wet and hot and hungry, crushed hers. He roughly grabbed her breast, kneading it as if it were bread dough, as different from Armand's light, loving caresses as it was possible to be.

Oh, God, give me strength to bear this for Armand! she silently prayed, willing herself to submit, although every part of her rebelled.

As if in answer to her prayers, an inner door behind a screen banged open and the queen marched into the chamber.

John turned toward Isabel with surprising—and guilty—speed. "I didn't summon you!"

The queen ran a cold gaze over Adelaide, who blushed with shame even as relief rushed through her.

"Does a wife require an invitation to enter her husband's chamber?" Isabel demanded.

"When he is the king, she does," John retorted. "Leave us."

The queen's shrewd gaze immediately wavered,

and she covered her pretty face with her slender hands. "Oh, you break my poor heart, my love! You parade your mistresses right before my very eyes!"

Her shoulders began to shake and she sounded as if she was sobbing.

"Oh, what am I to do?" Isabel wailed. "You said you loved me when you stole me away from Hugh the Brown, and you made me love you, but now you must hate me to do this to me! And you blame me for losing Normandy, too, as if I were your general and not merely a woman and your wife!"

"Don't take on so, Isabel," John said with slightly less annoyance. "Lady Adelaide isn't my mistress."

"If she's not yet, she wants to be! Every woman at court wants to take you away from me! Why else is she here, alone with you?"

"I've come to plead for my innocent betrothed, and to tell your husband who the real conspirators are," Adelaide said. "The king has just graciously agreed to a trial by combat."

Isabel uncovered her face, which was conspicuously dry, and looked from Adelaide to John. "This is so?"

"Yes," John snapped. "So you see you have no need to be jealous."

Apparently remembering she was supposed to be upset, Isabel sniffled and gave him a woeful look as she went toward him. "I cannot help it. I love you too much."

Seeing a chance to get away, and hoping there

would still be a trial by combat even if she fled, Adelaide began to sidle toward the door.

"I try to be a good wife to you," Isabel said to John meekly, "doing whatever you ask, and yet you torment me with these other women."

"Those women mean nothing to me," John said gruffly as he held out his fleshy arms.

As he engulfed his young wife in an embrace that was almost sickening to see, Adelaide eased open the door and got herself away.

ELOISE WAS WAITING for Adelaide as she came out of the king's chamber. By now, several other curious nobles, including the maliciously delighted Hildegard and grave Sir Charles, had joined the *routiers* there.

When Adelaide saw the inquisitive faces of the courtiers, and the leering lust in those of the *routiers,* she felt the pointed prick of pride. She'd allowed herself to be humiliated by John for Armand's sake, but she would maintain her dignity before these others.

She lifted her chin, straightened her shoulders and said not a word in justification or explanation as she greeted Eloise warmly and led her away from them.

"Is the king going to free Armand?" Eloise asked anxiously as she hurried after her friend.

"No. Did you find Godwin?"

"Yes. Randall's writing the message for him to

take right now. Walter de Chevron had absolutely no objections to sending him, and he's giving him an escort, as well, to make sure he arrives safely. Poor Walter's very upset by all this. He likes Armand and more importantly, he knows the earl trusts him. He's certain the earl's going to be very angry when he hears what's happened, and in one of his own castles, too."

"Good," Adelaide said with a grateful sigh, taking some measure of comfort from the steward's support as they entered the courtyard.

A few of the soldiers not currently on watch or patrol lounged near the chapel and watched them as they passed. A thin, spotty-faced young fellow gave her a friendly grin and others nodded a greeting. They didn't have to tell her they believed Armand was innocent. If they didn't, they would have scowled or ignored her completely.

Likewise the servants they encountered regarded them with sympathetic amiability, although they also gave the ladies a wide berth.

She couldn't blame them. They had their own concerns, and the guilt or innocence of a nobleman or woman not their master, or allied to that family, must take precedence.

"What of Armand's oath?" Eloise asked. "Did John just dismiss that completely?"

"Yes. I believe he puts no faith in oaths or loyalty. Why would he, after he's betrayed his own so often?" she asked bitterly. "But John's agreed to a trial by combat."

"Sweet heaven!" Eloise cried, coming to an abrupt halt. "Armand will be killed!"

The servants and soldiers, not surprisingly, stared at them.

"Armand can surely defeat any man John sends against him," Adelaide said staunchly.

"It's not that I doubt his skill," Eloise explained, wringing her hands. "Randall told me he was very badly wounded in Normandy."

"Mother of God!" Adelaide took hold of Eloise's arm and pulled her onto the chapel porch, away from the eyes and ears of others in the courtyard. "He never told me he was wounded!"

Even when they were alone and intimate…. But then she remembered, as suddenly and vividly as a thunderclap, how she'd heard those limping footsteps in the garden and, expecting to find Randall, had met Armand instead. "His leg?"

Eloise nodded. "His right knee was badly damaged by a mace blow, and left untreated for weeks while he was imprisoned. And he was shackled with his arms over his head for days at a time. His arms are still weak from his ordeal, Randall says, and his knee gives him a great deal of pain."

He should have told her…confided in her…. As she should have told him from the start about her vow not to marry, and why she had made it.

"Had I known…"

If she had, she would have done anything John asked to spare Armand and would never have proposed a trial by combat. "It's too late," she said as the weight of despair, as heavy as lead, settled upon her. "I've already promised John five hundred marks to ensure the trial."

"The amount of Bayard's ransom?"

"Yes, and the king showed me a letter, supposedly from France, claiming that Bayard's in league with Philip."

Instead of looking shocked, dismayed or incredulous, Eloise looked angry. "That's ridiculous. Bayard's no more a traitor than Armand. Randall trusts them both absolutely."

And apparently that was good enough for Eloise. It was good enough for Adelaide, too, and it should be for John and everyone else. Yet she knew John would only be satisfied by a trial by combat now.

Nevertheless, Eloise's staunch belief in the innocence of Bayard de Boisbaston brought Adelaide some much-needed comfort. "I'm sure Bayard's as honorable and trustworthy as Armand," she agreed.

"Can't we do something to stop it?" Eloise asked anxiously. "How can Armand win if he's injured?"

Perhaps if she went again to John and offered…

But what then? Giving herself to the king would not clear Armand and Bayard from suspicion of treason in many men's eyes and likely not even the king's. It would only buy them some more time before they were accused again, and John wouldn't be willing to take her body in lieu again.

Nor would Armand want a woman's body and her honor to be the payment for his freedom. Later, he might even resent the loss of the chance to clear his name himself.

"Armand will win," Adelaide assured her friend. "No matter if he's injured, or who fights against him. Because he's innocent."

FRANCIS STARED incredulously at Richard as they stood in that nobleman's expensively and sumptuously furnished bedchamber. Richard always traveled with what he considered necessities. "She's denounced me as a traitor to the king himself?"

"Yes, she has," Richard replied as he adjusted his belt to a more flattering position. Francis might turn into a mass of fear because of Adelaide's accusation, but he would not. "Surely it's no surprise she'd point the finger at you after your behavior toward her."

A look of alarm came to Francis's eyes and Richard realized he'd have to tell him more, lest the idiot do something stupid. "It isn't only you she's accused. She called me a traitor to my face. But I'm not panicking because there's no need. She's so besotted with Armand, everyone will believe she's casting accusations like seeds on a farmer's field, hoping one takes root and saves him."

"Oh, yes, no need to panic," Francis charged in return. "Then where the devil's Oliver? He wasn't in his bedchamber, as you said he'd be."

For the second time that morning, Richard experienced the icy grip of fear. He'd considered Francis the weakest member of their conspiracy and taken steps to ensure he knew very little of their plans, but he'd trusted Oliver. "His clothing was still there?"

"I'm not his body servant, so how should—?" Francis sucked in his breath and glared at his companion. "You think he's gone! Where? Why?"

He grabbed Richard by his lemon-yellow tunic. "Has that Irish cur betrayed us?"

Richard knocked his hand away. "Calm yourself," he ordered, still not willing to believe what Adelaide had told him. She was in love with Armand; she'd say anything, hoping to hit the mark, and she'd obviously seen him talking with Oliver in the past. "He's probably in the village with a whore. Or here, in one of the lady's chambers, with a different sort of harlot."

"I asked the maidservants if they knew where he was," Francis said. "They don't."

"So perhaps not a lady's chamber. There are plenty of other places a man can go to be with a woman."

Francis's hand went to the hilt of his sword. "*Somebody* told Adelaide and Armand about our plans. It wasn't me, so either it was you or Oliver. Was it you? Is that why you went to the king this morning—to set him against Armand and then denounce me? Is that why Oliver's fled—to avoid arrest because you betrayed us both? Or have you killed him? Are you planning to kill me, too?"

"Don't be a fool," Richard snapped, crossing the room to stand in front of the narrow window. "It's Armand I want dead. He's as loyal as the earl, so he has to be taken out of our way. Whatever my lady says, the king can be convinced she's only trying to save her lover. More importantly, *they have no proof,* or we would already be arrested. So for God's sake, calm yourself! Act like a knight and not a frightened woman."

Even as he spoke, more dread darkened Richard's thoughts. For now, they were safe, but John was a suspicious, capricious man. He might very well throw them in the dungeon and charge them all with treason just as a precaution.

"What if Armand convinces the king he's right and we're the traitors?" Francis demanded.

Anger and fear for his own fate overwhelmed Richard. He rushed toward Francis and pinned him against the nearest wall. "Do you *want* to be caught?" he growled as he held him there, his arm against Francis's throat.

Francis struggled to breathe and his face turned red, but still Richard didn't let go. "For God's sake, why don't you just walk into the courtyard and tell everyone our plans? Damn you for seven times a fool, you shouldn't even say the word *traitor,* because we're not! John is not the rightful king. Arthur was, and now that he's been murdered, the throne belongs to Eleanor, and to the man she marries."

Breathing hard, Richard released Francis and stepped back.

"And she ought to marry you, I suppose?" Francis rasped as his hand sought the dagger in his belt.

"I'm not that stupid," Richard retorted, swiftly drawing his own dagger and putting the tip at Francis's throat. "Don't make a mistake, Francis. We are in this together, come victory or defeat, and without me, you're like a blind man stumbling around in the dark."

Francis scowled as he held his arms out in submission. "If I'm accused and you betray me, I won't be going to the gibbet alone."

No, he'd babble like a baby. Thank God he knew so little, although they never should have brought him into their plans at all. He shouldn't have listened to Oliver, who'd insisted Francis would be an asset, or an easy, ignorant dupe to cast away if the king grew suspicious. They'd be able to outmaneuver him, Oliver assured him, should Francis turn on them.

Now he feared Oliver had outmaneuvered them both. "Neither one of us is going to be charged with treason," he said. "I've already seen to that by accusing Armand first. As for Oliver, he's somewhere in Ludgershall. You're worried for nothing, so sheath your dagger."

"You first."

"Very well," Richard agreed, doing so. Francis would never dare to kill him. He was too rich and too powerful, and so were his friends. "I'll go back to the king and ensure the lovely Lady Adelaide hasn't managed to persuade him that her betrothed is innocent."

"That's another thing," Francis said. "I'm sure she can be very persuasive, especially if she's willing to do whatever John wants."

"So we'll just have to make sure she's kept away from him. De Bréauté will see to it. God knows I've paid him enough. And while I'm doing that, you find Oliver. Search the castle and the village, and don't give up until you find him."

JOHN KEPT Richard waiting outside his private chamber for what seemed an age. Richard made light of the delay with the *routiers* on guard there, bantering about women and wine, but all the while, his mind raced, examining everything he'd said and done at court, trying to think of any possible mistakes he'd made that might work against him.

The worst was trusting Oliver, and as every minute passed that Francis didn't appear to tell him Oliver had been found, his fear that he'd been tricked by that scheming Irishman grew.

And what of the part that Oliver had played in their plans? Was the archbishop dead, or dying, or was he alive and well and Marcus in chains? He should have heard of the archbishop's illness, at least, by now.

Damn Oliver! The best he deserved was a slow and painful death.

"The king will see you now."

Richard started at the servant's announcement, then hurried into John's chamber.

John sat in a chair by the window, with Queen Isabel beside him like a little doll, holding his hand.

"A very disturbing story has reached me, Your Majesty," Richard began with an incredulous, and slightly affronted, air. "I understand Lady Adelaide has accused me of treason, and my friend, Sir Francis de Farnby, as well."

"She has," the king agreed with an amiability that did not alleviate Richard's fears. "Lady Adelaide was most impassioned in her defence of Lord Armand, and most adamant that you two were traitors."

"Of course she would blame and discredit me," Richard replied. "I was the one who arrested Armand—on your orders."

The king didn't seem moved by that reminder. "She was most sincere."

"No doubt she believes that everything Armand says is true. Like many women in love, she'll believe any lie her lover tells her."

"Lady Adelaide seems too clever a woman to be so overcome by love," the queen remarked. She smiled and patted her husband's plump hand. "Still, we women are so soft-hearted, perhaps it is as you say."

"Has she offered any evidence against us?" Richard asked. Surely she hadn't, or he and Francis would already be in the dungeon.

"She says she overheard you and Sir Francis plotting a conspiracy to murder the Archbishop of Canterbury and the Earl of Pembroke."

Richard laughed. "That's the most ridiculous thing I've ever heard!"

"I agree," the queen said, giving Richard a smile that made him quite certain that his attentions to her, which had occasionally ventured beyond the bounds of courtesy to something both more personal and exciting, had been worth the effort.

Pleased that he had the queen on his side, he grew more bold. "Whereas, Your Majesty, you now have evidence of the strongest kind against the de Boisbastons."

"I wouldn't say that," the king replied. "You brought me a letter that apparently damns Bayard de Boisbaston, not his brother. I would say your evidence against Lord Armand is no stronger than his evidence against you—that is, nothing substantial at all."

"Majesty," Richard protested, "it's been obvious from the moment Armand arrived here that he's your enemy."

"It's been obvious he's angry because of his imprisonment in Normandy," John replied. "Yet he's sworn another oath of fealty, something a man of his pride doesn't do lightly, and which he will likely never break."

Richard glanced at the queen, who was watching her husband. "Sire, many a traitor has sworn an oath only to break it at his convenience."

"You don't have to tell *me* about the dishonesty and duplicity of men," the king said, frowning, and Richard remembered with a sickening feeling that John wasn't exactly a model of fidelity and trustworthiness himself.

The queen stroked the king's hand and said something soothing that Richard couldn't hear.

Fortunately, John relaxed a little. "So what we have, my lord, is a stalemate, and one that must be broken, for I've no wish to delay my journey to Salisbury any more than necessary. Therefore, I've decided to put the matter to God, in a trial by combat, which will be held tomorrow. Since Armand has accused both you and Francis, one of you must meet him in battle."

Had that been Adelaide's doing, or was it John's idea? No matter. Even if he were skilled in arms, Armand de Boisbaston was not the sort of warrior he wanted to meet in single combat.

Francis was a greedy, ambitious dolt, but he could fight. And Richard remembered something else— he'd seen Armand limping as he left the hall at night, like his crippled, milksop friend. If he'd been wounded in Normandy—and there was every possibility he had been, given the fighting in Marchant before Armand had finally surrendered—there was a good chance Francis might actually win. "I believe Sir Francis will welcome the opportunity to clear his name and settle a more personal score, as well, Your Majesty."

"Very well. Sir Francis it will be." John smiled with an unexpected shrewdness that made Richard's blood run cold. "And you may tell him Lady Adelaide goes to the victor."

CHAPTER TWENTY-ONE

ADELAIDE APPROACHED the king's chamber, and this time, de Bréauté made no move to stop her, although he smirked as he opened the door.

John sat at the large table covered with rolls of parchment, vessels of ink and several quills. He glanced up when the door opened, then leaned back in his chair as Adelaide walked into the room. She said nothing as she placed the bag of coins worth five hundred marks on the table before him.

"Thank you, my lady," John said, reaching for it, his eyes gleaming like a miser's in a counting house. "I've spoken to Lord Richard, who was aghast at your accusations, and most firmly refutes them."

"He would," she replied. She hadn't expected him to do otherwise. "Will he be doing combat with Armand?"

"No. Francis de Farnby will be Lord Armand's opponent."

Adelaide didn't hide her smile. Richard was a clever man, and clever men were surely more dangerous fighters. Francis was neither clever, nor brave.

Even wounded, Armand would undoubtedly be more than a match for him.

"And in the meantime, sire, you will permit Armand to leave his cell," she said, and although she addressed the king, it wasn't a request.

Instead of taking offence, the king laughed. "Why not? If he didn't run from the siege of Marchant, I don't suppose he'll run away from Francis de Farnby."

IMPRISONED AND ALONE, Armand sat on filthy straw, his knees drawn up and his arms wrapped around them, staring at the locked wooden door. Once more he was imprisoned, and alone.

Yet this time, he didn't feel alone, because this time, he had Adelaide on his side. She would be a formidable advocate, and he thanked God with all his heart she was no meek and mild maiden.

How could he ever have thought he wanted some weak and placid bride? Adelaide was his equal in courage, in determination, in intelligence and resolve.

No, she was superior. He couldn't have traversed the tricky paths of court as she had for so long. He couldn't have played the courtiers like pieces on a chessboard. He would have murdered John if he'd had to fend off the king's advances, and wound up a convicted traitor.

Now, thank God, he also knew where Bayard was, if anything in that letter could be trusted. Bayard was alive and safe, too, and he hoped, enjoying an easier captivity than he himself had endured. He'd heard of the Duc d'Ormond. He was said to be as chivalrous as William Marshal, so he should treat his prisoners well. Genial treatment had been the accepted manner of dealing with knights waiting to be ransomed, until John had let the knights of Corfe starve to death.

Armand looked up at the small window high above his head—one other difference to this imprisonment that made his heart lighter.

Footsteps sounded outside his cell. For an instant, he felt fear and panic, remembering the beatings he'd endured in Normandy. Then he thought of brave, bold Adelaide and his hope returned.

The door to the cell creaked open. Holding a torch, Falkes de Bréauté entered the dank chamber. "How the mighty are fallen, eh, my lord?" he asked as he regarded Armand with a mean and vicious smile.

Again Armand felt that terrible panic, but again he thought of Adelaide, and his love and faith in her gave him strength. "John's favor comes and goes like smoke upon the wind—something you should remember, Falkes."

"Out of my way!" a wonderful, familiar voice cried, and then there was Adelaide—beautiful, amazing Adelaide, who looked as out of place in that terrible hole as a flower among the tidal flats of the Thames.

She rushed into his open arms, the scent of her delicate rosy perfume like a breath of spring. She had come, just as he knew she would.

"Adelaide, Adelaide," he whispered, holding her close, loving her even more.

"I've come to take you out of here," she said. "I've convinced the king to let God decide who's speaking the truth. There's to be a trial by combat and I know you'll win!"

A thousand questions burst into Armand's mind—first and foremost, what Adelaide had done or promised to convince the king to allow the trial and to free him from this cell—but those questions could wait until they were alone.

Ignoring de Bréauté, Armand let Adelaide lead him from the cell and up the slimy, slippery steps to the room in the keep that served as an armory for storing arms and the padded gambesons the soldiers and archers wore. Adelaide didn't speak, but the tight grip of her hand told him that she was not as calm as she looked or acted.

"We won't go to the hall," she said as they crossed the yard toward the apartments. He was relieved. He had no desire to be stared at, or asked a host of questions. He would much rather be alone with her.

Servants, stableboys, grooms and soldiers silently watched them pass, and more than one surreptitiously tugged a forelock, straightened in salute or, in the case of the maidservants, smiled their encouragement. Gratitude for their silent good wishes welled up inside him and gave him yet more confidence.

Entering his chamber, they found Eloise already

there, standing beside a table spread with a white linen cloth. On it was a tray bearing a trencher of brown bread holding a large piece of roasted beef swimming in a thick gravy. There was also a pease porridge and a carafe of wine. Candles lit the chamber, for it was nearly dusk, and the basin on his washstand was full of steaming water.

He smiled his thanks and made directly for the basin, where he washed his face and hands, brushing back his hair. He heard Adelaide and Eloise conversing quietly as he dried his face, but when he turned back, Eloise was gone.

"I assume some of this was her doing?" he asked, raising his brows and giving Adelaide a smile.

Obviously a bit overcome, she gestured at the table. "All of this was Eloise's idea. She didn't tell me she was going to do it. She must have brought all these things while I was taking the money to the king."

"Money?"

"I had to bribe him for the trial."

He should have foreseen this, Armand thought, struggling to contain his anger. It wasn't Adelaide's fault John was what he was. "How much?"

"Sit and eat and I'll tell you everything."

She did, and when Armand heard about her narrow escape from John's assault, he brought his goblet down on the table so hard, it nearly split asunder. "That stinking—"

"It doesn't matter," she interrupted, reaching out to

take his fisted hand in hers. "Isabel came to my rescue, although I doubt she thinks of it as such. The important thing is, I escaped unharmed."

"For which John should be thankful, or oath or no oath, I'd kill him myself." Armand got to his feet, too agitated to sit. "God's blood, that man's a villain! And to think he's our king."

"To whom we must be loyal, or the alternative is anarchy."

"But at what price?" Armand demanded, torn between distress and the need to abide by his sworn word.

"As long as John has good men about him, I can hope he won't utterly destroy the country—men like you and William Marshal."

"Unless John accuses us all of treason," Armand muttered, looking out of the window to the clear sky and a bird winging its way past.

Adelaide put her arms around him. "For all his greed, John isn't completely stupid. He knows he needs good men like you and the earl. And Bayard will yet be ransomed. Eloise just told me Randall's gone to get more money from his father."

To beg on his behalf. "Although I'm grateful, I wish he hadn't," Armand said, rubbing his forehead. "His father's a miserly old lout who takes it as a personal affront that Randall was born crippled."

"As much as Randall cares about you," Adelaide replied, "that wasn't his only reason. He's also gone to tell his father that he and Eloise are going to be married, and he needs money to pay the king for his permision."

For a moment, Armand forgot his own predicament. "Randall deserves a bride as kind and honest as he is."

"They love each other very much," Adelaide said softly.

As he loved her, Armand thought, reaching out and drawing Adelaide into his arms. He sighed and held her close. "I must not be the only man changed by love in Ludgershall, and if he can get the ransom money for Bayard, I'll accept it with thanks. And I welcome the chance to meet Richard in battle."

"You won't be fighting Richard," she said, gazing up with a pleased smile. "Your opponent will be Francis de Farnby."

That was not welcome news to Armand. Before Normandy he would have laughed and thought he had an easy task to beat any man who came against him. Not now, though, not when his arms still lacked their full strength, and his knee ached if he simply stood too long. And whatever other qualities Francis lacked, he wasn't an unskilled fighter.

Yet he didn't want to add to Adelaide's worries. "Francis has only fought in melees, for prizes and for show," he mused aloud, gaining some confidence from that remembrance. "He's never been in a real battle. He's never learned the hundred little tricks and feints that can save your life."

Despite his efforts to be reassuring, a little wrinkle

of worry appeared between Adelaide's shapely brows. "After I left the king, Eloise told me you were injured in Normandy and your wounds were left untreated. I didn't know—"

He silenced her with a brief kiss and sought to ease her fears. "I may not be at my full strength, but I'll defeat him. After all, I'm not the traitor, so surely God will help me win."

Adelaide smiled at him with all the courage and determination he'd come to expect from her. "I have faith in God and you, Armand," she said.

And then she turned away and covered her face with her hands, the first outward sign of vulnerability she had ever shown.

He cupped her shoulders and turned her back to face him. Gently he pulled her hands away. "Adelaide, don't worry. I'll be safe. I'll win."

"It's not that," she whispered with a catch in her voice. "I have faith that you can beat Francis de Farnby in a contest of arms.

"I love you, Armand. I love you more than my honor, more than my life, more than anything. I love you so much, I'll break my vow and be your wife, if you will have me. I always thought that I would be losing my freedom if I married, but now I know I'll never be more free than I can be with you."

Joy, excitement and a determination to triumph on the field of combat roared through him. "Do you mean that, Adelaide?"

Her smile gave him her answer even before she said, "Yes, Armand, I do. I'll marry you."

With a happy cry, he picked her up and twirled her around.

She laughed, then gave him a shy, delightfully wistful smile. "I hope Gillian and Lizette will forgive me."

"Will they be so very angry if you break your promise?" he asked. "Won't they understand that you fell in love? And there will be some benefit to them if we marry. They will have me to protect them, too."

"But *I* was the one who thought we should make that pact. It was my idea."

"Then perhaps it's best if you're the one who decides to break it."

She twisted the dangling ends of the ties of her girdle in her hands. "If we marry, you'll become the master of Averette. Gillian will probably hate me for that."

That was a concern he could easily assuage. "I have my own estate to run and that's plenty for me. I'll be happy to let Gillian rule Averette."

He had his reward for that minor sacrifice when Adelaide looked at him as if he was offering her the world. "You'd do that?"

"Gladly," he said. "It's you I want, not your family's estate."

Her eyes shining with love, she caressed his slightly stubbled cheek. "Oh, Armand, how could I *not* love you?"

"Then you do love me?"

She laughed softly, and this time, there was only happiness in her lovely eyes. "If my words are not enough, you have proof of my love in the breaking of my oath, for unless I loved you fully, completely, with all that I am and hope to be, I would never marry you."

"What can I offer to match that?" he asked, humbled by her declaration.

"You have already given it—your respect. You treat me as I never believed a man would treat a woman, as an equal, a partner and confidante worthy of your trust." The expression in her eyes changed to one of smoldering desire. "But if you must give me more proof of your love, I can think of something."

Her meaning was no great mystery, and the heat of passion kindled within him. "Really, my lady?" he asked, his voice rough with desire. "What might that be?"

"Do I have to tell you?"

"No, I don't believe you do," he murmured as he pulled her into his arms.

He kissed her tenderly at first, like a young and innocent lover, lightly and softly. Teasing her, it seemed, until her anticipation grew. She held him close, pressing her body against his, her mouth demanding more.

She was his, in love and soon in law. She was his, and always would be, as he would always be hers.

Together and equal. Lovers and friends. A union not of power and servitude, but mutual respect and trust.

Armand stopped teasing and led her to the bed. Standing beside it, they slowly, deliberately helped each other out of their clothes. They took their time, savoring every moment, every touch, every look, every caress.

Until the heat of passion overcame them.

Kissing him, Adelaide eased him down upon the bed and then, with wanton, blatant desire, straddled him.

Armand let the sensations of her touch, her weight, her hair, wash over and arouse him. She was his, and he was hers, now and forever, and no matter what the future held.

Adelaide licked his skin, her tongue making an excruciatingly delightful journey from the waist of his breeches up his belly to encircle his nipple. Everything but need and excitement, joy and desire, fled. He groaned aloud when she sucked his nipple into her mouth and gripped her harder when she laved it with her tongue.

Capturing his mouth, she placed her palm on his shaft. He squirmed beneath her delicate, hesitant caresses and moaned when she encircled him and began to stroke up and down.

"You like this, my lord?" she asked in a breathless whisper.

"Armand. My name is Armand," he gasped.

"I think you do, Armand," she murmured as she made a trail of light kisses down his torso and inched backward. "I think you like it very much."

He could only groan in response as his mind screamed with a question— Was she going to…?

By heaven she was! She opened her mouth and took him inside, the moist warmth of her surrounding him. It was all he could do not to buck and squirm until he half rose and pulled her forward.

"Enough," he gasped. "Let me love you. I *need* to love you."

Her eyes dark with longing, she raised herself and guided him to her. Leaning slightly forward, she reached for him, her gaze holding his as she lowered her ready and willing body onto his.

With a groan of gratitude, he thrust inside her. She was moist and slick and ready for his length, eagerly accepting him, raising her hips to meet him. Her eyes closed in an ecstasy that matched his own, her hands splayed beside his head, she began to rock.

Their desire and need increasing, their passion bursting as brightly as a torch in the darkest cave, they moved as one. Waxing and waning, rising and falling, they rode the ocean of their passion, skimming the surface, feeling the pull of the currents of their yearning, each attuned to the other as if they were but one body, one appetite, one hunger needing to be satisfied.

Armand could wait no longer. He lost all control and, thrusting hard and fast, filled her with his seed.

Throwing back her head, gripping him tightly, her nails dug into his flesh as she, too, cried out, her body clenching as she shared the moment of release.

She was his, and he was hers.

Forever.

"ME?" FRANCIS CRIED angrily as he stood with Richard in a corner of the hall, well away from anyone who could overhear them. "You told the king *I* would fight Armand? You stinking dog! I'm not your lackey to be put in harm's way!"

"God's blood, man, are you blind?" Richard demanded. "Haven't you noticed anything about Armand de Boisbaston except his attention to Adelaide? The man favors his left leg when he's tired. He was in chains for months, and likely wounded before. You'll be more than a match for him."

"So you say," Francis muttered. He downed the rest of his wine in a single gulp. "Easy enough for you when you've put *me* in danger. If you're so convinced he'll be easy to beat, why don't *you* fight him?"

"Because you're a better warrior than I am," Richard admitted with seeming reluctance. "Or would you rather take your chance in a court of law on a charge of treason—and that's if you even got that far. John might send some *routiers* to kill you before a trial, and you know they won't make it quick. Those men enjoy what they do.

"And, as an added reward," he said, saving the

reason that would surely most tempt Francis for the last, "the king will give you Adelaide when you win."

To his surprise, Francis didn't look pleased.

"What, you no longer want her?"

"Not since Armand's had her."

That was a slight problem, but there were still plenty of reasons Francis should accept the challenge. "Then think how impressed the barons will be when you defeat Armand de Boisbaston, especially those who complain that you didn't go to Normandy. This will be a way to prove your courage and ability."

"Who dares speak against me because I wouldn't waste my life on that hopeless campaign?" Francis demanded.

"It won't matter once you defeat Armand. That will silence any wagging tongues."

"Even if I succeed, John will surely still suspect us," Francis pointed out, proving he wasn't completely stupid.

"No more than he suspects everybody, but he'll trust you more than many. He may even bring you into his counsel, and send you on important diplomatic missions, as he does his most trusted household knights. Think of what you can accomplish then—the riches and allies you can gather for yourself and our cause."

"You realize that if John raises me up, I might not want him cut down," Francis said, watching Richard carefully.

"You would be even more vital to the new king if you bring knowledge and your allegiance to his cause. That will not be something to be taken lightly."

"It's not as if I have any real choice, do I?" Francis grudgingly conceded. "I have to fight Armand or be considered both a traitor and a coward."

"But there will be plenty of rewards when you win."

Francis's expression told Richard that the dupe was growing shrewd. "And when I win, I'll use them."

CHAPTER TWENTY-TWO

WHEN ADELAIDE awoke at dawn after a fitful sleep, the first thing she saw was Armand, magnificently naked in the early-morning light, his fingers interlaced as he stretched his long, muscular arms over his head. She lay still and silent, the better to admire his broad shoulders, his back, his taut buttocks and powerful legs.

Surely this man, this warrior, would defeat Sir Francis de Farnby. Even weakened, and despite his wounded knee, Armand must and would triumph.

He walked to the basin and splashed cold water over his face. The water dripped from his chin and nose as he glanced over at the bed. "You're awake," he said as he dried himself off.

Holding the sheet to her breasts, she sat up, her back against the pillows. "How does your knee fare this morning?"

He squatted and straightened. "Not badly."

It was obviously not completely well, either, for she caught the wince that flashed across his face, although he tried to hide it.

He flexed his right arm, squeezing the muscle of his upper arm. Then his left.

"And your arms?"

"Stronger than they were when I left Normandy."

She wondered if he was saying that only for her benefit, then decided that if he was, she would not question it. "When is the trial to be?"

"After the fast is broken."

"Then we can go to mass together," she said as she rose from the bed.

He went to her and took her hands in his. "Adelaide, will you marry me this morning? Before the trial, before mass?"

Adelaide didn't answer right away. Although her decision had been made and she was sure it was right, there would be no going back once they had stood before the priest on the chapel steps and pledged themselves in marriage.

Armand misunderstood her hesitation. "If you'd rather not tie yourself to me before the trial, I'll understand."

"No, no!" she assured him, embracing him. "I want to marry you more than I've ever wanted anything. So yes, Armand, I'll marry you this morning, and gladly. Gratefully."

She raised herself on her toes to kiss him. "Because I love you with all my heart, and I want to be your wife."

HOWEVER CERTAIN Adelaide and Armand were about the step they were about to take, the priest was much less confident.

"This is…this is most irregular," he prevaricated when they stood before him in the chapel before mass was to begin.

Armand wasn't going to let the priest's doubts or misgivings dissuade them. He had won Adelaide's heart, and as he lived, they would be wed.

As for the possibility that he might die that day, he would entertain no fear, although if he did die, he could be sure his widow would do all she could to save his brother from a similar fate, and he could think of no better custodian for his estate.

So he was calm, but firm, when he replied to the priest. "As you know, we have the king's approval to marry and as I suspect you also know, the lady and I are already married in one sense. We wish to acknowledge our union before God. And should He chose to let me fail today, I don't want to die in a state of sin."

Armand's gaze faltered for the briefest of moments, for he would betray no fear or dread before this man, or Adelaide, who squeezed his hand, and staunchly said, "Although Armand is innocent of treason, I would have his spirit free and clear of guilt or worry, Father. Will you not do this for us, to bring us out of sin into marriage?"

"As I wish others at court would do," the priest said, suddenly decisive. "Thus I shall hear both your confessions, and afterward, when the court has come to mass, I will bless your union."

A LITTLE WHILE LATER, after Armand and Adelaide had confessed to the priest and received absolution, they stood on the steps of the chapel watching the king, queen and the rest of the court approach.

Holding Armand's hand, Adelaide scanned the growing crowd for Eloise, and quickly found her. Eloise immediately guessed the significance of the priest on the steps of the chapel with them, and her look of surprise gave way to one of delight. Adelaide returned her friend's smile, and for one sweet moment, she forgot the trial to come—until she spotted Sir Alfred among the crowd, frowning and bleary-eyed.

Hildegard, not surprisingly, regarded them with open disdain. Sir Charles, Sir Edmond and Sir Roger, however, nudged each other and grinned their approval while Lady Jane looked pleased and ignored her mother's querulous demands to know what was going on.

Richard and Francis, perhaps not surprisingly, were nowhere to be seen.

"Good morning, my lady and my lord," the king said as he came to a halt. "What have we here?"

Armand stepped forward. "Lady Adelaide and I wish to marry today, Your Majesty."

"What, this morning?"

"Yes, sire."

"I haven't heard that there's been any formal betrothal contract signed."

"We require none," Adelaide said. "All that I have will be my husband's, as the law requires."

"And all that I have I shall share with my wife, as honor demands," Armand added. He lowered his voice, speaking to the king as one knight to another, giving the man such respect only because he feared John might yet refuse. "Sire, I wish to marry Lady Adelaide before the combat to come."

A murmur of approval went up from those gathered there, except for Hildegard and Lady Ethel who, finally having figured out what was afoot, muttered darkly about the lack of morals among the young in this degenerate age.

John looked as if he'd like to refuse, yet he grudgingly agreed, perhaps because of the mood of the crowd, or maybe he thought Armand wouldn't last the day. "As you wish. Far be it for me to deny a man what could be his last request. But should you fall, your widow will marry Sir Francis."

"What?" Armand cried, while Adelaide could only stare, too appalled to speak.

"Why should you care what happens to the lady after you're dead?" John asked. "Your estate will not go to de Farnby in any case. Since you will be a convicted traitor, it will be forfeit to the crown. The lady, however, will be some compensation to Sir Francis for your false charge." He regarded Adelaide coldly. "As for you, my lady, you have had your way for far too long."

She heard the finality in the king's voice and realized there would be no hope of avoiding marriage to de Farnby if Armand died.

"You still wish to marry her?" the king inquired of Armand.

"By God, I do," Armand declared. "Never more than now."

"Then marry her if you will," John said, "but do it quickly, priest, for I am getting hungry."

The priest began his blessing. As he did, Adelaide had no doubts about her decision to marry Armand. Whatever her sisters thought or whatever the future held, she would always consider herself among the most fortunate of women because she was his wife.

As ARMAND and Adelaide were becoming husband and wife, Francis stood in Richard's deserted bed-chamber, cursing under his breath. That lying, scheming, duplicitous fiend had fled like Oliver, leaving him to face Armand de Boisbaston and the consequences of the trial alone.

ALTHOUGH ADELAIDE KNEW it was her dread of what could happen afterward that made her wish the mass had taken longer, it still seemed far too brief.

Eloise hurried up to them, smiling through her

tears, as they left the chapel. "You're married!" she cried, embracing Adelaide. "I'm so happy for you!"

"You had best take care with whom you associate, Lady Eloise," Hildegard said as she passed by, "or you might wind up in a dungeon."

"I'd rather be in a dungeon with my friends than enduring *your* company," Eloise retorted.

Hildegard huffed and stalked away toward the hall, while Lady Jane hurried up to them, momentarily abandoning her mother.

"I'm so sorry about the trial," she said when she reached them, blushing as she addressed Armand. "I'm sure you're innocent."

"Thank you, my lady," he said with sincere gratitude.

"Daughter!" Lady Ethel called out. "Didn't you hear what I said? Leave those…those…*people* and come here!"

"In a moment, Mother," Jane answered before addressing them again. "I wanted to tell you that my maid said that Lord Richard rode out at dawn. She saw him herself."

"Jane! Come *here!*" her mother ordered.

As Jane turned to go, Adelaide put her hand on her arm to detain her.

"Thank you, Jane," she said sincerely. "For that, and for your friendship, too."

Sniffling, Jane scurried away as a cry went up from the barbican. "Knights! Armed and armored, and coming at the gallop!"

Armand immediately drew his sword. Foot soldiers rushed up the stairs and ladders to take their places on the wall walk. The queen gathered up her skirts and started to run toward the massive, round keep near the barbican, followed by most of the ladies of the court.

Not Adelaide.

Although she had no weapons, and no skill to use them even if she did, she wouldn't leave Armand's side until it was absolutely necessary.

"Who is it? Are we under attack?" John demanded from where he stood.

"It's the Earl of Pembroke!" the sergeant-at-arms cried from his vantage point, and with obvious relief. "Open the gates! Open the gates for the earl."

Adelaide's heart leapt with joy. Surely the earl would agree that Armand was innocent and there would be no need for a trial to prove it. His support would absolve Armand in the eyes of the other nobles, too.

The great wooden gates swung open to admit the earl, riding at the head of an armed body of knights. They entered the courtyard in a flurry of hoofbeats and the jangle of bits and other accoutrements. Godwin, likewise mud-splattered and exhausted, rode close behind Marshal. The servants, who'd huddled together in the hall or kitchen or apartments, began to peek out of windows and doors, watching the cortege.

After surveying the courtyard, the wall walks and

the people milling about, the earl dismounted. He was tall and well-made, with the bearing of a man certain of his own worth because it had been proven countless times. He wore his mail, which weighed sixty pounds at least, as if it were nothing.

Marshal nodded a greeting to Armand, then walked directly toward the king.

He'd likely already noted the queen coming out of the keep, her curious ladies with her. "My liege," Marshal said, bowing his head when he reached John.

"My lord," the king replied. "What brings you home in such haste? Is there new trouble with the Welsh?"

"No new trouble, sire. Indeed, I believe Llywellan will take Joan for his bride," he said, speaking of John's natural daughter, and the marriage agreement they were trying to promote.

"Then why come here at all?" ·

The earl, who had to look down at the king, didn't take his steadfast gaze from John's face. "I've been informed of the charges against Armand de Boisbaston."

Adelaide held her breath and reached for Armand's hand, while John raised an imperious brow. "And?"

"And I have come to see the outcome of the trial for myself."

Adelaide's joy dissipated like air from a deflated bellows. He wasn't going to tell John the charge was ludicrous? That Armand was loyal and there was no need for a trial?

Armand squeezed her hand. "He shouldn't interfere," he whispered. "If he does and I lose, he'll be in danger of being accused of treason, too, because he's my friend. We have to let this play out, Adelaide. For the good of the kingdom, there must be a trial by combat between Francis and me."

Adelaide cared about the kingdom, and the fate of everyone in it, but she cared about Armand more, so she was sorry the earl had not told John the trial was unnecessary.

John smiled when he, too, realized that the earl was not going to protest his decision. "You must be famished, my lord," he said, reaching up to place a companionable arm on the earl's broad shoulder. "Come and break the fast with us, and tell us the news from Wales before we settle this matter of treason."

A SHORT WHILE LATER, after a meal neither of them could bring themselves to eat, Adelaide and Armand stood in his chamber. The time had come to gird him for battle.

Armand knew what he must do, and he was ready to do his utmost to succeed. Adelaide's future and Bayard's life, as well as his own, depended on how well he fought today.

For the first time, he was truly grateful his father had been a demanding, unforgiving teacher, forcing his sons to train and fight for long hours regardless of the weather. Thanks to his father, he was surely more prepared than Francis for the battle to come.

"Kiss me, Armand," Adelaide said, her voice quivering only a little as he went to the chest containing his mail and armor. "Kiss me once before you put on your armor."

"Gladly," he said, again marvelling at her strength and courage.

It would also be a little moment of forgetfulness before the battle to come.

A rap on the door interrupted their embrace and the Earl of Pembroke sought permission to enter. Armand could tell that Adelaide would have preferred that he refuse, but as much as he adored Adelaide and appreciated her company, he welcomed the familiar presence of a man of war.

"I thought you might need some assistance," the earl said as he strode into the small chamber, "or would you two rather be alone?"

"No, no, please," Armand said, moving away from Adelaide, and hoping she would understand that if he grew distant, it was necessary to his preparations. As he armored his body, he must armor his mind, putting away all thoughts of everything except defeating Francis de Farnby.

He gave Adelaide a tender, loving smile. "I doubt you could manage the hauberk."

She made no protest. "And you must be sure that your mail is on properly," she said, "and that everything is done as it should be, so you don't have to give it a second thought. The earl will also be able to tell if your mail or helmet's been tampered with."

"Think Francis will to try to cheat, eh?" the earl asked.

"Do you doubt he might?" Adelaide countered, quite willing to stand up to the most famous knight in the kingdom if he couldn't appreciate the potential dangers Armand faced this day.

"Sadly, I agree that Francis de Farnby is more than capable of such dishonor," the earl replied. "After I've helped Armand, I'll check his horse's accoutrements for tampering, too. I'm loaning him one of my best."

Adelaide felt a weight slip from her shoulders, even as she realized Armand appeared more burdened.

He had such responsibilities, and he'd already endured so much. *Please, God,* she silently prayed, *protect him!*

"I assume this lovely young lady is your wife?"

Armand blushed like an embarrassed youth at the earl's question. "Oh, yes, forgive me, my lord. Lord William, this is Lady Adelaide, my bride."

"Trust you to find the most beautiful girl in England," the earl said with a fatherly smile. "And you've done well for yourself, too, my lady. Armand's a fine fellow. Bit proud and stubborn—I would have surrendered that castle weeks before he did—but loyal to the bone, and that's a rare quality these days."

Armand frowned with consternation at the mention of loyalty. "Although I appreciate your support, my lord, you shouldn't have come. If I lose, you—"

"My position will be no more precarious than it's been since I was born," the earl replied with a shrug.

"Yet you and Armand continue to put your life at risk for a king who's not worth such a sacrifice," Adelaide said, giving vent to some of her anger and frustration.

The earl regarded her with eyes that were world-weary, and as embittered as her own. "John is no prize, I grant you, but I've lived through one war of succession, and don't wish to experience another. Only a few gain from such a war, and seldom those who should."

"Yet John murdered Arthur, his own nephew, and with his bare hands."

"Did he?" the earl countered. "I have no proof. If anyone with certain knowledge and the proof to back it up came forward, that would be different. And Arthur was a boy more foolish even than John. He would have given England to Philip."

"While John has given him Normandy."

"For now. That may change."

"But surely that proves John isn't fit to be king!"

"I have no admiration for John," the earl said. "I respect the rank he holds more than the man—John has seen to that. At one time, I had great hopes for him, as did his father, only to see them dashed. But can you say another will be any better? Who would take his place? Eleanor? A girl can't hold the throne. The man she marries, whoever he may be? It could be years before a victor emerges, and in the meantime, many good men will die, and the land will suffer, and so will all the people, whether high-born or low.

"When all is said and done, John is the lawful king, God's chosen ruler, however we may wonder at God's plans. And in truth, my lady, few men have had a life like John, with such trials and temptations. So while he lives, he has my support, and since you, Armand, have sworn your oath to him, I know he has yours, too."

"Yes, my lord," Armand agreed.

"And you, my lady?"

She nodded, but in her heart, she added a condition. Whatever God's inscrutable plans, if Armand died today, she would do all in her power to bring about an end to John's reign. And if she was forced to marry Francis de Farnby, she would kill that traitor rather than submit.

"Good," the earl said, satisfied. "And now we must make haste to arm our champion. Where's your gambeson, Armand?"

Adelaide went to the chest and drew out the tunic padded with goose feathers. For the majority of foot soldiers, this was the only protection they had in battle; for a knight, it was the padding he wore between his shirt and mail.

Armand put it on and checked the buckles in the front before fastening them. As he did that, the earl called for the mail for his legs. Adelaide fetched the two pieces of chain mail with leather thongs for tying, trying not to notice the many dings and dents in the metal rings that had been repaired, each one a reminder of a past blow.

"Not the hosen?" the earl queried as he placed the guards on the front of Armand's shins and reached around to tie them into place.

"No, I can't take the weight on my legs since my knee was injured."

"How did that happen?"

"Mace blow."

"Ah," the earl sighed, nodding. "Experienced that a few times myself. How long ago?"

"Before I was captured."

"And no doubt you've treated it with care and delicacy, afraid to put your weight on it or move it much?"

"Yes."

The earl straightened, coming eye to eye with Armand. "Not always the best way with such injuries. Sometimes moving it helps more. Bend it now."

Armand did, and Adelaide could tell he was trying not to wince. So, too, could the earl, but instead of expressing sympathy, he ordered him to bend it again. "And keep bending it while I get your hauberk."

Adelaide watched, chewing her lip, as Armand obeyed, and slowly, a smile spread upon his face. "By God, it's getting better—not so stiff and sore."

The earl snorted a laugh. "I'll wager you haven't seen a physician since you were freed, have you?"

Armand shook his head.

"Proud idiot," the earl muttered. "Thought he'd tell you he'd have to cut it off or something, I'll wager."

"I knew it wasn't as bad as all that," Armand protested. "I haven't had time. I've been trying to raise the ransom for Bayard."

"There's a fellow even more proud than you," the earl noted as he went to the chest and lifted out the chain-mail hauberk, with a coif to cover the head and gloves for the hands attached at the neck and wrists. Slit up the center of the front and back to make it possible to sit on a horse, the hauberk was very heavy, yet the earl picked it up as a maidservant would a shift. "I've heard Bayard's in the custody of the Duc d'Ormonde. He has the freedom of the castle, if not to leave."

"So Lord Richard claims," Armand grimly replied. "I hope that's the truth, but I wouldn't be surprised if Richard wrote that letter himself."

"It wasn't from Lord Richard I heard it," the earl replied as he lifted the mail over Armand's head and helped adjust it in place. "I had it from another knight recently come from Normandy."

Armand's shoulders relaxed and he closed his eyes. "Then it may be true, after all. Thank God."

Adelaide, too, was happy to hear the news, for Armand's sake, but she was too worried about the trial to come to be relieved.

"The duke's a good man," the earl went on as he tied the leather thongs around each of Armand's wrists to keep the sleeves of the hauberk from slipping over his hands, which were not yet in the gloves. "He hates Philip, but unfortunately he hates John more. Thank God he values honor and chivalry. It's a pity he's not an ally."

"I'm glad to know Bayard's not suffering as I did," Armand said as he drew the coif over his head.

The earl helped him adjust the ventail, the flap of mail that went across his neck and chin to protect them. He tied it into place just above Armand's left temple.

Adelaide knew what must be put on next and went to fetch the surcoat lying neatly folded in the chest. It was dove-gray, nearly the same color as his mail. "I can help with this," she said, going to Armand.

He put his arms through the sleeves, and his head through the opening. She pulled it down and helped adjust it, then stood back to survey him.

It was almost like looking at a stranger, or a statue made of silver, except for his all-too-human, familiar face, and the determination etched upon it. How she loved him! And how she feared the next time she saw him, his gold-flecked eyes would be closed in death.

The earl brought Armand his swordbelt, and as Armand buckled it on, Adelaide fetched his helmet. It, too, bore scars of battle. Trying not to notice them, she helped him put it on and fastened it in place under his chin so that most of his face was covered by the ventail and noseguard. Then he put on the gloves, which were in two sections—one for his thumb, the other for the rest of his hand, the palm covered with a piece of leather to better grip his sword.

The earl nodded approvingly. "Ready, my lord?"

"Ready, except for one more thing—a kiss from my beloved bride."

When she pressed her lips upon Armand's cheek, no tears blurred her eyes or fell on her pale cheeks. No lump settled in her throat; no knot tightened in her stomach. She felt instead a comforting calm, the certain knowledge that God would watch over this nobleman she loved and help him, because their cause was just and he was good.

"I will pray that God will bless you and keep you, my lord," she said softly, "but I'm sure you'll win."

CHAPTER TWENTY-THREE

As ARMAND WAITED FOR the king to signal the beginning of the trial, he wished he felt as sure of the outcome as Adelaide and William Marshal seemed to be. Although most of the weight of the heavy lance was resting on his stirrup, and his shield was looped around his neck and chest, he was all too aware of the weakness that lingered in his arms.

At least he wouldn't have to hold his shield with just his forearm unless and until the battle was taken to the ground. If both he and Francis were unhorsed and fit enough to continue the battle, they would have to keep fighting with sword or mace.

He didn't want to use his mace. He was more confident with the lighter sword, especially after being imprisoned. Nevertheless, his mace was looped around the cantle of his saddle in case he required it.

At the opposite side of the meadow, Francis was likewise mounted on a powerful destrier. Armand knew Francis preferred the mace. It required only physical strength and a little accuracy to bash an opponent on the head or to numb his arm.

The river was on Armand's left, while the castle loomed on his right. The ground beneath his horse wasn't slick with wet, but it wasn't exactly dry, either. Although that added an element of danger for the combatants, the king hadn't delayed the trial. After all, to do that would cause further disruption to his plans. And rather than face the inconvenience of chairs sinking into the mud, John had decreed that he and the rest of the court would witness the trial from the wall walk, even if that meant everyone had to stand for the duration.

Like Armand, Francis already wore his helmet, so Armand couldn't see his face. But he could read the man's body—the stiffness in his shoulders, the way he sat so straight in the saddle and his hand twisted on the shaft of his lance. Francis was even more anxious than he, and why not? He had as much at stake as Armand now, and considerably less experience.

A horn sounded from the battlements and both knights looked toward the king, who was holding one of Queen Isabel's silken veils. Raising it would mean they should couch their lances and prepare for battle. Letting it go would be the signal for them to charge.

Armand's gaze swept over the wall walk until he found Adelaide. He couldn't see her face, but he was sure it would betray no fear, only a calm resolve and absolute belief that he would win.

Please, God, let justice prevail and give me the victory, he silently prayed, gripping his lance tightly. *Yet if it be Your will that I fail, protect my beloved.*

The king raised the veil.

Looking forward between the twitching ears of his warhorse, Armand lowered his lance and settled it between his ribs and elbow. Trying to ignore his protesting muscles, he held tight to his horse with his knees, his heels slightly turned out. He looped his reins once more around his gloved hand and tilted his head from side to side to lessen the tension in his neck.

The destrier knew what the movement of the lance foreshadowed. It snorted and refooted, ears back, impatient as his rider for the charge to begin.

The veil fluttered from the king's hand.

With a shout, Armand punched the horse's sides with his spurred heels. The horse gave a great leap and broke into a gallop, its powerful body surging as it went straight toward their opponent. Bending forward, Armand gritted his teeth, readying himself for the blow of Francis's lance on his shield as his own collided with its target.

If he was blessed and lucky or both, Francis's lance would miss him completely, or glance off his shield. If he was not, the lance would rip his shield from his body and pierce his armor. The force alone could shove him from the saddle and send him tumbling to the ground, where he could suffer broken limbs or a fatal wound to his head.

If Francis struck true.

They met with a bone-jarring crash of wooden

lance and shield. Armand nearly fell, but he managed to hold on with his knees, swaying like a drunken man for what seemed far too long.

Francis was not so fortunate. With the speed and strength of Armand's horse to propel his lance, Armand hit Francis's shield with enough force to split it and push him from his horse.

Only when Armand raised his lance and turned his horse did he hear the excited roar of the crowd.

The roar grew as Francis got to his feet. Not seriously injured or dead, then.

Since Francis was unhorsed, the battle must continue on foot until one or the other cried mercy, or was killed. Armand tossed his lance aside and threw his leg over the destrier, the stiffness and pain of his knee forgotten, overcome by the need to win this battle. He found new strength in his arms as he smacked the horse's rump to send it from the field.

Having lost his shield, Francis now held his sword in his left hand, although that was not the hand he favored. In that hand, he held his mace, its leather thong around his wrist. As he walked forward, he began to swing the iron rod with the round, barbed iron ball that could break a man's bones even if he wore mail.

Armand slid his left arm through the inner strap of his shield so he could move it where it would do the most good. He reached across his body for his sword, his leather grip tightening around the hilt as he pulled it free. The blade gleamed dully in the sunlight that warmed his mail and helmet, and he reminded himself to breath deeply, to conserve his strength and let Francis come to him.

Francis approached with deliberate steps, swinging his mace in ever-increasing arcs, his mouth a grim, hard line below his flared nose guard.

"You know what becomes of Adelaide when you lose, don't you?" he asked with a sly, vicious smile. "She'll be mine, to use as I will."

Francis truly was a fool to deliberately goad a man already determined to win, who knew his life, as well as that of his beloved and his brother, hung in the balance.

This was another sign that Francis had never fought in a battle when winning or losing meant life or death, not ransom or reward. Or that those left behind would suffer if he lost.

"Nothing to say, eh, Armand?"

Francis was right—he had nothing to say. All his energy was concentrated on winning, and this man's talk was no more than the jabbering of a beast who didn't see its own doom approaching.

"It was kind of you, Armand, to break her in for me, but I'm sure there are things she has yet to learn. It will be my pleasure to teach her."

Two more steps, Armand thought, readying himself. Two more steps and Francis would be close enough.

Francis halted just out of reach of Armand's sword. Like two stags in a wood in spring, they faced each other, each one wondering who would be the first to strike.

Wait him out, Armand told himself. Let him move first. Let the momentum of his blow take him off balance for that one necessary instant.

The movement of the mace caught his eye. It was a mere fraction of an inch, but it was enough to warn him and tell him that Francis had not the patience to wait. So Armand was ready for the sudden upswing of the vicious, barbed weapon and dodged out of the way of its downward arc. If his arms were stronger, he might have taken the blow on his shield, to get in closer to his enemy, but today, he couldn't risk it. The shield was weight enough.

As Francis recovered, Armand saw his chance. Francis likewise wore no hosen, so Armand brought his sword slashing down not on Francis's well-protected head or shoulder, but at the exposed space between his knee and the hem of his hauberk. It was a narrow opening, not more than a hand's width, but a deep cut there could be fatal.

He missed, and the force of his own blow sent him stumbling forward while Francis wheeled around and cried, "A low blow! You *are* a coward!"

"This is to the death," Armand reminded him through his clenched teeth as he regained his balance and faced him. "This is not a pretty fight to impress the ladies and brag about over wine. One of us will die here, today, or later, meeting a traitor's terrible end. I do not intend that it be me."

"You *will* die!" Francis shouted as he rotated the mace in his right hand, like a scythe of death in the reaper's hand. In his left, his sword was at the ready.

He was going to have to rid Francis of one of those weapons, and soon, Armand thought as he crouched slightly, steadying himself, again determined to force Francis to make the first move. A sharp pang in his knee made him wince, but he kept his focus on his opponent and the swinging mace.

This time when Francis struck, Armand let his shield and left arm take the force of the blow. His weakened muscles meant he couldn't hold his shield up for long, but it was enough to let him steer the terrible ball away and downward, while he brought his sword around, up and under, to strike hard at Francis's wrist. Although it was protected by mail, the wrist, like most joints, was a point of weakness. Armand had found out exactly how weak when he'd been shackled.

His hope was fulfilled, and Francis dropped his sword. Armand swiftly kicked it out of reach.

Then Armand saw the bright red stain of blood just above Francis's knee. He *had* cut him. Not deeply, perhaps, but enough to give him pain. Now they were even there, he thought, and his confidence began to grow.

Nevertheless, he must still be cautious. A single mistake could mean the end for him, and a terrible future for Adelaide, and Bayard and his country.

Since Francis had only his mace, he would be feeling more vulnerable. The exhaustion was creeping up on him, too—Armand could tell by his enemy's stance, the line of his mouth, the grip on the haft of his mace, and especially because he was silent.

Unfortunately, the weight of the shield was proving to be too much for Armand's arm to bear. Both arms were in agony, and he would never be able to penetrate Francis's mail if he held his sword in one hand. He needed the strength of both.

So he lowered his left arm and let his shield fall.

UP ON THE wall walk, Adelaide let out a gasp of dismay when she saw Armand's shield drop to the ground. She'd been thrilled when Armand sent Francis's sword skittering along the grass, but now feared Armand was badly wounded. He was certainly in pain, and getting weary; she could tell that by the slump of his shoulders and the way he crouched. Francis was weary, too, and he seemed to be limping a bit, perhaps because of the fall from his horse—but was he injured enough to be vulnerable?

The two men circled each other, Francis with his mace, Armand gripping his sword with both hands, the tip lowered as if it were too heavy for him to lift any higher.

Her silent prayers grew more fervent and pleading. Armand couldn't lose. He had to win. Please, God, he had to win!

Suddenly, Francis gave a great bellow like an enraged ox, raised his mace and ran at Armand. He brought his weapon back behind his shoulder, clearly intending to swing it down on the weary Armand's head before he could dodge the blow.

Adelaide cried out, but she didn't look away.

With a speed and dexterity that seemed impossible, Armand leaned away from the blow and simultaneously brought his sword upward. Francis screamed like a pig being slaughtered as he stumbled forward and fell.

Armand's aim had found its mark, in the pit of Francis's arm, where the rings of the sleeve and body of the hauberk rubbed against each other, wearing them down so that they were slightly thinner. It was, except for the face and that hands-breadth above the knee, a very vulnerable spot.

DRAWING IN great rasping breaths, Armand hunched over, his left hand on his knee, and his right still clutching his sword. It had taken all of his strength and determination, as well as Francis's own momentum, to cut through Francis's mail and draw blood.

Francis struggled to his hands and knees. The mace was still tied to his wrist, grasped in his gloved hand.

Perhaps the wound was not very deep, after all, Armand thought as he once again prepared to defend himself.

Francis didn't stand. Still on all fours, he pushed off his helmet and raised his glaring, hate-filled eyes to Armand. "You've won, Armand. I can't raise my arm," he gasped, his face a pale, livid white.

Francis blinked as sweat fell into his eyes, and blood dripped from beneath his arm to stain the grass below. "I'm going to swoon, and you'll win, but you haven't killed me. They'll bring a physician to tend to me so that I can be executed later. Hanged, drawn and quartered, to be made an example. My head on the Tower to be picked at by crows."

His eyes glimmered with unshed tears. "Have mercy, Armand. If I must die because I want another king, don't let it be like that. For the love of God, I beg you, kill me here and now."

Francis de Farnby was their enemy. He'd wanted Armand dead, and Adelaide in his bed. He'd conspired to kill the Earl of Pembroke and the Archbishop of Canterbury, good men even if John was not.

Yet as Armand looked at Francis de Farnby, he found not hatred, but pity in his heart, and he would have granted his request if he could. "I have not the strength to get another blow through your armor."

"My face, then," Francis begged, staggering to his feet. "Run your sword through my face."

"Oh, God," Armand murmured, a plea and a prayer combined. "I won't. I can't. I'm no executioner."

"Do it!" Francis ordered, his voice rising as he tried to straighten, his mace dangling from his wrist as he clutched the arm hanging limp at his side.

When it was clear Armand would not, Francis found the strength to raise the mace. He started to charge Armand like a demented creature. "Then by God, I'll kill you! With my last breath, I'll kill you!"

Silently begging God's clemency, Armand braced himself, lifted his sword and did as Francis wanted.

WHEN ADELAIDE saw Francis fall and Armand remain standing, joy filled her heart and a cry of mingled triumph and relief burst from her lips.

He had won! He was safe! And proven innocent.

"Well, that's done. And thoroughly done," the king muttered, addressing the grim-faced Earl of Pembroke beside him before he turned to Adelaide and spoke over the excited murmuring of the courtiers. They'd been mostly silent during the battle— even Hildegard—but once it was over and Armand clearly the victor, they gave vent to both their feelings and their opinion of the battle.

"God has passed His judgment," the king called out. "Armand de Boisbaston is innocent of treason."

Without a word, Adelaide turned and left the battlements to go to her beloved, for not even the king's command would have stopped her.

CHAPTER TWENTY-FOUR

ARMAND HEARD Adelaide calling his name and, with a deep sigh, turned away from the body lying on the ground. He didn't feel like a noble knight defending his honor or his king. He felt like a murderer.

"You're safe!" Adelaide cried, throwing her arms around him. "Praise God, you won! Now everyone knows you're not a traitor."

He had no strength left in his arms to embrace her in return. Instead, he laid his head upon her shoulder and sighed with a deep weariness of body and of soul.

"It's over," Adelaide whispered, her lovely voice audible over the throbbing pulse sounding a tattoo in his head. "My beloved husband is safe."

So was she. Oh, thank God, so was she. He found the vigor to slip his arms about her slender waist and hold her close.

He became aware that more people were crowding around them. He heard the earl's gruff voice, and Eloise's excited chatter. He could discern Sir Charles's praise, and Sir Edmond's comments about the virtues of the sword over the mace, and Sir

Roger's agreement. They were all anxious to congratulate him on his triumph, but out of the corner of
his eye, he saw Francis's squire and servant taking
away his body, and he felt no great delight.

He held Adelaide for as long as he could, until the
king's voice rose above all the others. "Lord Armand
de Boisbaston!"

Armand let go of Adelaide and wearily faced the
man he loathed, and yet to whom he was still bound
by his sworn oath. Behind John, he could see the
queen and the Earl of Pembroke—beaming like a
proud father—and Eloise, who was both smiling and
shedding tears, and Lady Jane looking vastly relieved,
as did several of the young men of the court. Even
Lady Hildegard and Lady Ethel were regarding him
with grudging respect.

His hand found Adelaide's and he grasped it as
securely as he could. No one's opinion or gratitude
or respect meant more to him than hers.

"Sire," he said, bowing his head.

"Lord Armand de Boisbaston," the king repeated,
"we consider that God has rendered His judgment,
and that accordingly, you are innocent of treason."

"Thank you, sire," he replied, although the grateful
words nearly choked him. "If you please, sire, I would
like to take my leave of you and the court. I must go
to Normandy, to learn the truth about my brother and
ransom him if he's being held against his will, as I fervently believe."

To his dismay, John shook his head. "That I cannot allow. I have need of men such as you at court, especially in view of this latest conspiracy against my lawful rule."

"But my brother—"

"May be loyal, or he may not," the king said. "We shall send Falkes de Bréauté to determine if your brother's imprisoned and in need of being ransomed, or if he's betrayed his oath and is in league with Philip. I will brook no objection, my lord."

Before Armand could reply, a man's booming voice called out from behind the crowd, "Sire! There's no need to send anyone to Normandy for news of Bayard de Boisbaston, or to doubt his loyalty, either!"

The crowd parted to let a dark-haired, mail-clad man pass. He was nearly as handsome as Armand, despite the long scar that ran from the corner of his right eye down to his jaw, and he strode forward as if he owned the world.

"Bayard!" Armand shouted, letting go of Adelaide's hand to rush toward him.

So this was Armand's brother and he was free and home. Tears of joy clouded Adelaide's eyes, then fell unheeded down her cheeks as she watched them embrace.

"Randall!" Eloise cried, running toward the slender young man who appeared behind them. She engulfed him in an overjoyed hug and when they kissed, Adelaide realized she need not doubt that beneath Randall's gentle exterior, there lurked a man every bit as passionate as her husband.

Armand let go of his brother and led him toward her. When he reached her, Bayard de Boisbaston gave her a smile that was every bit as devilishly attractive as Armand's or their illegitimate half brother's.

"This is my wife, Adelaide," Armand announced with a pride that made her blush.

"Wife?" Bayard repeated, a wrinkle of puzzlement between his dark brows. "Randall didn't tell me you were married."

"We were wed this morning."

His brother laughed—a deep, rollicking sound as full of vitality as the man himself. "You always were full of surprises."

He winked most impertinently at Adelaide. "You look happy enough now, my lady, but if you ever grow weary of this fellow, I offer myself in his stead now that I am free."

"I thank you for your offer," she just as insolently replied, "and I shall give it all the consideration it merits."

The king loudly cleared his throat, drawing everyone's attention. "We had heard, Bayard, that either you were imprisoned and waiting to be ransomed, or that you were in league with Philip and enjoying the hospitality of the Duc d'Ormonde."

"I was a *prisoner* of the duke," Bayard replied, as

grave now as he'd been merry before, "and I *was* waiting to be ransomed. Fortunately, the duke's a chivalrous fellow, so I wasn't kept in his dungeon. I had to give my word I wouldn't leave his castle, but otherwise, I was free to go where I would."

"How, then, are you here?" John asked, his question echoing Adelaide's own, and Armand's, too, to judge by the curious expression on her husband's face.

Bayard's roguish grin returned. "You may have heard, sire, that the duke has a pretty young wife. It seems she took a fancy to me—not that I ever touched her. She's far too young and flighty for my taste, and married to boot, although she made it clear she welcomed my company. The duke became…how shall I put it? *Concerned* enough that he waived the ransom entirely. I believe if I'd stayed any longer, he would have been offering *me* money to leave."

He laughed again with such good humor, everyone within earshot smiled, too.

Except the king, who held out his arm to his pretty young wife. "I see. You are welcome again to our court. Come, Isabel. The noon meal awaits."

The queen dutifully took the irate king's arm and started toward the castle, trailed by her ladies-in-waiting, including Hildegard. While Hildegard looked back over her shoulder at Bayard de Boisbaston more than once, Isabel—no doubt wisely—did not.

"Randall's been telling me some other astonishing

things," Bayard said after they had gone. He looked around, his brow furrowing again. "Where the devil has he got to?"

Eloise and Randall must have slipped away, Adelaide realized, leaving the three of them alone.

"By the saints, Randall is quite the dark horse," Bayard declared. "Meets me on the road near here and tells me in no uncertain terms we've got to hurry to Ludgershall. He then regales me with the most fantastic talk of conspiracies and betrothals and amazing young women and—"

"We'll explain everything later," Adelaide said as Armand began to sway, his face pale and drawn. "Armand needs food and drink and rest."

Bayard put his arm beneath his brother's to help him, despite Armand's protests that he wasn't completely feeble.

"Randall said you'd gotten mixed up with a very forceful woman," he noted as they started toward the castle. "I see that was no lie."

LATER THAT NIGHT, Bayard sat on a stool in Adelaide's chamber, his long legs stuck out in front of him and crossed at the ankles. His arms were likewise crossed as he leaned back against the wall so that the front legs of the stool weren't touching the ground, just as Armand had done when he'd spent the night there before.

Armand sat on the end of the bed, with Adelaide

beside him. "So while I was in that stinking cell with my arms shackled over my head and imagining you in a similar situation," he said, "you were being treated like a prince by the Duc d'Ormonde?"

"Not exactly a prince," Bayard replied, albeit with a look of remorse in his brown eyes. "But a damn sight better than you."

He moved forward so that the feet of the stool came down on the stone floor with a bang. "I didn't know what had happened to you, Armand, or I would have escaped from the duke's castle and ridden hell-bent to save you."

Adelaide could well believe that—he seemed the sort to do such a headstrong, impetuous thing, like try to rescue his brother single-handedly.

"I'm just glad you're safe," Armand replied.

"Now thanks to you, we're all out of danger," Bayard said. "John won't dare question our loyalty again."

Adelaide wasn't so sure about that and neither was Armand, for he muttered, "Not for a while, anyway."

Before the mood had time to sour, Bayard's eyes brightened with curiosity. "What about this alleged half brother of ours? Adelaide told me about him while you were sleeping. I remember that woman and her child. Do you really think that was him?"

"He looks like you when he smiles," Adelaide said.

"And he's got the family charm," Armand replied. "I had some anxious moments thinking he was trying to steal Adelaide away from me."

"As if he had any chance at all!" she protested.

"Well, how was I to know that? You certainly gave every impression—"

"If you two are going to start quarrelling," Bayard said, half rising, "I'll leave you to it."

"No, we're not," Armand said, reaching for Adelaide's hand. "I'm in no mood to quarrel with anybody, unless it's the king."

"I'm with you there," Bayard agreed, becoming serious. "I hate the rogue."

"Yet we've sworn to be loyal to him," Armand said. "I've even done it twice."

Bayard shrugged. "Once or ten times makes no difference to a Boisbaston, so there's nothing to be done now but obey as best we can and keep him safe. As long as he has the earl to ride herd on him, he might improve."

"If only there was some way to put limits on his power," Adelaide mused aloud. "Some kind of law, or treaty or contract."

"No king would agree to such a thing," Bayard said, shaking his head. "Certainly not John."

Armand frowned. "He might if he thinks he has no other choice. And many of the nobles who balk at rebellion and war might be more inclined to try to persuade him to sign such an agreement."

"Perhaps—if someone could suggest it without running the risk of being charged with treason," Bayard said. "Don't *you* get any ideas. Once is enough for that."

"I agree," Armand replied. "Still, I wouldn't be surprised if John never trusts me. I think that's why he wants me to stay at court, to keep an eye on me."

"I'm not so sure of that, my love," Adelaide said. "I can believe he wants you close by because you're one of the few men he can trust at all, now that you've sworn your oath again and triumphed over Francis de Farnby."

"If only Richard hadn't fled, and we'd been able to arrest him!" Armand said with regret.

"We've made a powerful enemy there, I'm afraid," Adelaide agreed.

"Since he's escaped and no doubt blames us for the ruin of his plot, your sisters might be in danger," Armand grimly noted. "We ought to warn them."

"I'll send Gillian a message," Adelaide agreed. "She has a good and loyal garrison at Averette. I'll write to Lizette to return there."

She hesitated, then added, "I'll also have to tell them I've gotten married."

Bayard was surprised to see that bold and beautiful woman blush when she said that. According to Randall, she'd kept the king and several predatory courtiers at bay for months, as well as working to solve a treasonous plot, yet she seemed oddly coy about her marriage.

But then, who could really understand women? Certainly not him. Nor did he particularly want to. They were wonderful creatures, especially in bed, but he had no desire to hear about their petty difficulties and minor concerns.

"I'll take the message, so you can be sure she'll get it and it won't be intercepted," Bayard offered.

That seemed the least he could do after all Armand and Adelaide had been through while he'd been wasting time fending off the advances of the Duc d'Ormonde's wife.

"Thank you," Adelaide said softly, smiling in a way that made Bayard think marriage—to the right woman—might be something to be sought, after all.

"Randall also said something about buried treasure?" he noted. "I gather he thinks it needs to be retrieved and taken to Averette. I'll do that, too, if you like."

Adelaide and Armand exchanged looks. "It's not really treasure," Adelaide said, "at least not of the sort you're probably imagining. It's a piece of jewellery that belonged to my mother. The king took it, and your half brother stole it back for me."

"What, right out from under the king's nose?"

"It seems, Bayard, that our brother is an exceptional thief," Armand said.

Bayard laughed. "What else would you expect, as we're exceptional knights? And speaking of exceptional, or at least unexpected, Randall told me he's getting married, too. Talk about a changed man! I gather he *told* his father he was getting married, whether the old trout liked it or not, and demanded money to pay John to ensure it would happen, as well as a sum sufficient to pay my ransom. I never thought Randall could be so bold, or so devious, either."

"Love can change a man, Bayard," Armand said quietly, smiling at his wife.

The way they regarded each other suddenly made Bayard feel like an unwelcome intruder.

"With that thought to rattle around in my head, I shall take my leave of you," he said, rising. "Randall and I rode like the damned to get here, so I'm tired, too."

He strolled to the door, then glanced back over his shoulder at Armand and the woman he had wed. "I'm glad you didn't die today, Armand."

"I'm happy that you're free, Bayard."

AFTER THE DOOR had closed behind Bayard, Armand rose, pulled Adelaide to her feet and ran his hands down her arms. "Time for bed, beloved."

"Time for *sleep,* husband," she corrected. "You still need to rest."

It *had* been a long and arduous day. Passion could wait, she thought, especially since they were husband and wife, although the look in Armand's brown eyes set her alight with desire like a spark to dry tinder.

"You may be right," he reluctantly conceded. "And there will be other nights for loving."

"Yes, Armand," she murmured as she wrapped her arms around him.

He laughed softly. "What, my lady? No argument? No resolute cry that I must not tell you what to do?"

"I don't consider that a command," she replied, love shining in her eyes. "So kiss me, Armand, and hold me in your arms as you fall asleep, and I will be more than content tonight."

"Is that an order, my lady?" he queried, laughter deep in his gold-flecked eyes.

"Only if you agree. I would have us equals in the bedchamber, if nowhere else."

"Everywhere else," he assured her. "I would have us friends and partners, as well as husband and wife. So I shall listen to your sage advice and do as you command. Tonight, I'll be content to lie in your arms until I fall asleep." His lips curved up in that devilish, seductive smile. "But tomorrow, after I'm rested, I may request something more."

"Which I'll be more than glad to give," she said as she led him to their bed. "To think I once thought marriage little better than slavery!"

"While I considered it a duty to be borne."

"We were both wrong," she said as she climbed beneath the sheets.

"Or else we learned otherwise because we found each other."

THAT NIGHT, they slept peacefully in each other's arms, and for many nights thereafter—although, truth be told, there were also many nights when gentle slumber came to Adelaide and Armand de Boisbaston only after another kind of embrace that wasn't quite so calm.

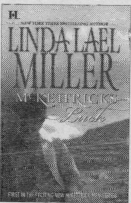

REQUEST YOUR
FREE BOOKS!

2 FREE NOVELS
FROM THE ROMANCE/SUSPENSE
COLLECTION PLUS 2 FREE GIFTS!

YES! Please send me 2 FREE novels from the Romance/Suspense Collection and my 2 FREE gifts. After receiving them, if I don't wish to receive any more books, I can return the shipping statement marked "cancel." If I don't cancel, I will receive 4 brand-new novels every month and be billed just $5.49 per book in the U.S., or $5.99 per book in Canada, plus 25¢ shipping and handling per book plus applicable taxes, if any*. That's a savings of at least 20% off the cover price! I understand that accepting the 2 free books and gifts places me under no obligation to buy anything. I can always return a shipment and cancel at any time. Even if I never buy another book from the Reader Service, the two free books and gifts are mine to keep forever.

185 MDN EF5Y 385 MDN EF6C

Name _____ (PLEASE PRINT) _____

Address _____ Apt. # _____

City _____ State/Prov. _____ Zip/Postal Code _____

Signature (if under 18, a parent or guardian must sign)

Mail to **The Reader Service:**
IN U.S.A.: P.O. Box 1867, Buffalo, NY 14240-1867
IN CANADA: P.O. Box 609, Fort Erie, Ontario L2A 5X3

Not valid to current subscribers to the Romance Collection,
the Suspense Collection or the Romance/Suspense Collection.

Want to try two free books from another line?
Call 1-800-873-8635 or visit www.morefreebooks.com.

* Terms and prices subject to change without notice. NY residents add applicable sales tax. Canadian residents will be charged applicable provincial taxes and GST. This offer is limited to one order per household. All orders subject to approval. Credit or debit balances in a customer's account(s) may be offset by any other outstanding balance owed by or to the customer. Please allow 4 to 6 weeks for delivery.

Your Privacy: Harlequin is committed to protecting your privacy. Our Privacy Policy is available online at www.eHarlequin.com or upon request from the Reader Service. From time to time we make our lists of customers available to reputable firms who may have a product or service of interest to you. If you would prefer we not share your name and address, please check here. ☐

BOB07

MARGARET MOORE

77003	BRIDE OF LOCHBARR	___ $6.50 U.S.	___ $7.99 CAN.
77040	LORD OF DUNKEATHE	___ $6.50 U.S.	___ $7.99 CAN.
77065	THE UNWILLING BRIDE	___ $5.99 U.S.	___ $6.99 CAN.
77095	HERS TO COMMAND	___ $5.99 U.S.	___ $6.99 CAN.

(limited quantities available)

TOTAL AMOUNT $ _____
POSTAGE & HANDLING $ _____
($1.00 FOR 1 BOOK, 50¢ for each additional)
APPLICABLE TAXES* $ _____
TOTAL PAYABLE $ _____

(check or money order—please do not send cash)

To order, complete this form and send it, along with a check or money order for the total above, payable to HQN Books, to: **In the U.S.:** 3010 Walden Avenue, P.O. Box 9077, Buffalo, NY 14269-9077; **In Canada:** P.O. Box 636, Fort Erie, Ontario, L2A 5X3.

Name: _____
Address: _____ City: _____
State/Prov.: _____ Zip/Postal Code: _____
Account Number (if applicable): _____

075 CSAS

*New York residents remit applicable sales taxes.
*Canadian residents remit applicable GST and provincial taxes.

HQN™

We *are* romance™

www.HQNBooks.com

PHMM0806BL